I0709922

Blood Bound

Blood Bound Copyright © 2025 by Daniel Dickinson

All rights reserved. No part of this book may be reproduced in any form or by any electronic or mechanical means, including information storage and retrieval systems, without written permission from the author, except for the use of brief quotations in a book review.

This is a work of fiction. Names, characters, places, and incidents either are the product of the author's imagination or are used fictitiously. Any resemblance to actual persons, living or dead, events, or locales is entirely coincidental.

Published by TigerEye Press and Daniel Dickinson

United States

ISBN: 979-8-9885796-1-8 (Paperback)

Printed in the United States of America

First Printing: December 2025

Blood Bound

By Daniel Dickinson

North Kelsa
Xonthian City
Wall of Ages
Fort Pointe
South Kelsa
Yenzu
Port Orlynns
Angelic Island

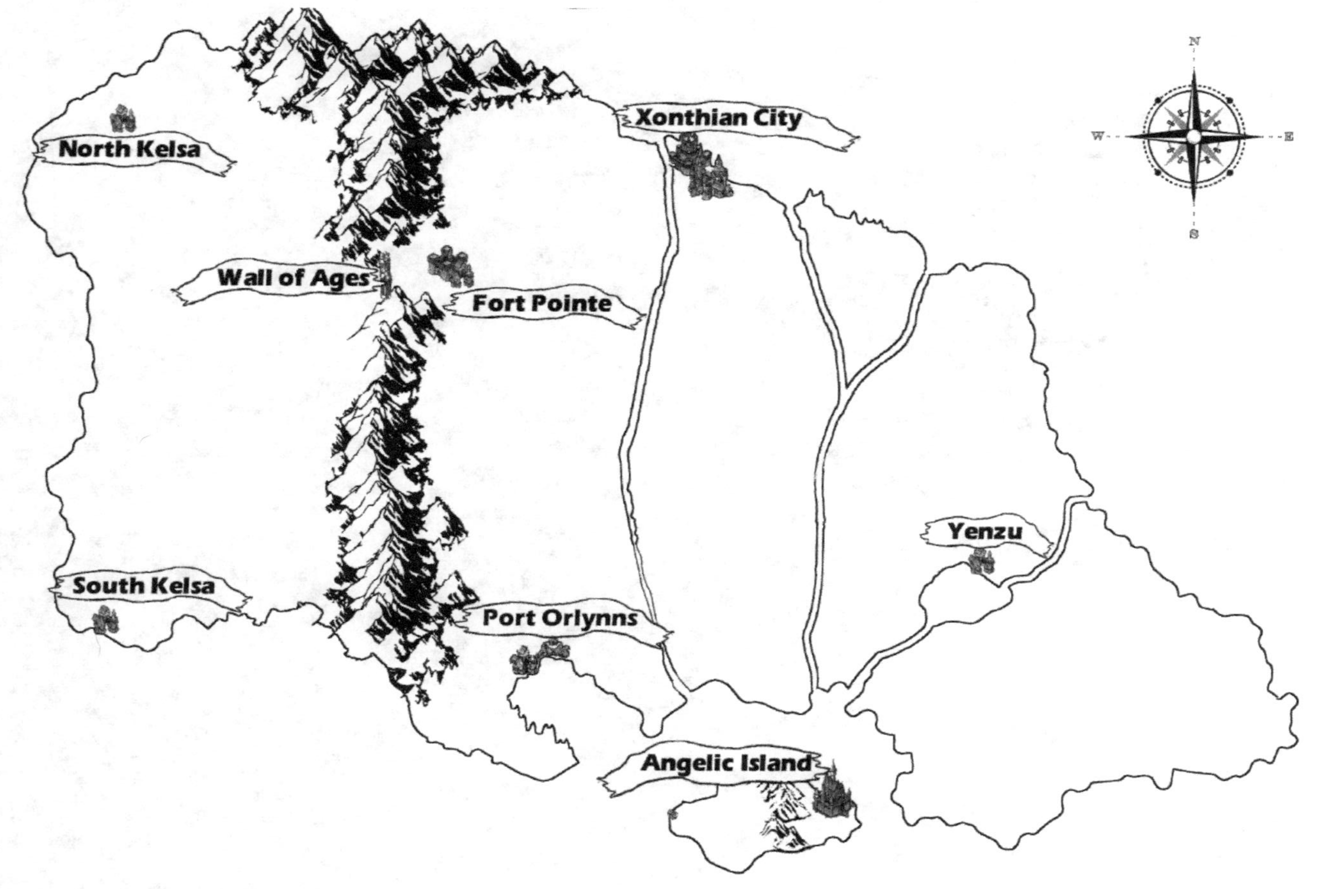

5

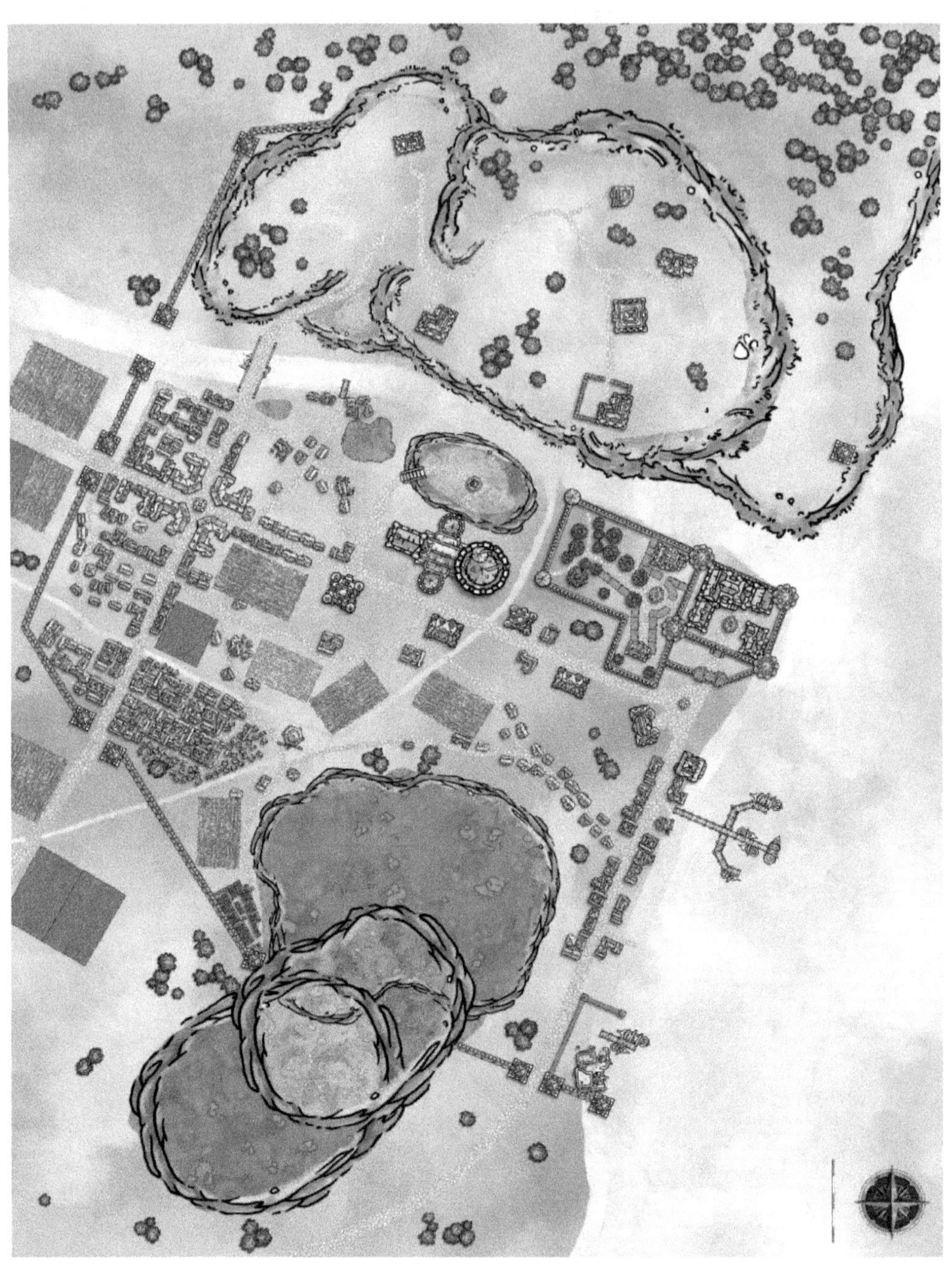

Prologue - Hunger

Bree watched with disinterest as citizens passed, heedless of her presence. She was just another vagrant, lingering on the periphery, lost in a sea of inhumanity. Just the way she wanted it. Spears of light penetrated the dark gray clouds, gracing the weary town of Fort Pointe with warmth. It was a solitary moment, a reprieve from the constant downpour. Men, women, and soldiers of every kind trudged through the muddy streets on their way to complete daily chores. The stench of animal waste from nearby farms mixed with the rancid, musty earth. Like an old wet blanket, it was smothering and heavy. The drum of the town was muted compared to the bigger cities: Xonthian City to the northeast and

Port Orlynns to the south. What she could hear were hushed tones laced with fear and uneasiness.

War had been waging not far from Fort Pointe for nearly a hundred years, yet daily life was a constant battle against starvation, shelter, and security for the short-lived humans who inhabited the area. Their faces were downcast, with sunken, sorrow-filled eyes. Taut skin covered their limbs, exposing frail bones as if a painter had stretched a canvas of flesh too tight over a frame. Threadbare clothes covered their bodies, barely held together with hemp rope and stitching. Bree huddled under a makeshift lean-to, made from broken crates and barrels from the tavern. Her cloak wrapped tightly around her thin body while her hood cast long dark shadows across her face.

Her stomach growled in a long moan of protest. The pain of it tugged at her, reminding her she hadn't had a decent meal in days. She missed her mother's cooking. By the hells, she missed cooking *with* her mom. All the chores, the mundane daily life, it all felt like a memory obscured by time. As if that life, the happy, loving life she once knew, was fading away into the abyss.

She glanced up to see a raven land on a crate, just out of reach. Its black, pearly eyes studied her, its head tilted from side to side, as if the other eye would judge her any differently.

"What do you want? I don't have any food," she said.

The creature cawed, then leapt into the air.

She watched as the creature ascended to the heavens. It's black, glossy wings carrying it upward and over the palisades of the city. Her mother used to say ravens only appeared when there was death about. Bree had spent enough time around the farm to realize they were smarter than that; it wasn't the death that drew them to the farm, it had been the free, abundant food source. The farm always had a stockpile of grain for the livestock. Her father had seen to that.

The faces of her parents lingered in her memory. Bree shook her head, shaking the visions of her past away and discarding them into the muddy, debris-strewn alley.

A scream of horror pierced the low hum of the city, snapping her attention in the direction of the wail. Guards and other onlookers bolted past her, splashing mud around them as they ran. Gooseflesh rippled up her arms and prickled the tiny hairs at the nape of her neck. Something in the depths of her subconscious urged her to rise and investigate the terror-filled shriek. With a sigh, she stood. The water that had collected on her cloak rolled down in rivulets. The long black fabric unfolded around her like a shadow, stretching its wings.

She followed the deafening uproar to the edge of town. The crowd was clamoring for a position in front of the butcher's shop. The barn doors that entered the slaughterhouse beside it were open. Guards were pushing onlookers back, forcing her to shove past them in order to see. She barely came up to the shoulders of most men, making her easy to miss in the crowd. The sight that awaited her was gruesome. A naked and bloody man was hanging from hooks, normally reserved for cattle and other large farm animals. Their metal curves pierced his lower thigh muscle, causing him to list to one side. From her position in the sea of onlookers, she saw the carotid artery had been ripped open, draining the man of his life, like some sort of swine.

Harsh whispers washed over the citizens, their eyes wide with horror. Mothers shielded children's views or dragged them away. Tears streaked down their mud-stained faces.

"Back, return to your homes, so we can clear this up," one of the guards commanded. "Someone get this man down."

Bree examined the body closer. Her keen eyes took in every detail, the bruises, old scars, and thinning hair, and the calloused hands from hard work. He was muscular and heavy-looking. Her brow furrowed together as she bit her bottom lip.

"I said move back!" the guard bellowed again, pushing one of the onlookers away.

The stench of blood hung heavy in the air, mixing with the pungent smell of wet earth and animal carcasses. Bree spat, clearing the taste of it from her mouth in disgust, and spun away from the gruesome scene. She had seen enough. This wasn't just a sick murderer playing a game. No man or woman could have lifted that body onto the meat hook. A dagger didn't cause that wound on the man's neck. This was a message.

Bree threw the hood of her cloak back. Long pale-gold hair fell around her shoulders, framing her youthful features. She glanced up at the tavern sign. The Stout Pony was situated in the center of town. It was a watering hole for travelers, merchants, and soldiers. The city was a staging area for the ongoing war near the Wall of Ages, several miles away to the west.

The Fire Isle Mages and their mercenary army on one side, while the two kingdoms and the Clerics of GateHar fought to keep them at bay. The invasion from the Fire Isle Mages had left much of western Xonthian in ruin. Although she doubted anyone alive today even remembered why the war had started, it had become a rallying cry against magic users, perpetuating hatred for their kind. Ironic, she thought, considering the Clerics were still able to use magic.

She sighed and watched as refugees and merchants from all over eastern Xonthian entered through the taverns door. The city was a popular stopover between all corners of Xonthian. Merchants often used it to gather news on the war efforts and sell what goods and resources they had, sometimes at a premium. Refugees used it as a brief respite before moving on to the larger cities.

The clouds above her had darkened with the setting sun, threatening to drown the city in another night of rain. Long dark shadows spread aethereal claws out along the muddy roads. The feeling in the pit of her stomach had grown. The sense of something lurking in the shadows prickled the nape of her neck, causing her to peer over her shoulder, although she knew nothing was there.

She pushed the door to the tavern open and walked inside. The smell of human refuge and unwashed bodies assaulted her nose. Thick smoke from tobacco and burnt food hung high in the rafters. She felt dozens of eyes on her as the door slammed shut behind her; she cursed herself for letting it announce her entry. Her stomach churned in panic. Those closest to the door glanced over but ignored her and returned to their watered-down stew.

Bree pushed her way through the crowd to the bar. Men stared at her and whispered lewd remarks to their friends as she sat down.

"Yeah, what do you want?" The barkeep, a thin, frail-looking man, asked.

"Information," Bree said.

The barkeep snorted in wry amusement. "Information around here costs money. Unless you're turning tricks somewhere, you look as poor as the rest of these sobs."

"I'd pay good silver for a private lap dance," a patron beside her sneered. He was missing several teeth and had a sickly yellow look in his sunken eyes.

The barkeeper laughed.

Bree took a deep, steadying breath. She peered sidelong at the man beside her; she didn't want to provoke him or give him any reason to keep talking. Why were men such feral animals? She turned her attention back to the bartender. "I'm looking for a stranger, someone who might have come in. Lanky, hollowed out features. Thinning hairline. Pockmarked skin. Seen anyone like that?"

"Why yes, I believe I have," the gap-toothed man chuckled. "He's upstairs right now."

Bree studied the man. Her stomach growled, and she licked her lips. The man took this as a sign to smile broadly, and he leaned over to whisper in her ear. "I can show you mine if you show me yours."

The man reeked of stale beer and unwashed male musk. Bree forced a brave face and buried the fear of losing control back under the hunger that gnawed at her insides.

"He is right, though," the barkeep said. "There was someone fitting that description here recently. I don't know if he's still here. If he were, he hasn't come down. That I've seen."

Bree didn't look away from the yellow-eyed man and only nodded her thanks to the barkeep. She slid a piece of silver across the bar top and stood. The barkeep's greedy hands snatched it up and hid it away under the counter. "Which room?"

"Last door on the right," the barkeep replied.

Bree glared at the beer-soaked man before whirling around toward the stairs leading up to the rooms. She climbed the creaking, wooden steps to the floor above. The hallway was dimly lit, with only one candle burning on a small table mid-way down the passage. Long black shadows flickered along the walls like ghosts dancing.

The coil of fear slithered in her belly. She sensed the presence of something not right. It gave her a feeling of dread and horror that was never visible, always lingering at the edge of her vision.

Bree felt the hair on her forearms stand on end as goose pimples washed over her. She placed a tentative hand on the door leading to the stranger's room and lifted the bolt. The heavy wooden door swung open with a creak that pierced her ears. The space beyond was empty except for a bed and a washbasin with a flickering candle. She crept inside, the soft soles of her boots barely audible in the still air.

She was so focused on entering the room and what possibly lay inside that she was oblivious to the yellow-eyed man from the bar suddenly appearing in the door frame. His thin body blocked what little light filtered in from the hall.

"I asked myself, did she pay me for the information I gave her? No, she hadn't," the man said as he slid inside the room, closing the door behind him. The man darted toward her like a snake circling its prey.

"You don't want to do this," Bree warned, hoping that the repressed fear didn't crack her voice.

The man stood within arm's length of her. She barely came to his shoulders. "Are you afraid? I'll be gentle if you don't fight it."

"I'm not afraid of *you*, but for *you*. I'm not here for you. I'm after the man who is staying in this room. Please leave," Bree said again, her eyes wide. Her stomach churned, and she couldn't tell if it was the fear and darkness she felt or the hunger that yearned to be free.

He peered down at her and smiled a toothless smile. "Your eyes are so mesmerizing, so dark, so... What color are your eyes?"

"Please, go back down-"

The man grabbed her arms and pulled her close, forcing his mouth over hers. His tongue lashed around her lips, trying to force its way inside. Before he could do anything further, Bree pulled away. Fury burned in her eyes.

"I warned you," she hissed, revealing her fangs to him. His eyes widened in horror.

"W-what are you?!" He yelled. The man turned and tried for the door, but her hand grasped his arm. She pulled him back into the room. The man's arm made a wet pop, and a scream of pain escaped his lips.

The man squirmed in agony on the floor. She kicked him, forcing him to become more compliant. She straddled his chest, her cloak settling around them like death's shadow. She leaned over and bared her fangs that dripped with saliva. She could almost taste the man's life essence. Her stomach growled in triumph.

"No, please!" the man sobbed.

She pulled his neck up and sank her teeth in, tearing the man's throat open. Blood poured into her mouth, and she drank deeply. She let the man's head drop back to the floor. She sat back and reveled in the warm feelings the blood gave her as it flowed through her. She stood and looked down at the man before turning away in disgust.

"Well, isn't this fitting," a voice said from the door.

Bree glanced up to see a lithe, well-dressed man watching her with mirth-filled eyes. He stepped inside the room, closed the door behind him, and then locked it with a click of the bolt.

"I'm glad I didn't have to look far to find you. I find it amusing you here in my room, though, feeding on some poor, hopeless soul. There's irony in that, don't you think?" he asked with a wide, toothy grin. His fangs were barely visible in the dim light.

Bree backed away. The feeling of fear and darkness overcame her senses. The hunger no longer muted the feeling of dread. Instead, she felt the vampire's power, like a wave of heat that held no warmth.

"Well, here we are. The hunter," the man said, waving a hand toward Bree. "And the hunted," He added, placing a hand over his breast.

"I can't let you leave here," Bree said, swallowing hard before wiping the back of her hand across her lips in a vain attempt to wipe away the blood.

"Who says I want to leave?" the stranger leapt at Bree and hit her with a punch that would have killed an ordinary man. She flew backward, crashing through the thin wall of the room and out into the muddy street below.

Bree's head swam at the surprise strike. Her ears rang loudly in her head as they throbbed painfully. Stars danced around the edges of her vision. She moaned as she tried to push the pain away. She glanced toward the hole in the wall and saw the stranger staring at her, a smile plastered to his smooth, pale face. He jumped down, landing in the mud with a plop.

"I suppose introductions are in order if we're to be fighting here in the street, like some sort of drunken brawl. My name is Varris. I know who you are, Bree. And I must say, it's a pleasure to meet the famed vampire slayer of Fort Pointe," Varris said with a bow. "You've been a busy girl, killing all our brethren. It's almost like you don't like our family. Well, do you?"

Bree rolled to her side and stood shakily. Her chest ached and burned with the sensation of pins piercing her flesh as she began to heal from the blow. "Your kind is a blight on this world."

Varris laughed hollowly and circled her, a viper ready to strike. "Me? That is hypocritical, don't you think? You're the one who just fed on that man up there."

"I'm not like you," Bree spat.

"No, I guess you're not, are you? You can walk in the sun, so I've been told. Among other things." He stopped and regarded her levelly. "You're still a monster, like us."

The sound of their fighting caused the tavern to empty into the streets, while others passing by stopped to watch. Whispers washed over the crowd as they began to speculate about the events.

"I'll stop you here, now," Bree said as she clenched a fist at her side, oblivious to the growing audience.

"You may," Varris grinned evilly. "But really, I just need to keep you busy."

"Wha—" Bree was interrupted by Varris's fist suddenly appearing in front of her. She managed to turn away, his blow grazing her shoulder as he brushed past.

Varris whirled around in an attempt to backhand Bree. She dodged it and punched the vampire in the side, sending him sprawling to the ground. He scrambled to his feet and attempted to kick her. She held a knee up, blocking the strike. With both fists, she punched him in the chest, feeling the vampire's ribs give beneath the blow. The sound of them cracking reverberated through her fists and up her arms.

The vampire lay in the mud. A smile spread across his thin face. "You're just as strong as the rumors said you were."

"What did you mean you're keeping me busy?" she demanded as she pressed a muddy boot against his exposed throat.

"I was the decoy," he grinned mockingly.

Bree closed her eyes and forced the anger down, allowing the sensation of fear and darkness to overcome her. At the edge of consciousness, she sensed another vampire. It was moving northeast. Her eyes flew open, and she glared down at Varris with a look of horror.

"Now you see, don't you," he laughed. "We wanted you to find us, or rather.... One of us. That man hanging in the butchery was a message for you. To get your attention. All the while, so an assassin can slip right past you."

Bree stomped down, cutting the vampire's laugh off and snapping its neck. She leaned over and ripped its throat out with her bare hands, causing blackened blood to spill into the muddy street. As she stood, she heard the horrific screams of the onlookers. The barbaric sight of her caused them to run in fear. She watched them as they scattered like cockroaches from a flame. They were oblivious to the truth of what happened tonight. She would no longer be welcomed in the town, where she kept them safe from her kind. They had seen her for the monster she was. She cursed herself for having fed off the man in the tavern. She was not like Varris, she told herself, although she knew it was a lie.

She reached up and pulled the hood of her cloak up over her head and disappeared into the shadows of the town, leaving behind the grotesque body of the vampire in the middle of the street. Varris went to great lengths to keep her occupied. She had to find the other vampire. The fear she felt bubbled in the pit of her stomach as she headed northeast out of town. Her hunger sedated, for now. In its place was a deep loathing for her kind. She glanced at the wooden signpost with an arrow pointing along the road out of town. Xonthian City was carved into it and painted in muted white letters. She drew her cloak around herself and set off down the road.

Chapter 1 - Trial of Life

Throngs of merchants pushed and shoved their way along the cobblestone road leading to Xonthian City. Tiger pressed his way through them toward the narrow entrance. A calm, early spring breeze carried with it the smell of the ocean that dulled the stench of the grime-covered people surrounding him. His father, a disciplined military man, insisted he kept a structured routine. He would be expected home soon; being late meant he'd have to run laps around the yard. The thought didn't appeal to him. He was tired from chasing pigs that belonged to a poor farmer. That was enough running for today. He had left his friends, Honey and Ryven, back at the farm. He had other obligations today; his father was waiting for him. Training never stopped. Tiger understood deep down his father's reasoning to keep training. Though he wished he could still get away sometimes. He wanted to live his own life. Tiger sighed, irritation building. The people around him needed to move faster; he really did not want to run anymore today.

Large gray towers loomed over his head, with a wall stretching out to either side of the road. He could see Paladins standing guard at the gate, their iron-clad hands gripping swords nearly as tall as him. He adjusted his well-kempt leather jerkin and stood straighter. They were enforcers of magic around the world. Although they could use basic magics themselves, they were absolved of any sin, unlike most other spell casters. They would undergo rigorous training and hold a rite of passage. Or at least that was what Tiger's father had explained. Unlike the city guards, the Paladins scared him. He always gave them a wide berth.

Tiger barged past an enlisted soldier who was shouting at a town guard. Warriors from every corner of the world lined the streets. The war that raged miles away echoed here at the heart of Xonthian. The more mundane City Guards attempted to keep the peace by shouting and pushing their way through the crowd.

"I want to go home to see my wife and kids!" a middle-aged man growled nearby.

"Sir, your country needs you here. Please return to your post," the guard said, pushing the man back toward the city gate. "Deserting is a crime the king does not want to have to prosecute."

"Then the King can fight the war! I haven't even seen active duty yet. Why waste my time?" the man said irritably at the guard.

Tiger thought he had a point, but decided against sticking his nose in the conversation. This was an instance where his father would say, "It was better to observe in silence than interject in ignorance."

The city guard glared at him as he pushed by. "Move!"

Tiger nodded, making sure his long black hair covered the pointed tips of his ears. The city guards might show outward restraint in his lineage, but the enlisted soldier certainly would not. Tolerance of others was not something soldiers were taught, or so his father had warned him. The city guards, and most of the town for that matter, were used to outsiders. Elves, Atticatten, the occasional dwarf. They travelled through the capital with enough frequency; the guards ignored them. Soldiers, on the other hand. Those were mostly mindless killing machines hired and trained for only one reason. Fighting in the war. Their ignorance showed when dealing with people from around the world. Or at least that's what he had heard, safe as he was, tucked away in Xonthian City. Still, he didn't need any attention. And although he was a young man of eighteen summers, he couldn't sneak past anyone; he was too tall. He kept his head low and pushed past them.

Tiger stumbled into a merchant, who glared at him and said, "Watch it, kid!"

The man's breath reeked of foul chewing weed. Tiger tried not to breathe as he apologized profusely. He bowed apologetically and hurried past the gate to the main street toward the city square.

Xonthian City stretched out before Tiger like a living, moving portrait of stone and wood. The buildings were weatherworn from rolling sea storms that washed over the coast. Their peaked roofs packed tightly together along the main thoroughfares that carved the city into quarters. These streets, wide enough for carts and lined with hanging lanterns, branched off in every direction, like veins from a heart, disappearing into the hazy edges of the horizon.

Smoke curled from chimneys, market stalls were open in bursts of color, along with the steady trickle of townsfolk. He noted the way the buildings changed as they stretched outward—modest homes near the edge, larger workshops, and trade halls nearer to the center.

The castle loomed ahead of him like a dark crown, its massive stone walls lined with tooth-like battlements. Purple banners hung from the towers, rippling slightly in the wind. The structure had a stern, almost resentful posture as if it had been built to endure, not impress. Tiger had always thought it looked less like a place of rule and more like a place that remembered too much. There was history in that cold stone.

And then there was the tower of GateHar that kept tugging for his attention, as it always did. Rising just before the castle, it speared the sky in a spiral of pale stone and silver inlay, catching the sun like polished steel. The tower seemed impossibly old, yet untouched by time, as though the years bent around it instead of through it. Its upper levels shimmered slightly in the morning light, half veiled by drifting cloud, reluctant to fully reveal whatever mysteries it held. There was an energy to it, subtle but constant, humming just beneath perception. Tiger looked toward the Stone Flame, where a small group of patrons was gathered at the front door. The tavern and inn sat in one corner of the main square, with a dry goods store, clothing, and a cobbler taking the other three corners. A large fountain sat in the center, water flowing down a white marble statue of the goddess.

"What's going on here?" Someone beside him asked. Tiger leapt upon the ledge of the base of the fountain to try to look above the crowd.

"Looks like Bo and his cronies are arguing with Carv," another onlooker explained. "Pretty heated by the looks of it."

Tiger jumped down and shoved through the sea of sweaty bodies to the tavern. The smell of so many people pressed together was overwhelming and threatened to smother him.

"I don't need to apologize for anything," Carv growled, pointing an accusing finger at the large, burly man in front of him, "You... YOU attacked my wife!"

Carv was a short, older gentleman, well-built, and completely hairless. Bo was the total opposite. He was tall, strong, and covered with dark brown curly hair. His companions, who were currently urging Bo on, were similarly built, though with lesser degrees of hair and not as broad.

"Are you going to take that accusation, Bo?" One of them jeered.

"You threw me out of the tavern for no good reason!" Bo shouted at Carv, "Your wife deserved it!"

"You deserve to be hung by the neck!" Carv growled, his fists clenched tightly.

A half-circle of onlookers was encompassing the front of the inn, eagerly watching the proceedings like a group of school children.

Should he run and get the guards? Should he intervene? He doubted the guards could be bothered by these two bickering idiots when they had a more significant problem of ensuring mercenaries cleared the city, and soldiers did not desert.

"You are an arrogant, sniveling old man!" Bo called, shaking a fist at Carv, "Let us back in, or you'll regret it!"

"No, I refuse to serve you anymore. Go find another hole to drown yourself in," Carv snapped back.

Tiger understood why people might get so angry. Carv's accusations, if true, would be enough for anyone to do things they usually wouldn't. What would he do if someone hurt a loved one, like his father? He hoped he would stand up against the aggressor, for honor, if nothing.

Just as Tiger ruminated on the thought, Bo lunged at Carv with a loud growl. The crowd, including his friends, stood stunned as Bo began to pummel the barkeep with closed, calloused hands. His associates took up defensive positions around the exploding brawl to keep the onlookers from getting too close, though needlessly, Tiger noted, as no one made a move to help the barkeeper.

Most of the onlookers quickly dispersed either to get help or more spectators. Tiger could not tell. But the crowd did thin noticeably. The merchants that made up the other three corners of the square, who had been watching from a distance, finally entered the chaos, trying to push their way toward Carv. The cobbler, a young, strong-armed man, swung at one of Bo's comrades but missed. The other two pounced on Bo, their fists flying in a maelstrom of flesh and blood.

Tiger stood transfixed in the commotion. His heart was racing, his legs unwilling to respond to his commands as he watched helplessly among the chaos.

A few city guards quickly pulled everyone involved away. People scattered like dandelions blowing in the wind. No one wanted to spend the night in jail.

Three guards finally pulled Bo off Carv's motionless body. They pulled him down the street, disappearing within seconds as a mob of people engulfed them.

Tiger looked around and found no one was tending to Carv, not even his business neighbors, who were being escorted away with Bo and the others to the holding cells. He crept over to Carv's body lying in the street.

"Sir?" Tiger whispered, though he did not expect a response.

Carv's face was bleeding profusely. Gashes on his cheek, forehead, neck, ears, and chin oozed red liquid like someone had squashed his face with a broad hammer. A large cut on his bald head bled massive amounts of blood and pooled on the gray stone behind the man's head. Aside from the apparent external damage, Tiger could only imagine what had happened on the inside. The head, his father had told him, was the warrior's greatest asset and the hardest thing to protect. He had told him stories of men hitting their heads and, although they looked uninjured on the outside, they had spasms and died within moments. Tiger had no misgivings about what would happen to him if he didn't help. And quickly.

Tiger's eyes darted around to see if anyone had spotted him next to Carv. No one had. The guards were still busy with the crowd and Bo's lackeys.

Tiger turned his attention back to the body in front of him. He could feel something. Life, maybe? It flowed in a chaotic swirl all around him. Like energy, he could touch physically. He wondered if he had just imagined things. He reached out a trembling hand toward Carv's blood-stained shoulder and felt the pulse of the man's body. It flickered under his fingertips, light and steady. Or maybe Tiger was feeling his own. Its rhythm was gentle, and he couldn't discern its owner.

Tiger began to feel pain and anguish just below the pulse of life. He looked at Carv's eyes and saw nothing but blood and purple flesh. Tiger's hand pressed against Carv's shoulder, and soft light began to radiate around his splayed fingers. At first, he had not noticed it. He was preoccupied with the barkeeper's face. Then, it started to grow in intensity, and as he turned to look at the appendage, Carv began to moan. Misunderstanding it as pain, Tiger tried to pull away, and like his legs a moment ago, his arms were unresponsive. He froze in place.

With detached astonishment, Tiger noticed the wounds on Carv's face began to close. The seeping crimson liquid dried up while the gashes across Carv's flesh closed as if stitched together by some unseen force. His eyes flickered open, and Tiger shot bolt upright. His legs suddenly filled with adrenaline, sparking them into action. He glanced around, his gaze settling on the peddler standing just inside his shop. The man said nothing, his eyes slowly settling on the Paladin opposite of him. Tiger swallowed the lump forming in his throat and pushed his way past the crowd before running toward home. His entire body was shaking with fear. He avoided looking up at the Paladins as he passed, knowing that if they suspected him of casting a spell of any kind, they would cleanse the world of his evil deed. Sweat dripped into his eyes, causing his vision to blur. He stumbled past them and into the street beyond.

He did not stop until he reached the gate to Hon'shu's estate. He swung it open and ran inside. His father was just entering the two-story home when he noticed Tiger dart up the path to the house.

"Gods! What's chasing you?" Hon'shu asked. Grey hair fell around broad shoulders, framing a proud-looking face etched with scars as well as wrinkles.

Tiger shook his head and forced a smile, "Nothing. It's nothing," he panted, "I-I, just wanted to run home."

Hon'shu arched a brow above his scrutinizing stare. In the end, however, he did not push the subject any further. "Hmmm... Get washed up then and join me for dinner."

"Yes, sir," Tiger replied.

As Tiger ran to the bathhouse, he wondered if what he had just witnessed had occurred. Magic was forbidden. How had he caused it? He splashed water on his face from a basin on the table. The rippling surface showed his youthful, smooth features staring at him anxiously. He gazed at the emerald eyes in the water and wondered what he had done. His life would depend on what happened next. If the Paladins of GateHar knew he had cast magic, the gods only knew what they would do to him.

Tiger pushed the fried potatoes absently around on his plate, then stabbed a piece of roast and ate it thoughtfully. His eyes focused intently on his meal, although he didn't see it. His mind was further away. It was no secret he was adopted; he knew nothing of his real parents. It never really mattered to him. His father would likely ship him off to the war. It was either that or eventually be found by the Paladins.

"Is something bothering you?" Hon'shu asked, setting his fork down before taking a sip of wine.

Tiger looked up too quickly, and before he could say, "No." Hon'shu was already scrutinizing him as if he could read his thoughts. In an attempt to circumvent the topic of how he used magic earlier in the day, he decided to bring up a statement that always resulted in an argument.

"I don't want to train anymore. Why do I need it?" Tiger said.

Hon'shu's chest rose and fell in quiet exasperation. "Because you keep getting in fights and because I may not always be there to help you or protect you."

Tiger dropped his fork beside his plate and set his hands on the arms of the chair in irritation. "I'm not going to join the war, or hells—"

"Watch your language."

Tiger sighed. "I've no interest in fighting. Even when I do end up in fights, as I've told you many times before, someone else starts it!" Tiger said.

"It doesn't matter who starts it. If you're the one who has inserted themselves into it, then you must be able to end it," Hon'shu said, steepling his fingers in front of him and regarding Tiger levelly. "Still, you will continue to train until you can beat me. That's a fair compromise and goal."

Tiger looked at his father with narrowed eyes. "I'll never be able to beat you!"

"No, why not?" Hon'shu asked with raised eyebrows.

"You're better than me," Tiger said, slapping his hands down on the table. "You'll always be better than me."

"Don't raise your voice at me," Hon'shu growled, "You will not get better if you don't train. However, that is not the answer I am looking for. If you can tell me the correct answer, you will no longer need training."

"I don't know," Tiger said, forcing the sparks of anger down. "May I be excused, please?"

Hon'shu nodded and watched as Tiger stormed off. His feet thudded heavily up the stairs, and slammed his bedroom door closed behind him.

The smell of stale beer hung heavy around him, as if the air was stained with it. He stepped inside and closed the solid-framed door behind him. The Stone Flame was closed in response to the recent mob and subsequent assault on its current owner. The common room, usually bustling with activity, sat silent. Carv sat at the bar, drinking heavily, his hands shaking from unspent adrenaline. His wife, a blond, average-looking woman, stood behind the counter, wiping a wet cloth down the barman's arm, washing away the blood that had dried there.

"Excuse me. My name is Iro. Iro Storm. I'm investigating the crime that took place outside."

"It's about time," Carv growled. "Bo needs to hang for this!"

"I'm sure he does. But that's not why I'm here."

Carv peered over his shoulder. "What do you mean?"

Iro cleared his throat and sat beside the barkeeper. He flipped the collar of his thigh-length jacket over to reveal a gold crown with four stars over it. The insignia of the Paladins of GateHar. "Pour me some whiskey, won't you…?" he said, glancing at Carv's wife.

"Krystal," she replied with reluctance. She did as instructed, setting the glass down a bit harder than was necessary.

"Thank you," Iro said with a smile, though it didn't reach his eyes. "Ah, good. Now then, to your question. I am here because of the miracle that happened after you were attacked."

"As I told the city guard, I don't know what happened," Carv said. "One minute I was unconscious, the next I was staring up at the sky." He took the bloody rag Krystal had set down to pour drinks and started to wipe his neck.

"So, you didn't see who was using magic?" Iro asked.

"No, I didn't," Carv said.

"And what about you?" Iro turned his attention to Krystal.

"I didn't know what had happened until I found him stumbling into the tavern. I was out back, preparing for today's services," Krystal said, tears of guilt pooling around her wide eyes.

"So, neither of you saw anyone cast anything, yet somehow here you are?" Iro said, glancing between the two tavern owners. He arched a brow. "Anyone else in the crowd I might want to talk to, that might have seen something?"

"Who wasn't there? Everyone was watching," Carv spat.

Iro stood and nodded. His gloved hand tapped rhythmically on the wooden surface, his eyes fixed on the tavern owner. He watched as Carv shifted from one foot to the other. After an uncomfortable amount of time, he finally broke the silence. "As you say, everyone was there. But no one was seen casting a spell." He walked to the door and put a hand on the handle, and before pushing it open, he turned to the two at the bar. "You two seen any break-ins? Notice any blood stains you can't account for?"

"What? No?" Carv said, his brow furrowed. "Why?"

"If no one cast a spell and healed you, or there were no clerics involved in your miraculous recovery, then it stands to reason that maybe you've been turned to a vampire recently," Iro said with a shrug, then chuckled. "But then again, you shouldn't be able to stand the holy light of the sun. Right?"

Carv shot Krystal a worried glance before the door closed behind Iro. The Paladin stood on the stone street, carts thundering up and down the avenue toward their destination. He took a cylindrical roll of paper,

stuffed with dried herbs, and lit one end. He began to puff on the other,

letting out a billow of smoke as his eyes scanned the chaotic scene around

him. The fight had occurred literally in the center of Xonthian City's

busiest street, yet no one saw anything. He took another drag and headed

toward the cobbler who was peering at him from across the street.

Chapter 2 – Reflections of Nightmares

T he leather, high-backed chair held Hon'shu comfortably, protecting his back from the void that threatened to open as if the past were a physical thing. A bottle of whiskey sat on the coffee table beside him, a glass already filled with the amber liquid clasped in his hand, ready to be consumed.

Hon'shu dreaded the evening hours. Try as he might though to make new memories, they failed to overwrite the ones that haunted him.

No one knew the personal battles he fought every night in the fire-lit study he was now sitting in. As far as he was aware, not even Tiger knew.

He thumbed the smooth lines engraved into the crystal tumbler, raised it to his nose, and inhaled deeply. The smell reminded him of peace, campfire stories, and hunting trips with his friends.

He placed the cool glass to his mouth, the smooth liquid touched his lips, and he sighed as it ran down his throat. He stared into the fireplace, hypnotized by the dancing flames.

Hon'shu sat and remembered his first day on the front line of the war against the Fire Isle Mages. How bloody it was, how savage the attacks were from both sides. The charred and ravaged remains of men and beast, the smell of sweat-stained leather, the blood-soaked mud, and singed flesh. The entire first week was enough to cause him to drink. He drowned his sorrows into oblivion and couldn't sleep without the aid of hard liquor after that. Those memories and many like them always came flooding back at night, as if the sun held them at bay. How had he gotten there? He wondered, watching the flames in the fireplace.

He recalled wanting to prove to his family and his peers that he was worthy of being a Swords of Justice soldier. He wanted to show everyone, including himself, that he was more than a highborn snob.

He left home and joined The Swords of Justice. They were strict and disciplined warriors and were, and still are, considered the most elite fighters in the Xonthians' army. They were fearless, savage soldiers who held honor in battle above all else.

Hon'shu remembered meeting his commander, a stout, ruddy man with scars up and down his arms and across his face. His eyes blazed with fury and focused hatred. Nevertheless, he admired the man and followed his orders religiously throughout his time at the front lines.

Hon'shu recalled how his sword sang its song of death as it darted in and out of the greenish Orc horde. A blur of steel, followed by the spray of gore, showered his senses. The red liquid that dripped down his face narrowed his vision. The blood he spilled daily could have filled rivers dozens of times. Yet, fear kept him moving during those first few weeks.

Hon'shu heard his commander howl a battle cry as he tore through the ranks. A spear ricocheted off the man's breastplate, just below the ribcage. The monster that had attacked him did not live long enough to see if his attack had done the commander in.

"Sir!" Hon'shu remembered calling, "There's too many. We need to retreat to the Fort."

"We NEVER retreat!" The commander yelled over the din of battle.

However, the more they killed, the more of them were raised the next day. Necromancers called forth the dead, replenishing what they had slain the day before. The Swords of Justice began to pile the corpses and burn them in great pyres to stem the undead tide. The foul, rancid stench of burning flesh could never be washed from his skin and hair.

"Our men need to heal," Hon'shu had said.

But nothing in all his training had prepared him for what he had seen at Fort Pointe and the Wall of Ages.

He learned early on that the Fire Isle Mages were the embodiment of all that was evil in the world and everything that peace-loving people feared. They were power. Absolute, tainted power. They had hired the Orcs and their kin, and along with the undead, laid siege to all humanity. Their innate ability to bend the very fabric of death caused the use of most magic to become outlawed. Mages that didn't hide their abilities were exiled to the Fire Isles or executed by the Paladins of GateHar.

Back on the battlefield, the commander picked up a discarded sword and embedded it into an Orc's chest, "There is no room for compassion on the battlefield! Now Move!"

Hon'shu fought his way through the Orcs and Mages. Men lay screaming or dying as blood pooled around them.

"Do you smell that?" a fellow soldier asked beside Hon'shu.

The acrid, electrical smell of energy focused on an area just before an explosion was forever etched in his brain.

"Smells like a lightning storm," another soldier said.

"Probably nothing. Let's move out," Hon'shu had told them before taking a few steps.

As he walked away, an explosion sent him flying forward. Molten liquid rained down on him. He ran his hand down his cheek automatically and realized what he thought was water was, in fact, blood. The head of one of the soldiers landed with a wet thump next to him. Its eyes evaporated and withered in their sockets. The man's ghastly stare penetrated his soul.

Months and years passed, and Hon'shu quickly rose in the ranks. So much so that when he reached the rank of colonel, he was brought before the king and made a General instead. He was given command of all the Swords of Justice, as well as recruiting and training.

After a few years of being the King's General, recruitment was higher, and the efficiency of the Swords of Justice was noticeably better. His last great effort to push the Evil Army and the Fire Isle Mages back from the wall affected him the most.

"You want to push the army against the Wall of Ages and take it back all in one campaign?" the king's advisor said incredulously, one day in the Throne Room.

"In essence, yes," Hon'shu had said, "I have been there; I have seen the blind tactics the enemy employs. This will work, my liege."

King Si'ann Alvis studied Hon'shu closely before responding. "What you plan would leave Xonthian City open for attack. Surely such an obvious move would give them pause."

"No, they will not expect it. If we make it look like we are defeated, they will fly forward in wild abandonment," He had assured them.

"Your majesty, you cannot possibly be entertaining the idea," The other advisor pleaded.

Hon'shu had begun to doubt himself. His chest became tight, and his breathing grew strenuous. This was more stressful than leading men into battle against the Orcs, Mages, and undead. He was not fond of the politics involved.

"Do it, but under one condition. You will lead them personally, General Hon'shu," the king had declared.

It only took a month before the battle plan was drawn up, and each commander under him was aware of the tactics. Once again, he found himself stationed at Fort Pointe, leading the Swords of Justice against the Evil Army and the Fire Isle Mages.

By the end of the following month, his battalions were moving south out of Fort Pointe, hidden in the mountains far from sight. Another more extensive group of soldiers had, under his direction, taken up defensive positions east along the road to Xonthian City and Port Orlynns to the south.

"Sir, the Fire Isle Mages are moving east just like you predicted," his scout had reported.

"Good," he replied. He had felt no relief from the news, and the most dangerous part of his strategy was not yet deployed.

The Swords of Justice had moved like a blade through the fields surrounding Fort Pointe, cutting their way through the lines of Mages, Orcs, and undead. Precise, swift, and merciless. Within a single few days, the army had severed the Dark Army's supply lines and driven a wedge deep into their formation. It was exactly as Hon'shu had planned. The timing, the terrain, the bait, it had all been near flawless. The orc battalions, disorganized and hungry, were caught between two fully armed columns of Xonthian's finest warriors. The undead that remained fell in ragged waves, cleaved down beneath steel and holy flame.

It was a perfect maneuver. A military success that would be taught in war colleges for centuries. They called it a turning point. They called him a genius.

But Hon'shu couldn't forget the cost.

He had seen it all. The fields they had crossed were not barren. They were once vineyards and villages, but now burned to ash in the wake of the retreating horde. And in those ruined fields, beneath the relentless sun and the stench of rotting corpses. The Swords of Justice had paid dearly. Men he'd trained beside. Officers he'd raised from squires. Dead. Torn apart by wild charges of berserker orcs. Ripped open by the poisoned claws of the necromancer's thralls. Some had bled out alone in the tall grass, unseen until the crows came. Others had lived long enough to scream for their mothers as medics tried and failed to hold their insides together.

There were moments he still saw when he closed his eyes. A boy no older than sixteen, half his face melted from fire; an older man clutching the hand of a friend already gone, whispering prayers through bloodied teeth. He remembered stepping over bodies to reach the command tent. He remembered realizing some of the fallen had followed his orders and had trusted his strategy. Only to be left behind as the abyss of decay took them.

And yet, they had succeeded. The Wall of Ages was reclaimed. The King had named him head military advisor, his voice full of pride and ceremony as if it were some grand reward for the slaughter.

But there had been no pride in Hon'shu when he accepted it.

Now, in the quiet hush of his living room, lit only by the dim, pulsing glow of dying coals, he watched the last flicker of flame collapse into ash. His arms rested heavily on his knees. They had done everything I asked, and they'd died for it. There would be no force in all the world that would wish that fate on anyone. He wondered if that was why he taught Tiger to fight. The boy had so much potential, so much desire to do what was right. The thought struck Hon'shu like a blade—his son, dressed in the armor of the Swords of Justice. It came without warning and stole the breath from his chest.

Fear clamped down on his heart like a vice. He could almost see it. His son's body was in the mud, eyes wide and still. The image twisted something deep inside him.

He had led men to their deaths. Given orders that changed the course of battles. But the idea of letting his own son walk that path?

That was something he didn't know how to survive. He prayed to the goddess, that whatever he did. It didn't involve fighting in an endless war. Hon'shu emptied the liquor from the glass in his hand and gazed into the expansive emptiness it left behind. He pushed the panic of Tiger joining the Swords of Justice down and subdued the shadow that veiled his heart. The decanter beside him, once full, was now nearly empty. His eyes grew heavy from liquor and long hours staring into the flames of the fire. Finally, he lay his head back and closed his eyes before drifting off into dreamless sleep.

Tiger came down the stairs to get a drink of water. He passed the study and noticed the crystal tumbler his father drank from sitting on the rug in front of the fireplace.

He entered the room. The fire in the stone fireplace was flickering ever so often as if the flame fought for life. The smell of the burning wood filled the room and reminded him of cold winter nights.

Tiger looked over to the leather chair and saw Hon'shu sleeping, his chest slowly rising and falling.

"Fall asleep down here, again?" Tiger whispered.

There was no answer. He didn't expect one.

Tiger walked over to the couch against the wall in front of the window and removed the wool blanket. He ran his hand along the soft fiber before unfolding it. He gently set it over Hon'shu's shoulder and tucked it around him.

"You're not alone. You don't need to fight whatever it is you're fighting on your own," Tiger whispered.

Hon'shu snorted and rolled his head to the other side.

Tiger kissed Hon'shu's cheek. "Good night, Dad."

Chapter 3 – Revelations of Death

Tiger's mind drifted like the clouds above him. The spiky blades of grass poked at his skin through the muslin shirt he wore as he lay on the small knoll in the backyard. Thoughts of how his life had suddenly become more complicated darkened his mood. His heart raced with muted panic and fear.

Last week, he had inadvertently healed a tavern owner. Now, he had to be careful. Any hint that he could use magic would bring down the wrath of the Clerics and their Paladins. The fact that they had not busted down the estate gates meant they either were not aware of what happened or Carv hadn't told them.

He folded his arms behind his head and watched the clouds pass by. The sun bathed him with warmth for brief moments before being covered by a blanket of light grey.

How did he come to this point in his life? What did he do to deserve this? He had always been careful to keep his elven heritage hidden. His mind drifted to better times as he gazed up at the clouds.

"Daddy?" Tiger recalled himself saying when he was a little more than five. "Why is magic forbidden?"

"It is forbidden because Mages use it to bring the long-dead back to life or use it in murder. It is no longer seen as a tool to improve lives but instead to take them," Hon'shu had told him.

"I will change that one day because I want to use it," Tiger had replied.

His father had only smiled at him then. Maybe he did not know how to respond to that statement, or maybe he knew something that Tiger had not. Tiger was, after all, half-elf. His blood gave him a natural affinity for magic. He could see in the dark, which was purely elvish in origin, as well as an empathy toward woodland creatures, among other things.

"Father! Look what followed me!" Tiger had exclaimed one evening when he was a little more than seven years old. "Can I keep him?"

Hon'shu had looked up from the campfire to see Tiger petting a large Dark Forest Panther. It was sleek black, with deep green eyes that had stared at the old warrior, its ears twitching at the buzzing of flies.

"Tiger, where did you find it?" Hon'shu had whispered carefully, not moving a muscle.

"He followed me on my hike around the forest. Can I keep him?"

Hon'shu slowly stood, reaching for his dagger by his side. "No, son, take him back. He cannot live with us in the city."

Tiger had not understood it then. Later that night, Hon'shu had explained to him that the elven people were more attuned to magic and that he had probably drawn the panther to him. Untrained as Tiger was in his abilities, other mysterious incidents would occur.

"Father, Cord's here!" Tiger said one evening when he was nine.

"How...?" Hon'shu had said just before a knock on the door reverberated through the house.

Tiger remembered running to the door and swinging it open to see Cord standing on the porch. Cord was eighteen or so years older than

Tiger was. He was a brother in all but name and visited as often as possible. He was also the one who had found him, abandoned on the side of the road. If it wasn't for Cord, he'd be dead and forgotten. Cord had brought him to Hon'shu in hopes the family friend would raise him as his own. Thankfully, Hon'shu had agreed.

"Hey, young one!" Cord had said that evening years ago, wrapping his strong arms around Tiger. "Good to see you!" His thick Port Orlynns accent was hard to understand at times, but Tiger always listened intently.

"You bring me a new story of adventure?" Tiger beamed.

Cord laughed, "Of course!"

Cord brought tales of his travels, and hours would be spent telling them to the young half-elven boy. The stories mainly consisted of his adventures through Fort Pointe on his way north or his account of daring sea battles on one of Cord's father's frigates. But, regardless of the content, it was always good to see him.

Tiger shook the cobwebs of memories from his mind. Past events faded away, like ghosts passing through the aether. He stood and walked down the knoll toward the house. The estate was a two-story home on High Born Hill, a secluded area west of the city where the city's politicians lived. Unlike their neighbors, however, Tiger and his father lived modest lives. Hon'shu believed in doing housework himself, stating it was degrading to keep hired help. Tiger learned to garden when he was young and helped his father maintain the estate where he could.

Tiger rounded a corner to find Hon'shu working on a bench, fixing the back, where the wood had split from age.

"Hi, Dad," Tiger said. "Need any help?"

Hon'shu looked up at Tiger and shook his head, "I have it in hand, thank you."

Tiger stood there awkwardly for a minute and then took a deep breath. Somehow, between lying on the grass and walking to the house, his mind had concluded he needed to talk to his dad about using magic.

"What would you do if I used magic?" Tiger asked, then quickly added, "Hypothetically, of course."

He hoped he sounded more neutral to Hon'shu than his own ears. In reality, he wanted to run away from Xonthian City and the possibility of being caught by the Paladins. He didn't dare tell his father that, however.

Hon'shu stopped working and sat back on his heels to look at Tiger.

"Has this got something to do with you running home last week?" Hon'shu asked. Clearly, Tiger's attempt at a neutral tone had not fooled his father's keen parental intuition.

"Yes," Tiger said softly. "I accidentally healed Carv."

Hon'shu studied him for a minute and then smiled. "Well, if that's all you did. I wouldn't worry about it," Hon'shu said, turning his attention back to his work. "To answer your question, however, I would probably see if the Clerics of GateHar would train you. If that's what you wanted, of course."

Tiger looked at his father's back, perplexed. "You wouldn't turn me over to the Paladins?"

"You didn't know what you were doing, right?"

"I guess not, no."

Hon'shu's shoulders shrugged before swinging the hammer down onto the wood pin that held the back of the bench in place. "Then why would I do anything but help you find a way to control it?"

"Because magic is outlawed," Tiger said.

Hon'shu stopped working and turned again to face his son. "It's outlawed, in a very specific way. Over the ages, people have incorrectly assumed that all magic is outlawed."

"I don't want to hurt people," Tiger whispered.

Hon'shu smiled and nodded. "I know. Maybe the Clerics could help you figure out how to use the magic you feel around you."

Tiger shrugged. His head hurt from the tension in his shoulders, and it felt like the world was suddenly resting on him. "I don't want to learn."

"Eventually, son, you'll have to choose your own path to walk, your own destiny," Hon'shu said as he stood, placing a weathered hand on Tiger's shoulder.

"What is my destiny? What path should I choose? How would I know what that is?" Tiger asked.

Hon'shu smiled. He knew wisdom rang in his son's words, "Son, the gods will show you that when you are ready. I did not know I wanted to fight in the war until I was given the opportunity to join the Swords of Justice," his father said, looking past Tiger as if seeing a memory sneaking up on them. "You'll know when it happens, it'll feel right."

Tiger fell silent. The future was as clear as mud in the rose gardens around the estate.

"Thank you," Tiger said after a moment of contemplation.

"For what?" Hon'shu asked after removing his hand from his son's shoulder.

"For not flipping out on me about the magic," Tiger replied.

Hon'shu erupted in laughter, lifted his calloused, rough hand to his son's head, and brushed the long black hair aside, revealing half-pointed ears. "It was only a matter of time until your elven blood felt the pull of magic," Hon'shu said with a mirthful smile that sparkled in his eyes.

Tiger laughed then and shook his head away from his grasp. "Yeh, yeh, ok. Fine," Tiger said with a trailing chuckle.

Bree slid quietly through the dark alleyway between the buildings. She caught the scent of a vampire in the air. She was following it as closely as she dared without being seen. She had hunted it northeast from Fort Pointe a week ago to Xonthian City and now she tracked it through the shadows of the vast cityscape.

Her long blonde hair flowed freely down her back. Her crimson eyes were intent and focused with concentration. She felt the evil creature slithering through the shadows ahead of her. Somewhere down the western avenue. She glanced at the fountain, the water gave a smooth, rhythmic cascading jingle as it flowed down over stone tiers, into a large basin. A statue of the Goddess GateHar stood in the center. She would have stayed and studied its beauty longer if it weren't for the tendrils of darkness that pulled at her. The creature's presence made her insides churn as if something slithered in her belly. The closer she got, the stronger the feelings became.

"Where are you headed?" she muttered to herself.

The evil creature moved further away, and she followed. She could not tell exactly where it was, but knew it was nearby. She used it as a beacon and tracked it carefully.

As she walked through the mostly empty streets, Bree barely noticed the occasional beggar or a sleepy guard passing by. They were nothing to her—she was nothing to them. She existed in the margins of the world, where shadows were home, and the cold, bitter taste of death lingered. Her life was a path carved by loss, by the endless hunt for those who would use their power to prey on the helpless. Her soul was a thing she kept locked away, hidden under layers of frigid determination. But at least she had one, unlike the creature she stalked.

She passed the cathedral, its looming structure casting a long shadow across the street. The sounds of the city seemed distant here, muffled by the weight of the stone and the sacred air around it. She barely spared the building a second glance. There were far more dangerous things to worry about than whatever sanctity the cathedral was meant to protect. The vampire she was tracking—he was a far greater threat.

"Ah, smart creature," she murmured, a rare moment of begrudging respect in her voice. She knew it was headed for Highborn Hill. She doubted the creature had any real chance of getting to the king, surrounded by Paladins and Clerics as he was. But the vampire wasn't after the king. No, the smarter move was to strike at one of his generals or advisors. Easier prey. The thought of the vampire slipping through the cracks, unnoticed among the elites, made her stomach twist with cold horror. She quickened her pace, moving faster now, darting from the darkness of one alley to the safety of another shadowed doorway.

She was close now. The city felt different as she neared the gate that led to Highborn Hill. It was a place of wealth and secrets buried beneath polished facades. She had never been one to care for those things. Power was nothing to her, just a mask for the monsters that wore it. She had seen enough power in her long life to despise its false veneer.

She reached the gate and paused, her eyes narrowing as she scanned the area ahead. The guards stood at attention. There would be no way past them without raising suspicion. Every inch of her being screamed at her to be careful, to remain hidden. She'd let the vampire think it was in control for now. She'd let it think it moved unseen, and then, when the time was right she'd strike.

"You hear the King will announce a new strategy for the war soon?" one of the guards said from under the portcullis.

"Naw, I doubt he will. It's probably just an attempt to boost morale," the other one said, stifling a yawn.

Bree pressed herself against the wall a few yards from the gate. No use but to go over it. Bree turned and leapt over the high stone wall in a single upward push. She landed on the other side with an eerie silence. She knelt for a moment to assure herself that no one had heard or seen her. Confirming that none of the guards had raised the alarm, she darted toward a copse of trees and then up the hill.

The vile vampire she was hunting had stopped moving, and the feelings in her stomach grew stronger as she drew closer. The hairs on the back of her neck prickled with anticipation. She jumped over another stone wall into the courtyard of a large mansion, where a single light flickered in a downstairs window.

She crept toward the house and spotted her prey dart up the wall into an open window on the second floor. She followed suit, leaving enough distance to avoid detection. Landing in the open window with practiced skill, she looked around the dark interior. The room was modestly furnished with a large oak bed, several drawers, and an armoire. Next to the dark dressing closet was a water basin, a pitcher, and a mirror on the wall above it.

She snuck carefully to the open door and peered into the dimly lit hallway, where she saw the creature's shadow disappear downstairs. She crept through the empty corridor to a large staircase that spiraled down, ending just before the front door.

Bree dropped to the ground floor and then bounded through the open door where the light was emanating from. Once inside, she saw the vampire. Standing over a corpse, blood pooling around the elder man's throat. A young man screamed. She remembered that sound all too well. It was a bloody, horror-filled scream. The kind a child would make as they woke, the lines of reality and nightmare blurring into one single, skin-prickling cry.

The youth lunged at the creature; his attacks were sloppy.

She was too late to save the man who sat in front of a raging fireplace, but if she didn't do something, the child would be next.

Tiger bolted up in bed, the sound of something crashing downstairs fading from his ears. He was not sure if he had dreamt it or if he actually heard it. Drowsiness caused reality and his dreams to blur into a single hazy memory.

"Father?" he said before darting from his room. The sound of glass breaking echoed through the floorboards.

He ran down the stairs to the study and saw his father's corpse fall to the floor. A man dressed in form-fitting black cloth licked his bloody lips while an evil grin played across his face.

"You are too late," he hissed through sharp fangs.

"Noooo!" Tiger yelled, his eyes blurry with tears. He grabbed his father's short sword that hung on the wall beside the door and lashed out at the monster.

The evil creature laughed mockingly, easily side-stepping Tiger's attempt to gut him.

Tiger shifted around with the tip of the sword, passing harmlessly by the vampire's midsection. He lunged forward and came down and then up with the sword, but missed. The creature was too fast. Tears stung Tiger's eyes. Fear and hatred filled his chest. He was having a hard time breathing despite all Hon'shu's training. He could not focus. He wanted to die too, his only family now gone, torn from the world by the evil monster in front of him.

"I tire of this," the vampire said. He knocked Tiger's thrust aside and backhanded him hard across the jaw.

Tiger's head snapped back, and he flew across the room, landing against the bookcase opposite the fireplace with a loud, bone-crushing thump. Stars danced in his eyes just before he lost consciousness. Tiger's last thought was of his father and how he hoped to see him soon.

Chapter 4 – Fate's Path to Destiny

The pain woke him. Every bone in his body felt like it had been crushed by a stampeding horse. His head throbbed, and the nausea was beyond control. He threw up last night's dinner onto the floor beside the bed. He hoped he had died, but the fact that he was in his bed, in pain and not encased in earth's firm embrace, proved his mortal existence.

He sat and tried to gain control of himself. His heart pounded loudly in his chest. Its rhythm soothed his racing mind as last night's horror came back to him.

"Father..." he whispered through sticky, vomit-coated lips.

Tiger stumbled to the bedroom door. *How did he get back up here?* he wondered.

Tiger's father was dead, and he was forced to relive all of last night's grim scenery in his mind. He tried to push it aside, but it did little good. It was as if a nightmare had burst from the darkest corner of his mind to mock him.

He headed downstairs to the study and braced himself before entering the archway.

The sight that greeted him was worse than any nightmare. Blood and gore were splattered from the wall to the ceiling and all over the brown leather chair in front of the fireplace. Tiger's father lay pale on the floor beside the small table. His whiskey decanter was toppled, and only a few sips remained in the glass container.

A pile of ash lay a few feet away in front of the bookcase where Tiger remembered landing. Hon'shu's short sword lay beside it where it had fallen.

"Ash? W-what happened? What's going on?" he walked to his father's corpse and dropped to his knees. Tears welled in his eyes again, and anger bubbled up from the depths of his soul. He held Hon'shu's blood-encrusted head in his lap. "Father..." he choked before crying harder than he ever had.

"Your father was a brave and honorable man," one of the city guards said, "I'm truly sorry for your loss."

The guards, along with a cleric, arrived early in the afternoon after passing neighbors heard Tiger's uncontrollable sobbing. They arrived to find the young man, cradling his father in his arms, covered in blood. Tiger was finally able to calm down enough to explain last night's events, leaving the cleric and the guardsmen visibly shaken.

"That explains the savagery," the city guard muttered.

The cleric's expression blanched. "If vampires are here in the city, that means the Fire Isle Mages have grown bold."

"How so?" the guard asked as he covered the elder man's corpse with a blanket.

They seemed to completely forget Tiger's presence beside his father's body.

"For a long time now, it had been rumored that the Fire Isle Mages had control or were being controlled by a powerful vampire lord. If they are attacking this far into the province, it must mean they've become desperate." The cleric walked over to a pile of ash on the ground. Everything was singed within a few feet. "The question is, however, who killed the vampire?"

"Well?" the city guard asked as he stood and peered down at him.

Tiger shook his head.

"Come, my son, let's take your father to the king and prepare a service fit for a noble," the cleric said, laying a solemn hand on Tiger's shoulder.

Hon'shu was draped in white cloth and loaded onto a cart. Specks of blood peppered the surface where they had been rehydrated by Tiger's tears. The walk back toward the city was long and lonely, despite the accompaniment of guards and the cleric.

People began to line the streets as word spread like fire through dry grass. He could hear them gasp as they realized who lay in the cart under the shroud. Hon'shu was a hero of the war, and the implications of his death would be felt around the kingdom. The Swords of Justice would no doubt be hugely demoralized once they found out.

Tiger was now an orphan. With his magical abilities starting to manifest, he needed his father more than ever. His heart filled with regret at the thought of not being able to tell him. The Paladins would kill him when they found out he healed someone. Any protection Hon'shu might have afforded him was now gone. The prospect of death suddenly did not sound so bad. At least he would be reunited with his father.

Tiger shuffled behind the cart, head downcast in shame, guilt, and loss. His heart ached. His senses became detached as if he was seeing his life through someone else's eyes.

The cart rounded the corner to the castle, where the guards stopped them briefly. Upon seeing the small caravan's contents, they were quickly ushered into the inner courtyard, where a few more guards greeted them.

Tiger had been to the castle several times growing up. It sat on the shores of the Irga Straight to the north. He looked around the outer curtained walls that encompassed the castle, court stables, and emergency armament, as well as the King's Guards barracks. Large buttresses reinforced the wall facing the water on both its northern and western façades. Waves crashed against walls and were noticeable even over the commotion their appearance had made. A large statue of the King Warrior Xonthian stood in the center of the courtyard, welcoming guests with an open hand, while the other held a spear. Even though he had spent some time in the castle, there were even fewer times he had been left to wander off alone. Despite that, he knew it inside and out. The most impressive part lay inside the main wall, where a large garden outlined by a stream ran from the outer wall into the city's waterworks. The castle itself consisted of the main body with two distinct wings. The northern wing that ran along the beach was the royal quarters where the king, his family, and close advisors lived. The other, the south wing, housed the servants and prominent guests.

"Please wait here a moment," one of the guards said before disappearing through a door that led to the Royal Wing.

A few moments passed, and the king, along with his wife and five-year-old son, followed the King's General, a man Tiger knew as Oskar Salomo and a spiritual adviser, Kendrick.

"Tiger, I'm so sorry for your loss," the king said, bowing slightly, "Please accept my sincere condolences."

Tiger felt lost in a hazy dream. Nothing seemed real. He only nodded to the king in reply.

A few hours passed, and then the preparation for Hon'shu's burial was completed. Tiger had said little during the arrangements, and the longer he sat, the more he felt stifled by his surroundings.

"Please excuse me," Tiger said politely before leaving the table where they were now talking about the consequences of his father's death.

He walked out to the garden and knelt in front of the statue there. It was a beautifully sculpted maiden with a crown of stars. He recognized her as the goddess GateHar. He was not normally a religious person, and he felt it was a futile act to kneel before a stone representation of the goddess. This time, however, he fell to his knees and looked up at the statue.

His father never guided him to the gods for answers. Instead, he had been taught that all men's answers lay within themselves.

"I beg you..." he whispered, "What should I do?"

There was no response.

"Please... Show me the way," his voice cracked in muted fear.

"Statues don't generally tell you which way to go," a soft voice called behind him.

Tiger stood quickly and spun around. It was the queen with Prince Si'ann Alvis the Third in tow. She was stout, but pleasant to look at. Her long raven hair sparkled in the early evening light, with slivers of gray shimmering in its depths, a sign of her age.

"Queen Arabelle," Tiger said politely.

"Directions can be subjective. There could be more than one way to reach a destination," she said, smiling softly. "I was not aware that you and Hon'shu were religious."

"We're not," Tiger replied.

"May I?" she asked, waving to a spot beside Tiger.

"Of course."

She took a few graceful steps beside Tiger and peered up at the statue. "The Goddess teaches all who listen that life is only one side of a coin. When I was young, I went to Angelic Island on a pilgrimage. While I was there, I spent several days in prayer. I don't even know why; it just felt right. Like it was something I had to do. Sometimes it's ok to seek guidance. No one will think less of you."

"What did the goddess teach you?"

A thin smile spread across her face. bitter in how it tugged at the corner of her mouth. "Life and death are a part of life. A part of the same coin. Without one, there can not be the other."

Tiger nodded in understanding, "I feel lost in an ocean of uncertainty," He explained, turning back to the statue of GateHar, "I... I don't know what to do... I shouldn't have to think about these things."

"I can't give you direction, but what I can say is that reaching your destiny begins with that first step," Queen Arabelle said simply, "Feeling pity for yourself will not help you."

Tiger knelt again in front of the statue and bowed his head, "My father said he didn't want me to join the Swords of Justice. But now that he is gone, maybe I should."

"Joining them could bring you great honor. Nevertheless, it could also bring about a swift death. Take heart in Hon'shu's wisdom, would he ask you to forfeit your life because of his?" She said, kneeling beside him on the grass, "There will be a time when you will need his wisdom. Don't squander his gifts by throwing away your life."

"I hate them."

"Hate who?"

"The Fire Isle Mages. They did this. They need to pay."

The queen set a hand on Tiger's shoulder and peered down into his green eyes. "Hate is not the answer. The war drains and weighs on us all. Only the gods remember why it even started. We're at a point where we can't stop because doing so would put our way of life at risk. Millions would die."

"Magic should never have been outlawed," Tiger muttered.

"Perhaps not. The kings of old did the best they could. It's our choice now to see it through."

Tiger had an overwhelming urge to run as fast and as far as he could, and the worst part was, he didn't understand why. Not then, not in the emotional typhoon he was wading through.

Before he could act on that impulse, a spark of recollection struck him. Magic. This was all because of magic, his source of pain, the world's problems. It was all because of the greed men had for magic. Cord had told him once how he found Tiger on the side of the road south of Xonthian City. Alongside him was a sword. Cord had warned that the sword could not be touched and that anyone who had tried had suffered an injury. He had the sudden urge to see it for himself. If it were as powerful as his stories said it was, then maybe it would take the pain away. This was, of course, assuming the Clerics and the Paladins had not already disposed of the enchanted blade. It was a chance he was willing to take. If he did not find it, he could continue to Fort Pointe and join the Swords of Justice. Doing anything was better than wallowing in pain and anguish.

Aside from this, he didn't know where he would go. He didn't want to return home. It no longer felt safe, and he didn't know if he could sleep in the house where his father was murdered. Maybe he could find Cord in Port Orlynns and live with him.

The queen leaned sideways and whispered. "Want to know what else she said?" she asked, jutting a chin in the direction of the statue.

The question snapped his attention to the present. "Yes."

"I was going to become queen and have a castle full of children running around. I would become the most blessed queen in history."

Tiger gave her a weak smile.

She giggled. "Where will you go?" she asked with concern before standing once again.

Tiger stood too and looked out over the wall to the setting sun, "South."

"There are lots of things south of here," she said, setting a gentle hand on his shoulder, and added, "Don't choose the wrong path, or it might consume you."

He nodded in agreement. "Thank you, your majesty."

She smiled brightly. "You're welcome. You'll always be welcome in the castle, Lord Tiger."

There was little in the way of memorabilia in the house. It had simple decorations and was moderately furnished. Despite the plain interior, every room held some type of fond memory for Tiger. The kitchen was where he and Hon'shu would make breakfast or dinner together. The study was where they would read or learn history. Every room he entered, to make sure there was nothing of monetary value, kept tugging at his heart.

He remembered breaking an Atticatten pot in the library once, at the age of five. He recalled the incident as if it were yesterday.

"Father. I'm sorry," Tiger had said solemnly to Hon'shu, who had come running into the study when he heard a loud crash echo through the house. "I'm sorry!"

It was valuable because not only was it a rare piece of work, but it held personal meaning for his father. Tiger felt so guilty for breaking it, guilt that plagued him for several days afterward and would return powerfully whenever he thought about it. Hon'shu tried not show any outward disappointment, but Tiger knew better and always felt his father blamed him for the loss.

The guilt he felt returned now as he stood in the study. He felt not only the loss but also the failure of having seemingly given up on his father. The dried pool of blood on the wooden floor brought back the night his father was murdered two weeks ago. It was like a flood of cold water sweeping him away. He had not slept in the house since. Mainly because he was reminded of the horror and how he was unable to avenge his father's death. The idea sat hard in the pit of his stomach.

Tiger walked over to his desk and rifled through the mahogany drawers, trying to avoid the feelings welling up inside. He did not expect to find anything of much value. Anything that did have significant resale value, like jewelry, gold, and armor, was kept in the Royal Vault. Tiger asked the king and his treasurer to hold onto those possessions until he could figure out what to do with them. Tiger knew some of the vault's contents. They were valuable, and he did not feel comfortable selling his father's prized possessions to the highest bidder.

Tiger pulled some documents from the drawers and set them on the desk, then scanned their contents carefully. Hon'shu's elegant handwriting made the reading easy. The pages consisted mostly of random thoughts on military strategy, supplies needed, and where they would be best utilized, as well as bills and a few lines of credit. He set the latter aside to settle the debt with the creditor after selling the house. The military strategy he stuffed into a pocket, making a mental note to add them to his journal later. The rest, he tossed into the fireplace.

"Leaving so soon?" a voice from the door called.

Tiger's heart leapt in his chest, and he turned to see a well-dressed man with a thigh-length black and blue coat standing at the entry to the study. "Who—?"

"Sorry, didn't mean to startle you, son. Name's Iro. My regards to your father," he said before taking a step into the study. "How'd he die?" The man's face held an air of authority. Gritty, but well-shaven and kept. His cold grey eyes set Tiger with an accusatory glare, as if he were judging him.

"Who are you?" Tiger said.

The man stopped and flipped his collar aside to show the insignia for GateHar. Tiger barely kept himself from stumbling away in fear.

Iro's thin lips parted in a sly smile. He had noticed Tiger's change in demeanor.

"A Paladin?"

"Indeed," he said, peering at Tiger as if he were judging him where he stood. "So, how'd he die?"

"H-he was attacked in the middle of the night, a vampire," Tiger said, swallowing hard before continuing. "A vampire killed him."

"Is that so?" Iro continued to survey the room as he paced along the fireplace mantle, his finger tracing the edge of the wood as if appraising it. "And where were you?"

"Asleep upstairs," Tiger replied.

"And did you come down to your father's aid?"

"Yes."

Iro stopped at the desk and opened a drawer. Tiger had already cleared them all out. He was fishing, Tiger realized. Wasn't he? The Paladin turned toward the stains in the carpet and jutted a chin at the two spots. Both were black, but the blood was unmistakable, while the spot where the pile of ash had been was grey and not as dark. "Is that where you found him?"

"Yes," Tiger said. His hands were sweaty, and he rubbed them on his pants legs.

Iro peered at him. "Couldn't heal him?"

Tiger's heart leapt into his throat. It took every ounce of will to keep from responding. Finally, after what felt like a lifetime, he said. "I don't know what you mean. I'm not a cleric."

"No, you're not," Iro said as he walked over to him and stared down the length of a hawkish nose. "By the looks of your ears, I'd say you're at least part elf. Is that true?"

"Shouldn't you be looking for whoever killed my father?"

"I think we know what happened to your father's killer," Iro said.

Tiger stared at the man, he was suddenly cold, as sweat trickled down his spine. "I don't know what you mean."

"If you're not a cleric, then that makes you a mage," Iro turned to peer at the ash stain in the carpet. "Only a mage could have burnt a vampire in its tracks."

"I'm not a mage," Tiger muttered.

"Then what are you?" Iro asked, a brow raised in question.

"I'm a grieving son who lost his father. I don't know what happened last night. I came down and found my father lying dead on the floor, and a pile of ash next to him."

Iro nodded before heading toward the hallway, he stopped in the archway and peered over his shoulder at Tiger. "You know Carv?"

Tiger swallowed the lump in this throat. "Yes?"

"Pretty interesting that he was healed, don't you think?"

Tiger paused, then replied. "I wouldn't know what you're talking about."

Iro snorted and walked down the hall, his heavy boots eerily silent as he disappeared outside.

Tiger stood in the study, his legs shaking as the fear of being arrested by the Paladin began to dissipate. The adrenaline suddenly leaving his limbs. He couldn't shake the feeling, however, that he had not seen the last of Iro. He wanted desperately to leave, even if the destination was unclear.

Tiger walked over to the short sword lying undisturbed on the floor where it had fallen. He bent down and picked it up, its silvery surface reflecting the evening sun that shone through the window beside him.

"The sword is an extension of the warrior that wields it. Don't ever let it fall to ruin, or so shall you," his father's words echoed in his head as if from the grave. "The sword shall be your grace, your vengeance, and your honor. Train it, and it will protect you and your loved ones."

Tiger clenched his teeth. "I must train myself to be better. I have failed you, Father."

He walked over to the sheath still hanging on the wall next to the door and replaced the sword. He grabbed both off the peg it hung by and left the house, leaving the estate behind for the last time.

Tiger walked across town to the military cemetery just east of the city. Its monumental statue of the first king and warrior the city was named after, Xonthian, stood before him, its massive form guarding the burial grounds. The glistening white marble served as a beacon to lost souls, calling them to him to rest forever in his presence. He rounded the statue and came to the crypt where his father was buried. He fell to his knees before the small stone plaque commemorating his father's achievements.

"I have to leave you, Father. I must find my destiny, and right now, the only way I know how is to first find out where I came from," Tiger said, bowing his head in prayer. "I'm going to find the sword you and Cord told me about. Travelers in the taverns still speak of it, and all agree it has not yet been removed by Paladins."

A dog crashed through the foliage beside the grave. He stopped and stared at Tiger. After a brief pause, the shaggy-looking creature padded its way to Tiger.

"You scared me," Tiger muttered.

The dog tilted his head at him, barked once, and then leaned in to smell the young grieving boy.

A smile tugged at Tiger's dour demeanor. "Go on, I'll be ok."

The dog looked up at him before bounding off toward the bushes and disappearing.

Tiger turned his attention back to the grave and placed his father's short sword down in front of the tomb, caressing the hilt longingly before sitting back on his heels, "I love you and am sorry for my failure. I'll be with you soon."

Tiger stood and marched off toward the distant horizon, leaving behind the last remnants of his attachment to Xonthian City. The road before him was as barren as the open sea and hungry to engulf his first step, like water washing away footprints in the sand.

Chapter 5 – Soul and the Sword

The days blurred together. Tiger began to wonder if he'd ever find the sword. The road, though well-traveled, offered little companionship beyond the occasional distant rumble of wagons or the fleeting shadows of passersby hurrying southward. As he sat on the side of the road, he heard the sound of voices approach. A group made up of women, older men, wounded, and hollow-eyed children clutching bundles of meager belongings. Their clothes hung in tatters, stained with the soot of burned villages, and their faces bore the etched lines of exhaustion and loss. They moved slowly, like ghosts fleeing the light of the sun. They paused when they spotted Tiger rummaging near the roadside foliage, his wild appearance mirroring their own dishevelment.

One of the men, a broad-shouldered figure with a scarred cheek and a limp, stepped forward warily. "You look like you've seen better days," he called out, his voice rough from thirst or smoke. "Searching for something? Best not linger here. The guards patrol this stretch, and they don't take kindly to loiterers poking around. We've been hurried along more than once already."

Tiger straightened, wiping dirt from his hands, his throat tight with the weight of his despair. He had no desire for talk, but the group eyed him with a mix of curiosity and suspicion, blocking the path as they rested. A woman beside the man, holding a toddler close, narrowed her eyes. "He's after that sword, isn't he? The ones the guards warned us about. They claimed the Clerics told them it's a relic of the old wars, tainted by Mage blood. Touch it, and you're killed, or severely wounded." The others murmured agreement, shifting uneasily.

Another refugee, barely older than the first man, spat on the ground. "Fool's errand. We've heard tales from travelers heading south of fools like you getting dragged off by patrols for digging around that spot. Called them threats to the peace, or worse, Mage spies. Locked away, if the stories are true. And for what? More power? The world's broken enough without stirring up more darkness."

Tiger felt a surge of irritation mingled with growing hopelessness. These people, fleeing the very Mages who had stolen his father, spoke of caution, while he only wanted. What exactly? Yet their words gnawed at him, echoing his own doubts that the sword's magic would repel him or end him swiftly, a twisted mercy. "I know the risks," he muttered, his voice low and edged with bitterness. "But some things are worth dying for."

The scarred man shook his head, gesturing for the group to move on. "Suit yourself, lad. But if the patrols catch you digging, don't say we didn't warn you." With that, they continued north, leaving Tiger alone once more, their warnings lingering like smoke in the air.

He continued his search. His clothes became clumped with dirt, and his hair was unkempt. He looked wild. After several more days of hunting, he dropped his pack beside his feed. He had only packed enough food for two weeks' worth of travel, and yet he was barely halfway to Fort Pointe. The dried meats and hard biscuits had dwindled to a few scraps, rationed so thinly that his stomach growled constantly. He sank to the roadside, pulling the pack open with trembling fingers, and stared at the remnants: a strip of jerky no bigger than his pinky, crusted with salt and mold spots, and half a biscuit. Stale. He broke off a piece, the dry crumb sticking to his parched tongue as he chewed mechanically, each swallow a reminder of the miles still ahead. The taste was ash in his mouth, fueling the gnawing thought that starvation might claim him before the sword ever did, his body wasting away like the hope that had driven him here. If he did not find the sword soon, he would have to give up and move on—or worse, starve on this forsaken stretch of road, his body left for the crows as another fool claimed by the forest's shadows. The idea fueled a desperate urgency; he couldn't fail now, not when every empty bite reminded him of the life slipping away. His father's dead body flashed in his memory, sharp, a shard of glass piercing his thoughts. Would his death be meaningless?

The sun was beginning to sink into the trees, causing the shadows to grow longer across the road. The overgrowth on the side of the road made the search long and tedious, and he did not know exactly what he was looking for.

Tiger pushed deeper into the brush, thorns snagging at his sleeves as he parted vines with dirt-caked hands. His breath came in shallow huffs, the last crumb of biscuit sitting like a stone in his gut. A distant clop of hooves echoed from the road, growing louder. He froze, and a flood of adrenaline suddenly shot through his veins. He fought against the urge to flee like a rabbit scared from hiding. Gruff voices carried through the trees.

He dropped low, flattening against the damp earth behind a tangle of roots. Pebbles dug into his palms as he peered through the leaves. Two guards on horseback trotted into view, their cloaks bearing the faded emblem of GateHar, swords glinting at their hips. One scanned the treeline, his eyes narrowing as if scenting trouble.

Tiger's pulse hammered in his chest. Sweat trickled down his back, mixing with the grime. He pressed his face closer to the ground, and the scent of rotting leaves filled his nostrils. The horses snorted, stamping closer, one guard dismounting to prod at a nearby bush with his boot—mere feet from where Tiger lay. A twig snapped under the man's weight, and Tiger's fingers clenched into fists, nails biting into skin. If they spotted him now, with his wild eyes and empty pack, they'd drag him off as the refugees had warned.

The guard grunted, remounted, and the pair urged their horses onward, their voices fading into the forest's murmur. Tiger waited, chest heaving, until the road fell silent again. Only then did he rise, brushing off the dirt, his legs shaky as the unused adrenaline burned away. Tiger was about to stop for the day when something glittering against a tree caught his eye.

He crawled through the foliage, pushing the plants and vines down under him. He managed to clear away a section around a wide birch tree. His breath caught in his throat as his eyes found the source of reflected light.

Camouflaged under green and brown plants and buried halfway up the blade shone a beautiful sword. The handle appeared to be aged ivory, with a tilted bell-shaped pommel at the end. Set at the slanting edge of the pommel was a gold-colored half-moon, stark against the silvery contrast of the rest of the sword. The cross guard was curved slightly toward the long blade in a wave shape that flattened into a table. At each end sat a claw-shaped blade, giving the entire sword a malicious appearance. Set in the center of the cross guard was an oval-shaped stone he recognized as Tigers-Eye, a brown and gold jewel that shimmered in the late afternoon light. Down the long blade of the sword were runic writings he had never seen before. They were pointed, flowing markings that almost resembled the elvish runes he had seen in books. However, whereas elvish runes flowed as if drawn with a single stroke, these consisted of short, measured strokes with carved patterns.

Tiger's throat became dry, and he found it hard to swallow. The sword that sprang up from the earth before him was even more breathtaking than Cord had described. He was suddenly glad the Clerics of GateHar had not seized it. He reached a tremulous hand out to grasp it, but froze inches from the handle. He recalled Cord's tale of how the sword held power beyond control. That anyone who attempted to pull the sword from the ground would be thrown back in rejection or killed on the spot. With the story echoing in his ears, he quickly grasped the sword. The rush of sensations was like nothing he had experienced, nor could he have predicted.

His head swam in a mass of confusion and light. Then, just as abruptly as it appeared, it evaporated. The world was suddenly vibrant and alive with color. He was not aware of how dark and grey it had appeared before. Where he saw only dread and darkness after his father's death, light once again shone. The shattered fragments of his heart began to heal as if a hand ripped open his chest and forced them to mend. He had no description for the connected feeling it gave. The gap left by his father's passing suddenly began to fill.

For the first time in weeks, Tiger became conscious of where he was, his eyes focused on the shrubs around him, seeing them but also seeing beyond them. He pulled the sword from its earthly grave, and the smooth blade sliding effortlessly out. He held it close, the eerie sensation of the sword's presence soothing his battered spirit, like a touch of a mother's hand upon a baby's cheek. TigerClaw. Was that the sword's name? How did he even know that?

He sat down on the edge of the clearing and laid the sword in his lap. He felt a rush of emotions bubbling in his heart: hope, fear, disgust, and hatred. Hope for a brighter future seemed to be within his grasp. Fear of how he could accomplish that feat tinged those feelings. The prospect of failure in that task weighed heavily on his shoulders. He felt disgusted with the world that had forced him to seek this destiny at the cost of losing someone he loved. He felt hatred, pure unbridled hatred. He hated the war and the Fire Isle Mages. He knew it was the Mages who had ultimately given the order to have Hon'shu assassinated, he hated them because of it. It was because of them that the war raged on around the world. He loathed their kind, their greed, and their lust for power.

Tiger knew now what he had to do, he had to see for himself the devastation. He vowed to himself that wherever he traveled, he would combat the deadly Fire Isle Mages and see that they pay for his father's death, even if it meant dying. He wanted revenge against all the Fire Isle Mages and all the undead hordes they commanded.

Flames licked hungrily at the air. Thier warm glow reflected off his newly found sword like the sun off polished steel. Gold light danced in his eyes, urging his soul to revel in the hatred of his father's killers. As he sat silently next to the fire he'd built, he was unaware of the shadow that shifted just beyond the reach of the firelight. Sharp eyes studied him. They saw the emotions that played on his face.

"Revenge is never as rewarding as one would expect," a voice said softly.

Tiger bolted to his feet, holding the sword in front of him, "Who are you?!" he demanded.

"A friend, I hope," she said soothingly. The woman was beautifully proportioned despite her thin build. She appeared young, with long blond hair. Her complexion was deathly pale and glowed in the fire's presence. But it was her crimson eyes that took his breath away. They radiated power and death underneath their youthful appearance, holding a kind of understanding that spoke volumes.

"What do you want?" He clenched his teeth and studied her fluid movement as she approached cautiously.

"To give you my condolences for your loss," she said with a slight bow of the head. Her body was tightly embraced in black cloth, and strips of various clothing wound around her entire body from neck to just above her boots. Her boots were torn slightly and matched the rest of her attire in color. A black cloak draped over her back as if darkness followed her every step.

"You've done so, now leave," he growled, leveling the sword at her.

"I don't wish you any trouble. If you will listen to me, I'll explain why I am here," she said, holding up a hand to show she was unarmed. "If it helps, my name is Bree."

"Make it quick," he said, unrelenting. He sounded cold, he knew, but after his father's death and being alone on the open road where bandits were known to attack, he didn't feel like giving anyone a chance.

Bree nodded and walked to the fire, where she sat down opposite Tiger, unfazed by his harsh words. She crossed her legs and began to tell him how she saw his father killed.

"I'm a vampire hunter, I guess you could say. I was hunting the vampire that killed your father. Unfortunately, I was too late. I apologize for that." Her voice held a clear tone of remorse.

"The pile of ash. That was you?" he asked, his quizzical mind momentarily forgetting the danger he could be in.

"Yes..." Bree began, "You see, I have an ability to control the air around me, even within others or objects," she said cautiously.

"Are you a mage?" he asked, once again leveling the sword in his hand at her. "You're not a cleric?"

"No," she said, "I'm something worse."

The hair on the back of Tiger's neck stood on end as she spoke, "What are you?"

Bree sighed, "Please understand one thing before I tell you, that, unlike anything you know or think you know about my kind, I am nowhere near as savage and primal."

"What does that mean?" he snapped. "Who are you?"

"I am a vampire," she said softly, watching him closely.

The blood drained from Tiger's face. He froze, whether from fear or panic, he could not tell. His brain urged him to attack now and not let up until one of them lay dead at the other's feet. His heart, on the other hand, told him to hold off. There was something in the way her eyes watched him. He saw compassion in their crimson depths. Vampires were notorious liars, cunning creatures that would talk you willingly to your death. She was not asking him to follow her to the abyss. She was not demanding anything. At least not yet.

"What do you want of me?" he said finally, after several moments of uncomfortable silence.

"Nothing," she replied with a shrug.

"You lie! All vampires want something in return," he said.

"As I said, I am not an ordinary vampire," she replied firmly, "If I were a true vampire, why would I have killed my own kind and moved you safely to your bed? If it is proof you seek, then let me join you. We can walk in the daylight if you so choose."

Tiger arched a brow at her last statement. Vampires were nocturnal and could not withstand the powerful rays of the sun beating down on them. Any vampire caught by the sun's deadly light would be painfully vaporized.

"Why do you want to prove yourself to me? You and your kind owe me nothing," he spat hatefully.

"My kind is why I walk before you today. I share in your hatred for vampires and the Fire Isle Mages. I have seen the destruction they have caused. It was because of them that I am the cursed soul you see before you," she said. "Please, sit, and let's talk."

"I don't trust you," Tiger said.

"I wouldn't expect you to. Would it help to know my name? My name is Bree, and though I rarely use my sire name, it is Sangmu."

Tiger glared at her. He wanted her to so much as twitch, and he would fly over the flames just to run his newfound sword through her unbeating heart.

"I get it, you're angry," Bree said. "Don't let that anger grow so much that you shut down people who only want to help."

"If you wanted to help, why didn't you kill the monster that attacked my father?" Tiger said, his voice cracking. Adrenaline was starting to fade away, leaving him shaky.

She shrugged, "I am sorry for that. I truly am. How would you like me to prove it?"

He blinked at her, "W-what?"

"I tell you what, let's sit here and talk. I won't move from this spot, and when the sun comes up, if I suddenly burst into flames and turn to ash, you'll be rid of me."

Tiger shifted uncomfortably. The sword was growing heavy in his arms, and his anger was fading.

"What's your name?" she asked.

He lowered the weapon and looked across the fire at her smooth face, "Tiger."

"Nice to meet you, Tiger," she said, smiling slightly. The gesture was enough to be warm, but not enough to bare her fangs, and it did not reach her eyes.

The vile, gut-churning darkness he felt from the vampire that killed his father was not present when he looked at Bree. Her sincerity was visible, and he sensed no deception from her.

"I apologize for the way I reacted," he said.

"You have every reason to act the way you did. I would have expected no less. I have been following you since you left Xonthian City and debated whether I should even make myself known to you," she said, looking up to the brightening sky above.

"Why did you decide to confront me?" Tiger said.

"Because I know the anger you feel in your heart and how it can consume you. The path you have started down doesn't lead to anything but more suffering."

"How do you know what I have chosen to do?" Tiger asked defensively, "You don't know me."

Bree shrugged. "I don't need to know you. Let me tell you more about me, and I think you may understand how I claim to know your intent."

Tiger sat across from her, leaving fire to burn between them, tendrils of a small campfire licking pre-dawn void, like a beast clawing its way from the darkness.

"I was a teen when I was taken, twenty years ago," Bree began. "In North Kelsa…"

Chapter 6 – Cattabree Sangmu, the Vampiress

Bree dear? Will you run out and get some eggs, please?" Bree's mother, Awelan, called from the kitchen.

Bree looked in from the door beside the tub of water, where her mother stood, and smiled brightly. "If I have to!" she said.

Her mom flicked water at her and laughed. "Go get me some eggs!" she replied.

Bree giggled and disappeared out the door.

"Eight of them!" she heard her mother add.

Bree returned a few minutes later and set the eggs down beside her mom. Bree's blue eyes sparkled with love. Her mom, tall and fair-skinned, with long blond hair and a freckled face, smiled adoringly at her.

"Thank you, can you milk Sooa, please. I didn't get to her this morning. I need milk," Awelan said. "The bucket is by the door."

Bree muttered as she walked over to the bucket and kicked it over.

"Bree!" her mother snapped, "That's enough of that."

Bree sighed, picked it up, and slowly left the kitchen again to fetch the milk. She hated milking the cows. It was boring, tedious, and smelly. She'd rather be daydreaming or watching the boys in a town sword fight.

The war started in South Kelsa, a week's journey south of where Bree lived. Between them was the Crossroads. This was more or less a rest stop for travelers and merchants on their way from South Kelsa to Xonthian City to the east, on the other side of the Wall of Ages. North Kelsa was of no strategic value to the Fire Isle Mages, who were coming in droves up from South Kelsa. The town where she lived was a simple town, with only enough farmland to support the settlement. People had settled here so long ago that most of Xonthian forgot they even existed.

The men of the town had formed a militia, and many of the older boys were training to join the war effort, or else make sure that if the mages should decide to invade their small town, they would be ready enough to defend themselves.

Bree's mind returned to the task at hand and milked the cow she was told to. She then returned the bucket of milk to her mom.

"Thank you, dear, you want to help me with dinner?" Awelan asked with a smile.

Bree sighed and nodded, "Of course."

The day turned into evening, and dinner was served. Night fell across the town, and everything drew quiet as it typically did.

"That was a great meal, my loves. Thank you," Faen said, with a smile. Bree's father looked between the two women in front of him, his brown eyes sparkling in the candlelight.

Bree grinned, "You're welcome. You can clean the plates."

Faen grabbed at his heart as if wounded, "No, please, not the dishes!"

Her father was of average size, with muscular arms that fit his craft of leatherworking. He was in charge of making armor for the militia when he wasn't fixing saddles or aprons for other folks around town.

The table bubbled in laughter, which was cut short by a knock at the door.

Faen chuckled slightly and stood from the table and went to the door.

He came back to the dining room with a stranger in tow. Bree looked at him and instantly felt uncomfortable at his presence. The man was skinny and pale, even in the bright, orange glow of the candles and fireplace. He wore tattered leather armor and a full steel breastplate, with an emblem she didn't recognize.

"This is Sergeant Todesfall, of the Xonthian Army," Faen said, introducing the man, "He's looking for a place to rest the night, and saw we had a barn."

Bree looked the man over again. His gaze shifted restlessly from one person to another, while a smile that never reached his eyes sat awkwardly on his pocked face.

"I won't be a bother," he said, "My horse and I will sleep in the barn, and be gone by dawn."

Bree's mother smiled and nodded, "Welcome to North Kelsa, Sergeant Todesfall."

Faen nodded and took the stranger outside to show him into the barn.

"I don't like that man," Bree whispered.

Awelan smiled and started to clear away the plates and empty mugs. "It'll be alright, dear," her mom said

Bree helped her mother put the remaining dishes away before turning in for the night. She gave her mom a kiss and her dad a hug and disappeared into her room.

She was just about asleep when she heard a scream that chilled her to the bone. It was terror-filled and unlike anything she had ever heard before. And then, silence. Not even the crickets could be heard chirping their lullaby outside.

She started to leap from her bed when the door to her room flung open. She saw the silhouette of the stranger; streaks of dark crimson ran down his limbs as if he had come in from the rain. The smell reminded Bree of the butcher shop, thick with death and blood.

Bree scrambled to the end of the bed and tried to run, but the man was fast. He grabbed her by the hair and yanked her back onto the bed, pressing his scarred face close to hers.

"You'll be a wonderful prize," he whispered, baring sharp, pointy fangs that dripped with blood.

He slapped her then, and her head snapped back, sending shards of white light flickering across her darkening vision. Just as she passed into unconsciousness, she was flung over the shoulder of the stranger, like a sack of grain.

The next thing Bree remembered was waking up sometime at night, bound and gagged to the back of a horse. The stranger sat erect in the saddle. The pain from the man's strike still reverberated through her skull, and she soon passed out.

Bree woke again to the jostling of movement, and she groaned in pain.

"Pipe down, you brat," Todesfall growled.

Bree looked up to see they were at the Crossroads, a place several days south of North Kelsa.

How long had she been out? she wondered.

The man carried her into the tavern, where several orcs and Fire Isle Mages were laughing and drinking.

"Well, look what we have here," one of the Mages said, looking at Bree and caressing her face.

Todesfall hissed at the man, and he backed away, "She is not meant for you."

"Bah, you vampire scum," the mage spat, "get what you came for and leave."

"We will leave when the sun sets tomorrow," Todesfall growled, "For now, I'll take my meal."

"Your mea—"

Todesfall leapt at the Mage and ripped into his throat. Blood poured from the man's wound as the vampire drank deeply.

The rest of the tavern watched in horror but made no movement to stop the attack. When it was over, Todesfall tossed the man to the floor and sat down next to Bree.

Her eyes were wide with terror. Tears streaked down her face, washing away the days of dirt that had collected around her cheeks and crevices of her eyes.

The next night, and for several nights after, the atrocities continued. An unceasing display of violence that echoed in her memory, no matter how many times she tried to look away.

The routine didn't change until they reached South Kelsa, a week or more after she had been taken from her home.

"Sergeant Todesfall," a Fire Isle Mage said, saluting the vampire as he passed, "We were told to expect you."

"Good, do we have a ship leaving soon?" Todesfall asked the man.

"Aye, we do. Leaves in the morning," the mage replied, grabbing the horse's bridle as Todesfall jumped down.

The vampire nodded and picked Bree up off the back of the horse and carried her toward the docks.

Even though torchlight lit the town's streets, there was darkness everywhere she looked. Doorways were hollow, windows held no warmth, and entire buildings were piles of debris.

They climbed the gangplank to the ship and then dragged her to the belly, where she was chained to the hull with cold manacles.

Rats skittered in and out of her cell as the ship began to move. The wood creaked and moaned with the stress, as if her shrill screams were being echoed by invisible creatures. She drifted off into fitful slumber, waking ever so often to the pinch of a rat gnawing at her skin. Or the pain in her shoulders from the restraints.

She was fed and given water occasionally throughout the trip, though not enough to keep her lips from becoming cracked or her stomach from growling constantly.

The voyage seemed to last an eternity. When it was finally over, she was dragged out into the bright sun, where her eyes were forced to painfully adjust to white-hot light.

"Where am I?" she asked weakly.

The Fire Isle Mage who had dragged her down the ship's gangway to the dock said nothing.

Bree's wrists were sore, and her skin was peeling from under the manacles' rough surface. She was led toward a massive stone keep, made from dark stone and built into the side of a mountain. The peaks spewed smoke, like a chimney built out of the earth. The smell of sulfur hung in the air, not enough to choke, but enough that she knew it was there.

She was dragged inside, where several women were, dressed in thin red robes that would have matched the men's if they were not so sheer as to be see-through.

"Where are you taking me? Where am I?" Bree growled.

"Shhh, we're going to take you to him. But first, we need to wash and bathe you. Clean yourself up," one of the women said as she led Bree further into the castle.

"Him?" Bree asked, "who's Him? Where am I?"

"You are on the Fire Isle," the woman said calmly.

Bree pulled at her chain, but it bit into her, causing her to stumble in pain.

"Don't fight it, you'll be worse off if you fight," the woman warned.

She was taken to a brightly lit room with a stone tub in the middle. Bree felt the chains drop away, and she instinctively started to rub her wrists. They bled in several places along the joint of her thumb where it attached to her wrist.

"Get undressed, please, or we will do it for you," the woman said evenly.

Bree looked at the woman, who was, all in all, a beautiful being. The others were too, with various hair and eye colors. She wondered how they could be here freely as they seemed to be, and not be in terror.

She looked over her shoulder at the door they had come through, but it was closed.

"Now, please," the woman said, more agitated than before.

Bree sighed heavily and did as she was instructed. The women took her old, ratty clothes and helped her into the tub in the center of the room, where they washed her from head to toe. When she was done, she felt much better than she had in a while. The water was the perfect temperature, and it felt good against her battered skin.

When she got out, she was dried off. She looked down at her wrists and saw that the wounds had healed.

"Wha-what happened?" Bree asked.

"The water is imbued with healing, soothing, just enough to help with whatever surface irritations may be bothering you," the woman said with a smile. "We're not savages or prisoners here."

Bree looked at the woman while her finger touched what had been cracked lips, but were now rejuvenated. "Is everything here magic imbued?"

"Mostly, yes," the woman said.

A bell rang from somewhere in the castle, and the women nodded, "It's time. Please put this on."

Bree was given the most beautiful silk gown she had ever seen. It flowed down her body, complementing her young, supple form. The gown was sheer and gold in color. It laced up the back in a weave of gold and silver ribbon.

After she was dressed, she was escorted to another room in the castle where a man was waiting. The entire room was a single circular wall. There were no windows, no doors that she could see, and aside from the desk in front of her, there was little else in the way of furniture. She did notice a twisting staircase behind him, which disappeared into the vaulted ceiling above.

His bony features were held together by taut, white skin, almost the color of alabaster. A wide grin played across his ghoulish face, showing long, pointy fangs. "Ah, you must be my new toy," the man said with a smile that held horrible promises, "You all may leave. She's fine here with me."

The concubines bowed and turned to leave.

"Tell me your name. I am Sangue Bebedor, Lord, of course. You can call me master," the man said.

Bree glared at him, "I'll tell you nothing."

He laughed hollowly and clapped his hands together, "Oh, yes, you'll do just fine."

Bree backed away, Bebedor didn't move, only watched her curiously. She turned to look at the door they had entered, but it was gone. The entire room was a single circular wall. There were no windows, no doors that she could see, and aside from the desk in front of her, there was little else in the way of furniture. She did notice a circular staircase behind him, which disappeared into the vaulted ceiling above.

"There is nowhere you can go, on this entire island, that I won't find you," Bebedor said.

"What do you want with me?" Bree said, tears welling in her eyes.

"To play with you," he said simply.

He moved to her so fast that she didn't even see him get up. His bony hand pulled her blond hair back, and he bent over her, inhaling her scent deeply.

"So fresh," he grinned, licking her lips, "so alive."

He allowed her to go free, and she darted for the only escape she saw. The stairs were made of marble, like the rest of the floor. She stumbled up and emerged into a smaller room with a domed ceiling. A four-poster bed sat in the middle with a table on one side and several chairs and couches.

"So eager," he whispered from behind her, a hand creeping over her shoulder.

She ducked away, then turned to face him, "I'll never give in! Let me go! "

"Oh, please, beg more. That's part of the fun," he replied with an impish grin.

He moved toward her again, and she started to make a dash for the stairs but froze when she noticed the rail that led down had dissolved and disappeared. She was trapped.

"No," she whispered in horror, tears streaking down her face.

"Yes," the vampire growled, inhaling her scent again, "So much fear, and anger. Simply intoxicating."

He caressed a finger down her chin, and she pulled away. But not far enough, his other hand caught her shoulder and pulled her to him.

She tried to kick him where her father taught her to kick when boys were getting too close, but it did no good. Her knee landed with a soft thump, but the vampire made no move of discomfort.

"Stay away!" she yelled.

His smile widened, and bearing his fangs once again, he held her tightly and began to untie her dress.

"No!" she screamed as she tried fruitlessly to hold it against her bosom. It did no good. His grip was like iron manacles, unyielding and cold.

"I'm sorry," Tiger caught himself saying before looking away.

"You didn't do anything, did you? Were you there? Hell, were you even alive then?" Bree said irritably.

Tiger looked at her, saddened, angry, and embarrassed. "No," he said finally in resignation.

"Then don't apologize," she sighed.

"Fine. Continue then, please," Tiger said, cheeks flushing in shame.

"After that first time, it was more of the same for weeks, even months later, it all blurred into one," she said, watching Tiger as he picked up a rock and thumbed it, before tossing it into the fire. "I never gave in; I fought every single time. In the end, it broke him."

Tiger glanced up with a puzzled look, "How do you mean?"

"Never giving in didn't give him what he wanted, which was to see me shatter, to become docile, to become his. I was never his. He grew angry with me one day, and that's when he turned me into a vampire. The pain was… Not what I expected, it was more of a release than anything," she said, taking a stick and shoving a log over in the fire. She watched the sparks fly through the air, then continued. "I remember waking up the next day in his bed, cold, hungry, and angry. I didn't feel dead, but I didn't feel alive either. I don't know what happened, but it seemed to me that I was trapped, so to speak. Something in me was trapped. Like I was caught between two worlds."

Tiger watched her through the orange glow of the fire. "What did you do?"

"When he came to bed again, my anger, rage. It erupted in a torrent around me. An explosive force, as I had never seen, suddenly burst from around me," Bree said through pursed lips. "It's hard to explain."

"Was it magic?" Tiger asked after tossing another log into the fire pit. It crackled angrily and then settled as the smoke engulfed it.

"No, I don't believe it was," Bree replied, shaking her head. "Anyway, after that, I didn't see him again. I presume he's dead. Or at least according to the rumors I heard, he is. I wandered the Fire Isles for a time, feeding off the Mages there. I found a ship headed back to the mainland and stowed away back here."

The sun finally broke over the tree line, bathing their small camp in orange, bright light. Bree cringed but did not attempt to hide from the warm glow. Tiger could see the pain the sun caused, but nothing further happened. After a few moments, Bree's features smoothed out, and she recomposed herself.

"You did all this, so I would trust you?" Tiger asked.

She nodded.

"I don't," he said finally. He stood, sheathed his sword, and picked up his pack.

"Where will you go?" she asked, watching him coolly.

"I'm going to Fort Pointe," Tiger said.

"That would be a waste," she whispered.

"What do you know of it?" Tiger growled, "You're a vampire. Like the one that killed my father!"

"What I know is human nature. I've spent long enough time in the shadows of the world studying how people behave. Sure, you could go to Fort Pointe, and they might allow you to join their ranks. In the end, it will be your death. You are still young; fate has given you a bad turn in life, but you must not give in to depression. You want revenge, but you can't seek it blindly."

"If I wanted vengeance, I should kill you where you sit," Tiger spat.

She shrugged. "That is up to you, of course. Kill me now and continue on to Fort Pointe. I won't stop you. Here, I'll make it easy." She walked over to him and held her arms out to either side, exposing herself to him. "Go on, do it."

He stared at her.

Sensing Tiger wasn't going to take up her offer. She lowered her arms and fixed him with a stern glance. "No? Then let's go back to Xonthian City. I will help you understand life, because who better than someone with a dead heart and frigid blood to teach you of life?" she said, a smile of irony playing across her lips.

Tiger looked in both directions along the road, then back at Bree. "Wait—how can I trust you're not just like the rest? Vampires are killers, mindless assassins for those Fire Isle Mages. That's what the priest said anyway. The one I faced looked feral. Like... Like a monster."

Bree's eyes darkened, her voice dropping to a whisper. "They are. Most of them, anyway. Turned into tools, stripped of their will, driven only by bloodlust. But me... Yet, I'm fighting it every moment. That hunger gnaws at me, whispering I'm no better than a monster. Yet here I stand, not lunging at you, not giving in. I'm less feral because I refused to break, even after he turned me. If I were like the others, you'd be dead already."

Tiger's grip tightened on his sword hilt, his eyes narrowing. "Prove it. How do I know you're not playing me, waiting for my guard to drop?"

"I've shared my pain with you—more than I've told anyone. The Mages use them as weapons, but I escaped that fate, as I said. Let me show you on the road ahead. Walk with me to the city gates, and if I falter, strike me down."

"As long as there is breath in my body, I will help you avenge your father. And know that you do not walk this path alone. I, too, want to see the Fire Isle Mages burn," Bree said. She turned toward Xonthian City and started to walk, leaving Tiger behind. He watched her as she started the long trek toward the future, Bree's figure growing smaller against the rising sun, her steps deliberate, unhurried.

She's a vampire, he thought, the word bitter like ash from the dying fire. Just like the one that tore Father's throat, leaving him dead on the floor. The memory flashed hot, like iron from a smith's furnace, the helpless rage he felt after. How could he walk beside one? Yet her story hung in the air around the camp, those threads of resistance, of not breaking. Her will to survive, despite all the evil in the world. The evil that had tried to undo her.

He glanced toward the road to Fort Pointe: the path promised vengeance—join, train, kill. But he would die there, that was certain. The fort's walls might shelter him for a time, but not quench the fire in his gut, not like the gleam in her eyes at burning the Mages.

A twig snapped under his boot as he shifted, heart pounding. *What if she's right?* he thought. *Going alone ends me before I swing a blade?* The sun rays grew longer, warming the air. Bree didn't falter, didn't glance back. That irritated him more than anything: her confidence, or indifference.

Finally, with a curse under his breath, Tiger adjusted his pack and took a step forward. Then another. He kept his distance, sword hand ready, eyes on her back like a predator watching for weakness. If she turned around, if the bloodlust won, he'd end it. But for now, to the city gates, he'd see what the road revealed. The future stretched ahead, uncertain as shifting shadows under the trees.

Chapter 7 – Shadows of Xonthian City

Could you get a place to live, any closer to the Clerics?" Bree muttered as they strolled down the street toward their new home.

"I'm sure I could have, if you want me to go look," Tiger replied.

"No," she growled.

"Good, because I don't trust you yet, not fully. Just because you can walk in the sun, doesn't mean you're not capable of killing me in my sleep," Tiger said, "I didn't want to come back in the first place. But I did so... We both made sacrifices coming back to the city."

She groaned as they ascended to their new residence, which was little more than a room. "I wasn't planning on staying with you anyway."

"No, but you'd know where I lived. Slept."

"Fair point."

The apartment was the size of Hon'shu's old study, with sparse furnishings and a stone hearth and table near the door. Bree took the bed near the balcony, which looked out into the streets below, allowing her to come and go without disturbing Tiger, who slept across the room from her. Their beds were modest mats, barely high enough off the ground to keep the bugs from sleeping with them. The sound of scurrying feet could be heard coming from the walls and floor at night as they slept, constantly reminding them that they were not alone.

"So, we're here. What now?" Tiger asked, tossing his bag to the floor beside his bed.

"I get you're angry, Tiger. You need to focus that anger toward becoming better," Bree said, smoothing out the sheets on her bed. "Better fighter, better person. You are smart, you have skill. You have your father's teachings, which make you something the Fire Isle Mages could fear, given proper training. And that's what we'll do together. Learn to control your emotions, to hone them into something focused."

"Why? For what end? I don't have anything I—"

Bree moved so fast beside him that he didn't have time to react. "You have more than most," she growled, fangs bare in irritation. "I would kill to be alive right now, to be normal, and to not have to feed off the living!"

Tiger blinked. His hand felt for the hilt of his sword, but she darted away before he could find it.

"You are a child. You have had everything given to you. You lost your parents, and so have many other children out on the streets. So have I. Do you see me wallowing in self-pity?" she asked.

Tiger bowed his head. "No," he said.

"No. You don't," she repeated solemnly.

"You're angry, I get it. But that doesn't achieve anything. Find a way to harness that, and you'll see what I mean when I said you have skill."

They stood in silence. Tiger looked up at her and walked to the door. He left her there in the cold, darkening room.

"I expect you to be gone when I return." The door slammed behind him as he left, echoing through the thin walls.

Bree bowed her head. What had she gotten herself into?

Tiger stormed his way east of the city. He wasn't sure where he was even going. He had to get out of the apartment. The sun was barely a thin line behind him, peeking over the horizon like a sleepy eye. Bree's words echoed in his mind; he wasn't a spoiled child. What had she meant by that? What was he supposed to do? What should he focus his energy on? He glanced up and saw the Swords of Justice compound. The towering structures beyond peered over a stone wall. He could hear shouts coming from the other side. He suddenly had an idea— he should see his father's close friend. Maybe he could still join the Swords of Justice.

As he approached the tall iron and wood gates, he was stopped by a pair of guards, barely older than he was.

"Hey, announce yourself, kid," The brown-haired one said. The other, with black, short-cropped hair, chuckled.

Tiger looked between them, "I'm here to see the commander. Commander Jule Sworren."

"Hey, Mira. Do you hear a buzzing sound?" the black-haired guard said.

The other laughed, "Sounds like a civvy whining."

Mira looked at Tiger and growled, "Get lost, kid."

Tiger ignored them, "I'm here to see Commander Sworren."

"Are you now?" The two guards looked at one another.

"How old are ya, kid?" The second one said, chuckling.

"Young enough to be home suckin' on momma's tit, hey Solice?"

The brown-haired guard roared with laughter.

"What the hells is all the commotion out here?" a gruff voice called from the gate as it swung inward.

"Sir!" both guards said in unison as they saluted.

Tiger recognized the commander from his visits to the castle to see his father.

Commander Jules Sworren was a stout, rough man with a sparse beard and short brown hair. He held the guards' gaze for several moments, then turned his attention to Tiger.

"Ah, Tiger. Please come in," the commander said.

Commander Jules waited for Tiger to pass, and then turned his piercing gaze back to the guards, "You two will report to latrine duty as soon as your guard shift is over. Is that understood?"

"Yes, sir!" the two guards said with a salute.

Sworren led Tiger to his office across the drill yard to a small one-room building.

"Have a seat, son," he said without preamble.

Tiger did as instructed and watched the man cautiously.

Sworren walked over to a sidebar and poured two glasses of amber liquid, then returned, setting one of the glasses down in front of Tiger.

Tiger took the glass and held it up in salute. He held the glass to his lips and inhaled the smooth, charred wood smell of the whiskey before sipping the glass's contents. It burned down his throat and into his chest, causing Tiger to cough involuntarily. Commander Jules chuckled.

"I'm sorry about your father. He was a good man, a great soldier, and an even better friend. I take it you're here to fill some kind of need?" the commander asked.

Tiger set the tumbler of amber liquid down on the desk between them and nodded. He swallowed hard in an attempt to clear his throat, "I'd like to train as a warrior, a Sword of Justice."

"Why? So you can rush off to the Wall of Ages?"

"Yes. I hope to fight there one day," Tiger replied.

Jules looked at him levelly. "Look, Tiger. Hon'shu was my greatest teacher. I'm here because of him. We fought at the wall. I may not know you well enough, but I do know him. And Hon'shu would not want you anywhere near that place."

"No, he wouldn't," Tiger said heavily, "But I must. The Fire Isle Mages killed my father, and I mean to see them suffer for it."

Jules sat back and steepled his fingers together, resting his elbows on the arms of the chair, "Revenge is not a good reason to join the army. In fact, at this point, I'd tell you to go home and come back when you've grown up."

"I won't do that," Tiger replied.

"No, I didn't think you would. I've seen the look in your eyes before. Saw it every morning in the mirror before I joined the Sword of Justice. Determination, purpose, wrath. I wanted to join the Swords for my country, for all its people. Not just one man," Jules said, a tinge of regret creeping into his voice.

"Hon'shu was my only family. He took me in, loved me, and cared for me. When I walk down the street, people stare at me. Do you know what that's like?" Tiger asked, brushing his hair aside to show a short, pointy ear. "I owe him my life, and if it ends up that I end this war too, then so be it. To get there, I need your help."

"You're humble too, I see," Commander Jules said. "Is that ego I sense, or high self-esteem?"

"Fine, I see you're not going to help," Tiger said, planting his hands on the desk as he started to stand.

Jules shook his head, "Don't get me wrong, Tiger, I plan on training you. I plan on taking the rest of your young adult life and wringing it into something resembling a Swords of Justice soldier. I just want you to understand I'm not doing it so you can run to the wall and throw your life away."

"I understand," Tiger said.

"Then report back here before dawn. We'll get you squared away and ready to be forged into sharpened steel," the commander said. "Dismissed."

Tiger stood and bowed slightly, then turned and left. Each footstep pulled him down to earth more heavily than the last, as if the weight of realization had compounded and was dragging him down into despair.

It was midnight by the time he returned to the apartment. Bree was gone. He would only get a few hours of sleep before drills started. He pulled his newfound sword close and fell into a restless sleep.

Chapter 8 – Misguided Youth

Tiger arrived just as the bell to line up clanged loudly through the drill yard. Solice and Mire had been replaced by two new guards, who only narrowed their eyes at him as he entered the gates.

As he did so, men ran to line up, which Tiger did as well. His heart was pounding with mixed fear and panic. Had he arrived too early? he wondered. He tried to find a place to stand but knew nothing of the drills, such as who belonged where or what he was even supposed to do. He had never felt so out of place and lost.

"What in the hells are you doing there? Get in line!" a tall, angry man said with a scar on his cheek and across his bare arms.

Tiger nodded.

"Do you have a problem?" the man yelled, stomping heavily toward Tiger. The man put a thick finger to Tiger's forehead and pushed. "I said, GET IN LINE! You respond with, 'Yes, Sir!'"

"Yes, Sir!" Tiger replied, anger building up in the pit of his stomach.

Before he could say or do anything else, the man turned his attention to the rest of the unit.

"This is why we do not take on spoiled kids from Highborn Hill. Not only is he a half-breed, but a soft-skinned one at that. They don't listen," the drill sergeant yelled.

"Yes, Sir!" came the response of the men lined up.

Tiger sank to the back of the line and found a spot where he fit in, hoping to hide in the back ranks.

"Don't fuck this up for the rest of us," a voice whispered beside him, "You get us extra cleaning duty or something, you'll regret it."

Tiger started to look to see who was whispering, but found the drill sergeant was watching him with a glare.

"Now, since you are all lined up, and time has been wasted, you all will take an extra lap around the compound! Get moving! Get your gear and run!"

"Yes, Sir!"

Tiger followed the rest of the unit as they ran by the master of arms, loaded up on a shield, sword, and pack filled with what felt like rocks, then proceeded to run the radius of the large compound.

By the end of the two laps, Tiger's lungs were on fire. His heart pounded loudly in his ears. He had no time to catch his breath, however. Men were lining up once again in the same spots.

Tiger stood as erect as he could, gulping in air as he was, when something in the back of his nose picked up a slight smell, something he had never experienced. It was the smell of rain. No, that wasn't right. How did it remind him of rain?

"Get down!" he heard the unit commander yell.

Before Tiger knew what was happening, an explosion of air threw him off his feet and back against some crates nearby.

Men scattered, lifting shields and swords as they did, as if preparing to fend off whatever it was that was attacking them.

That smell again, Tiger thought as he stood and grabbed the sword and shield that he was assigned. The large, wooden disk was heavy, and it threw him off balance.

Another explosion rocked the drill yard. This time, more of the men had been flung aside, as if an invisible hand had swept through the ranks. Some crashed into one another, and others landed in the dirt with bones cracking.

Tiger's ears were ringing; he looked around, hopeless and afraid. He glanced toward the rest of the unit. They were starting to form around one another, like a circle of blades and shields.

He started to follow their lead when a firm hand grasped his shoulder. "You're already dead, half-breed."

Tiger looked up to see the fierce brown eyes of the drill sergeant boring into him. Then he noticed the man in white and silver robes beside him, a Cleric of GateHar.

The cleric had cast the spell that had caused the explosion. It was all a test. Tiger thought to himself, the blood draining from his already pallid features.

A whistle blew twice somewhere nearby, and the unit began to relax, sheathing weapons as they formed up once more.

Tiger felt a sharp shove, snapping his head back; he stumbled forward and landed face-first in the dirt. Tears welled in his eyes as pain shot up from a gash on his chin.

"You maggots are all dead. Not one of you detected the telltale sign that magic is about to strike a spot or area. On top of that, the half-breed here got himself killed by leaving the protection of the others. Another lap! Now!" the sergeant growled.

Tiger stood, picked up his gear, and started after the rest of the unit.

When they returned to the drill yard, the sergeant was standing with his arms crossed. The unit lined up, breathing heavily and sweating profusely.

"Drop, twenty-five pushups. Now!" The sergeant yelled as Tiger finally fell in line. Tiger tried to catch his breath, but before he could protest, a boot struck the back of his knee, and he fell forward. He caught himself, barely avoiding scraping more flesh from his chin.

"He said now," the voice beside him hissed.

Tiger stood and grabbed the shirt of the man who had kicked his leg out from under him. With a savage, angry growl, he punched him.

The two began wrestling, each one vying for a position to get on top to pummel the other. Tiger, being the less experienced ground fighter, found himself easily pinned. A large fist slammed into his nose, and he saw stars with a sickening crack.

He felt more than saw the unnamed assailant being dragged off him.

"If you have this much energy for wrestling and fighting like dogs, then you all will get another lap after your pushups. Is that understood?" the sergeant yelled, the words breaking through the ringing in Tiger's head.

"You two, report to Commander Sworren for your punishment," the sergeant yelled.

Tiger was dragged along with his antagonist to the commander's building. They were thrown to the ground in front of the door where the sergeant had entered, who then returned a few moments later with Commander Sworren following behind.

The look of warmth and compassion Tiger had seen the day before was replaced with a scowl and intensity that made the sergeant seem like a puppy.

The sergeant returned to the rest of the unit to oversee their pushups and lap around the compound. Tiger stood in front of the Commander, blood dripping from his nose and chin. Anger burned any sense of pain away.

Sworren circled the two a few times, hands behind his back. A viper coiled and ready to strike.

"You two came here. Why?" he asked.

Tiger started to answer, but was cut short by the sudden glower in Sworren's blazing eyes, "I don't CARE why you came here. NO ONE here cares. But why are you in my yard, in my drills, and in my company of elite soldiers? You will act like men worthy of the title Swords of Justice. Do I make myself CLEAR?"

"Yes, Sir!" the two said in unison.

Commander Sworrens continued to encircle the pair, his eyes never left them, "Now, since you two enjoy each other's company, you will both push the stones around the compound, for the rest of the day. If either of you stops, you will go again, and again, and so on. So, I suggest you two swallow whatever pride you have. Because if you don't, you will beg for the stones when I'm through."

Sworren came to a stop and looked between Tiger and the man beside him, "Do I make myself clear!?"

"Yes, Sir!" they responded.

"Then why are you two standing here? Go!" Commander Sworren shouted.

Tiger ran to the large boulders set aside and started to push. It didn't budge. The rock was even with his shoulders; it didn't look that heavy. It was perfectly round— it should have moved.

The man beside him laughed and began to roll his stone away at a strained, consistent pace.

Tiger tried again; but it moved slightly, then rolled back into its resting spot. Laughter echoed back from the man in front of him. Anger welled in his stomach again, and he pushed harder. A grunt escaped his lips, but it was no use as it rolled back into place.

"You have to be smarter than your opponent, if you ever hope to survive here," Tiger heard Sworren's voice say with pity.

Tiger looked at him, but he had already turned away and walked back to his office.

Anger, pain, despair, failure, and humiliation churned in Tiger's gut like a raging sea. He wanted the waves to wash him away, to drag him into the shadowy depths. He bowed his head in defeat, and as he did, he noticed the boulder was sitting in a half-ring of wood, with one end blocked by a wedge.

Shame flushed his cheeks even further. He was forgetting one of his father's first lessons: "Your mind is the greatest weapon you have.

Imagination and thinking about the problem will always get you out of a bind."

Tiger kicked the wedge aside and began to push once again. With each step, the stone moved an inch, then a foot, then further. The weight of emotions began to charge his muscles as they strained against the boulder.

Pushing the rock along the outer yard only got harder as his energy drained. Sweat dripped into Tiger's eyes. He blinked it away, grunting with each shove. It rolled forward an inch, then another. A shadow fell across his path, causing Tiger to look up.

"I don't begrudge you any, my friend," the soldier said. "Those things are heavy. Takes some getting used to."

Tiger grunted in response but didn't stop.

The soldier kept pace beside him and continued. "Name's Gim. Sorry about Aldrani, bugger has always been short-tempered."

"Lucky. Me," Tiger managed to murmur between pushes.

"Yeah, his parents are vagabonds or something. He'd sell his own mother for glory. Or coin. Hard to tell. Either way, best avoid him if you can."

"Right."

The taller soldier nodded, his grey eyes lingering on Tiger before turning away. "Good luck with the boulder! It gets us all in the end."

Tigers snorted. "Indeed."

The irony of using his anger to fuel his pushing the rock wasn't lost on him. The conversation with Bree when they had arrived suddenly snapped into memory.

"You're angry, I get it. But that doesn't achieve anything. Find a way to harness that, and you'll see what I mean when I said you have skill."

Life was the boulder, and it was heavy. If he let his anger get the best of him, in the end, it'd just roll right over his body and crush him.

As the day wore on, the skin on his hands grew thin and started to bleed as he pushed the boulder continuously along the path that encompassed the compound. Dirt made its way into his boots and dug into the soles of his feet. Each step sent a sharp pain through him, like shards of glass.

Night had started to fall when Sworren stepped out just as Tiger rounded the corner to the drill yard.

"Tiger, that's enough for today. Come by my office in the morning, before drills start," the commander said.

Tiger started to nod, then stopped. "Yes, Sir," he said solemnly and pushed the boulder into the spot where he got it. The other boulder was also in its place, indicating the other soldier had also been relieved.

By the time Tiger had made it back to the apartment, Bree was gone again. It didn't matter, he thought. It was better that he slept alone. It was one less thing he had to worry about. He didn't want to fret about being bitten by her, and even though his sword was close at hand, he wasn't sure he could wield it.

He sat on the edge of the bed and pulled his boots off; he knocked the dirt and rocks out over the balcony, then sat back down. Blood had coated his feet, mixed with the dirt and rock of the training yard. He washed them along with his hands and then wrapped them in aloe. A trick his father taught him after some of his training sessions. Drained from more than just physical exertion, Tiger fell into his bed and slept like a rock.

Tiger knocked on the commander's door. Every muscle in his body, from head to toe, burned as if it had been ripped apart and put back together. The skin on his hands and feet was wrapped as tightly as he could without cutting off circulation.

The commander's door opened and admitted him into the sparsely furnished room.

Tiger stood before the commander's desk at attention. He didn't want to push the boulder again so soon. He was on his best behavior this morning.

Commander Sworren noticed Tiger's posture and smiled, "Well, I see you learn quickly. Good. You may sit."

"Yes, Sir," Tiger replied as he took the offered seat.

"Tiger, I don't know what you think I can help you accomplish, but bringing anger into this regiment will not get you very far," the commander said, holding a hand up, as Tiger started to speak. "Let me finish."

"Yes, Sir," Tiger replied.

The commander sat down across from Tiger and held his hands together, elbows propped on the edge of the desk, "Life is not fair, and you've got to know that by now. There will be worse people than those men out there. Being angry at them will get you as far as pushing that rock did when the wedge was in its way."

"Yes, Sir," Tiger said slowly, unsure what else to say.

"Those men out there, angry as they are for one reason or another, are family," the commander said as the bell for drill rang dully outside. "Yes, you are an outsider. You will have to work extra hard to be welcomed into the unit. Your grudge against your gods and fate has no place here. Bringing them with you will not help your cause."

Tiger stood and bowed slightly. "Yes, Sir."

The commander only watched him a moment, then nodded, "Good."

Tiger opened the door and stepped out into the cool air of the morning. The men were lining up, which Tiger quickly followed, taking his place in the back.

Drills proceeded without any problems. Tiger pushed through the pain of yesterday and forced all of his anger into accomplishing each task with minimal discomfort.

Lunch was called, and the men were ushered into the mess hall where they were given what Tiger could only describe as mushy meat and watery potatoes. He took his tray and started to look for a spot. When he found one, however, his heart sank when he realized it was next to the man who had tripped him yesterday.

Tiger sighed and bowed his head. He swallowed hard as if swallowing the anger he knew was there on the surface back down.

He walked over to the table and looked down at the empty seat, then at the man across from him.

"This spot's taken," he spat.

Tiger looked up. Everyone else was already sitting.

"Look, I don't want any more trouble. Truce?" Tiger said, setting down his tray on the table.

The man looked at Tiger, then the tray, and then swatted it to the ground with a loud clang.

Tiger growled and started to make for the sitting man, but was surprised to find the man was up and jumping across the table before Tiger could even react.

"What in all hells?" the drill sergeant bellowed from his seat.

Tiger held his hands up over his head and did all he could to keep from fighting back.

The sergeant pulled the man off Tiger and looked down at the tray of food scattered across the floor.

"You two again?" the sergeant said, "Fine, you get no food today. And while we're enjoying an easy day of sword practice outside, you two will be in here cleaning every inch of the mess hall."

"Yes, Sir!" Tiger replied, narrowing his eyes at his assailant.

Tiger and his antagonist sat by the kitchen door and watched everyone eat and head outside. Plates, trays, food, and drinks were tossed everywhere. Hearing that the pair were being punished meant that everyone contributed to the punishment. The previously clean mess hall was now a wreck, like a party had been thrown within the last hour.

Mops were brought out with buckets of water, and the pair set about cleaning from opposite sides of the room. Two guards were posted by the door.

Tiger assumed this was to ensure they didn't kill each other. He wasn't sure, though.

After they had cleaned the mess hall, dinner was served, and the process was started all over again. By the time they had finished, the sun had set, and men were returning to their bunks for the night.

Tiger put his mop away with the other man following close behind. The guards escorted them from the hall and were sent about their nightly routines. Tiger and the man left the compound quietly, worn out from the day's tasks of cleaning everything twice.

As Tiger staggered along the street, he passed very little traffic and realized it was later than he thought. As he rounded the corner toward the apartment, he saw his nemesis from the drill was a few yards ahead of him. He sighed and looked back down at the street.

A shadow caught Tiger's peripheral vision. He looked but saw nothing. He shrugged, believing that it was a trick of the lights, or his mind was seeing things. He glanced back down the road and noticed the man from training vanished. He thought nothing of it until the dull pain of something smacked the back of his head, causing him to stumble forward.

Bree wasn't following Tiger; she happened to be passing him when she caught the smell of the man in front of him. He was tall and lanky, with muscles hidden under a layer of half-worn clothes. His brown eyes were sunk in narrow sockets, and his thin lips pressed together in suppressed frustration. She wasn't even meaning to follow the young man, but when the stench of anger, pain, and violence suddenly assaulted her sensitive nose, she had to get a closer look.

The stranger darted down an alley beside the road, and as Tiger passed, he threw a broken crate against Tiger's skull.

Tiger stumbled forward and then fell to one knee. She bolted for the attacker and grabbed him by the throat. Terror and panic suddenly clouded the man's sharp, featured face.

Tiger moaned and felt the back of his head where a lump had begun to form under thick, gooey blood.

He stood and turned to see Bree holding the man from the drill an inch off the ground, his boots scraping the stone, trying to gain enough friction to stand.

Tiger looked at Bree, then the man, then back at Bree. Would she feed on him? Was she waiting to see what he'd do?

Time dilated to a crawl as all these questions and more whirled through his still pounding head. Tiger was angry, and so was this man, Tiger thought. If he was going to make it in the Swords of Justice, he had to be seen as worthy. Bree just gave him that opportunity, whether she realized it or not.

"Halt, vile creature!" Tiger said, "By the power of my elven blood, I command you."

Bree arched a brow at him, "You-" she began.

Tiger cut her short with more words, mostly gibberish, then he began waving his hand in the air as if he were casting a spell.

Bree stared at Tiger as he spouted nonsense, waving his hands around in circles, as if swatting at flies. She looked at the man in her grasp, and then back to Tiger, an idea dawned on her. He was trying to save this man. But why? She decided to play along, however, to see where this charade went.

"You dare command me?" Bree finally said, setting the man down slightly, but not letting go.

"Please, don't hurt me!" the man croaked.

"Silence!" Bree hissed, showing him all the horror of her fangs.

Tiger held a hand out. "I command you, let. Uh, him. Go."

Bree raised her brow again; Tiger didn't even know who this was. He stumbled for a name, she thought. Or was he being dramatic?

"Now!" Tiger demanded.

"Fool, you do not command me without the name of those you wish to save!" she laughed playfully. If she were honest, this masquerade was amusing.

Tiger walked toward Bree and the man, then whispered, "What's your name, quick, I can't hold her forever."

"A-Aldrani… Aldrani Joro! Please, don't let this thing eat me!" Aldrani stammered.

Tiger nodded solemnly, "I command you release Aldrani Joro and return to the shadows whence you came!"

Bree hissed, dropped the man, and covered her face as if in pain, then turned and disappeared into the shadows nearby. He swore he saw her covering up a smile.

Tiger started to laugh but held it back as he saw how much terror was in Aldrani's eyes. He held a hand down to the man and helped him stand.

"That was close," Tiger said, "Good thing I'm a half-breed."

Aldrani nodded fervently, "Thank you. I'm… I'm sorry I attacked you."

"We're starting over tomorrow. No more jabs, okay? I can always summon the creature back, I have seen it, I know it now," Tiger said.

"No, gods, please. Yeah, peace between us," Aldrani said.

"Good," Tiger said with a pleasant smile.

"Walk you home?" Tiger offered.

"N-no. I'm okay from here." Aldrani said.

Tiger shrugged. "Good night, Aldrani."

He watched the man disappear down the road, then turned to the shadows and said, "That was quite the show."

Laughter echoed through his ears as Bree walked up beside him, "Summon me, huh?"

Tiger shrugged again. "It will keep him off my back now," he said.

"I wasn't about to let some thug attack you."

"Thank you," he said. "You picked up on that little skit pretty quick."

"We work well together," Bree pointed out.

The silence between them grew. Tiger sighed and rubbed the back of his head. "I best be getting home, I'm beat. Literally and figuratively," he said, laughing at his joke.

Bree nodded. "I'll walk with you if that's okay."

Tiger yawned. "You'll be carrying me if we don't go soon," he added.

They started down the dimly lit road, Tiger's body aching with every step. He glanced sidelong at Bree, her form silhouetted against the faint glow of streetlamps. She moved with that effortless grace, like she belonged in the shadows as much as the light.

The silence stretched between them, comfortable at first, but then it started to feel awkward. Thoughts swirled in his head—how she'd jumped in without hesitation, she could have ignored his plight. She could have killed him at any time since they returned to the city. Home wasn't far, but the idea of parting ways at his door felt... wrong, somehow. Not just because he was beat up and half-asleep on his feet, but because having her around felt. Different. Maybe his priorities were misaligned; could she forgive her kind? Probably not. But then, she hadn't done anything to him. The creature that killed his father had, and he was dead.

Bree broke the quiet first. "You doing okay? I heard the Swords of Justice training was brutal."

Tiger chuckled, though it came out more like a wince. "Yeah, nothing a hot bath and a week's sleep won't fix. Thanks again for the backup. I owe you."

She waved it off. "Besides, it's not every day I get to act in some play or story. Whatever you want to call it."

He smiled at that, the corners of his mouth lifting. His mind wandered again—to the empty apartment waiting for him, the creaky door that echoed too loudly in the quiet. And her? Where did she go after nights like this? The thought nagged at him, pulling him toward words he wasn't sure how to speak aloud.

As they turned the corner onto his street, the building loomed ahead, its windows dark like closed eyes. Tiger slowed his pace, rubbing the back of his neck again, that awkward habit kicking in. His heart picked up a notch, words tumbling in his brain like rocks in a creek. Spit it out, he told himself. It's just an offer. No big deal.

"Uh, Bree," he started, his voice catching like he'd swallowed dust. He stopped walking. "Listen, it's late, and... well, I mean, if you don't want to head all the way back... Where are you staying exactly? Anyway, y'know, you could stay. There's an empty cot. It's not much. No funny business. Just... safer, maybe?" He trailed off.

"Not afraid I'd snack on you?"

"If you wanted to do that, there would have been plenty of times on our journey back to Xonthian City."

Bree nodded. "I could have."

Crickets filled the canyon-like silence that loomed between them, echoing through the empty streets like a symphony.

"I'd have to see if it's okay with the gutter trash and feral cats in the alley. But a cot does sound comfortable."

Tiger chuckled. "Alright."

They walked the last few steps to the building's entrance, where Tiger fumbled for the iron key in his pocket. Bree followed him inside, her footsteps light on the worn stairs that creaked under their weight.

The space felt smaller than usual, cluttered with the remnants of his solitary life: a stack of books on the table, a half-eaten meal forgotten on the counter. "Cot's over there," he said, nodding toward the corner where a simple bedroll lay folded against the wall. "I'll grab some blankets."

She unrolled the cot and settled onto it, pulling her cloak around her like a shield. "Thanks, Tiger. This beats the alley."

He nodded, easing onto his own bed across the room, every muscle protesting the movement. Exhaustion pulled him quickly into the depths of sleep.

Chapter 9 - Daylight

The smell of freshly baked goods assaulted Tiger's nose as he walked down the road from his apartment, causing his stomach to roar in hollow rage. The sun was partially hidden behind clouds, warming his skin before cooling again when the clouds shifted to shroud it, as if the sun was playing a child's game with the thick pillow of clouds.

Since there were no drills today, he was free to wander the city. He decided that he needed to gain the trust of the people around his apartment. He and Bree didn't have a lot of money, so they needed to rely on the good nature of those he assisted. Having steep discounts from good neighbors helped significantly. He looked up to see the general goods store. The bushels of fruits and vegetables piled around the shop sat next to baskets of grain and other dried goods.

"Good morning, sir," The store clerk said cheerfully, "How can I help you?"

The store clerk was a short, chubby woman with long brown hair. Her pudgy face was set atop broad shoulders, with a button nose peeking out under round blue eyes.

"Good morning, Hazel," Tiger said as he adjusted the TigerClaw that hung comfortably on his back.

"Oh! Tiger… Was it?" she asked, her face brightening as she saw him closer.

On more than one occasion, Tiger had shown polite charm toward her and had also helped stock the shelves when she was feeling under the weather. His patience appeared to be paying off.

"Yes, ma'am," Tiger said.

"Hungry, dear? I can hear your belly from over here! Have an apple while you shop," she smiled wider, showing her somewhat crooked teeth.

Tiger flashed the woman a smile and bowed grandly, "You honor me, m'lady."

She giggled and fidgeted with her apron shyly.

Tiger grabbed an apple from the bushel next to the door and began to eat it delicately. He turned back around and saw a shadow shift slightly from the corner of his eye, catching what he thought was a tail. He tried to track it through the shelves of honey, hanging bundles of corn and garlic, but lost it somewhere in the back room.

He shrugged, passing it off as a trick of his mind. He turned his attention back to shopping for breakfast. He picked up some dried jerky and fruit and set the desired goods on the counter. As he did, though, he saw a sleek and steady hand reach for the store clerk's gold pouch, which hung just under the counter.

"Hey!" Tiger called, making a grab for it.

He startled the store clerk, who jumped back and tripped over someone behind her. She landed with a heavy thud and slammed her head against a nearby barrel. The owner of the offending hand, also startled, bolted from behind the fallen woman, making a direct dash for the front door.

The blur of movement finally set into his mind as he whirled around toward the door. The hand and the body attached to it came into focus as she darted past Tiger. An agile Atticatten body disappeared out the door, her tail sweeping behind her.

Tiger froze for a moment; he had never seen an Atticatten. The tail and pointy ears he caught a glimpse of on top of her head were a clear sign of the woman's heritage, or at least he thought it was a woman. He shook his head to clear it of the awe and sprinted for the door and out into the crowd.

Mischievous, agile, and reclusive. Atticatten were known to travel, but rarely stayed in one place too long. Tiger had seen a few around the city before. They were mostly merchants, traveling and trading from Yente to Cettera, and here to Xonthian City. They were notoriously finicky, however, and were known to take back deals or swindle honest tradesmen. Not because they were evil, but because it amused them. As if they played with their prospects before agreeing to a deal. Of course, this was all second-hand stories, told between friends around a campfire.

He shook his head and focused on the crowd of people, but failed to catch sight of anyone resembling an Atticatten. He growled and cursed himself for being surprised, though he doubted that even if he had been ready for a chase, he would have caught her. They were infamously fast and cunning. He had only heard of their kind through stories but had never seen one until now.

He turned and went back inside, where another patron had already come to the aid of the store clerk. She was stirring awake in the bearded man's arm, who was just as confused as she was.

"Wha—?" She moaned, rubbing her head where she bumped it.

"Someone tried to steal your purse," Tiger said, kneeling beside the storekeeper.

"I thought you were trying to attack me," she replied, standing shakily with his and the stranger's help.

"No, m'lady. I apologize for scaring you. Please allow me to pay for the apple and the other goods, and I will be on my way," he said. Reaching into his pouch, he produced several silver pieces, more than enough to cover his purchase.

She did not seem to notice the extra amount. She was still reeling from the whirlwind of events. Tiger bowed slightly, took the jerky and dried fruit, and then left.

Who was that? he wondered, trying to recall more details of the Atticatten he had seen flash by him.

Tiger turned down the main street toward the seedier east side of town. Hastily, he ate the dried fruit before pushing the remaining beef jerky into his pocket. He rounded the corner to the slums where an overwhelming scent of human waste wormed its way into his nostrils. His senses were becoming flooded by the taste of foul air.

The slums of Xonthian City ran along the eastern road, which ended at the East Gate, before dumping out into the farmlands that surrounded the city. The area was composed mostly of ram-shackle huts, with the occasional wood and stone building that was the main architecture of the city. Most of the slums were comprised of refugees from western Xonthian and those fleeing the war.

Tiger did not fear coming here. In fact, in his current state, he looked no worse than most of the other riffraff that lived in the shadows of the city. Waifs begged on the street corners for food or anything else they could grab. Tiger instinctively pushed his gold pouch into his pants, hiding it still tied to his belt, in the waist of his breeches.

He was not sure what he hoped to discover here, but as he walked further into the underbelly of the city, he found what he was after.

Talking to a mud-caked young girl was a sleek and beautiful Atticatten woman. A long beige tail protruded from the lower portion of her spine, swaying casually behind her. Cat-like ears twitched attentively on the top of her head, apparently listening to the crowd around her. The hair on her head flowed down to her shoulders in waves of dark brown. She wore a tight, form-fitting green body suit that barely left anything to the imagination. She had matching, fingerless gloves on her hands with well-manicured, sharp nails, clearly visible in the morning light.

Tiger walked toward her inconspicuously to avoid being noticed. As he drew closer, he could make out the conversation between the woman and the girl.

"I'm sorry, I don't have any food for you today, maybe later, okat?" the Atticatten woman said

"Okay," the little girl said, dejected.

The Atticatten woman stood up just as Tiger stepped next to her, a smirk playing across his lips that he could not contain.

"You!" The woman said with a scowl just before turning and darting down a dark alley made up of wood and stone multi-story buildings.

Tiger was ready for the chase this time and was hot on her heels. She disappeared through the darkness between houses and lean-tos. Laundry hung from lines spanning the gap between the buildings. It made it difficult to keep her in sight and navigate the labyrinth of abandoned crates and boxes. He leapt over a woman who had crawled out of her hovel to see what the commotion was, causing him to narrowly miss the clothesline overhead.

The Atticatten disappeared into the crowded street beyond, but Tiger was able to find her quickly and continued the pursuit. She jumped over a small stack of crates set in front of another alleyway. Tiger crashed through them like a bull running through a fence, stumbling only slightly. He hoped there was nothing in them or hidden on the other side. He cursed his clumsiness.

As he opened his eyes to see where the Atticatten had gone, he found himself in an alley, sandwiched between walls on one side and two-story businesses, homes, and warehouses on the other. The narrow alley was devoid of any inhabitants, including the woman he was chasing.

"What in all hells?" Tiger mumbled to himself.

He walked down the shadowy alley in hopes of finding any sign of her passage. The smooth walls of the buildings glistened in the dim light that filtered down from the sky above. The passage was long and narrow, with no obvious exits. A few yards in, it forked in opposite directions. He looked down each passage in turn but saw nothing other than trash and a few crates scattered among the debris.

"Which way did she go?" he growled.

Tiger glanced in each direction again and decided to turn left. He walked along the alley for a few more feet, his eyes scanning the walls ever so often in hopes of finding a door, but there was nothing. Tiger was about to give up when something caught his attention a little further down. As he approached, the slight mismatch in the color of the stone wall of the building was visible to his keen eyes. Anyone else looking or passing by would have missed it.

"What's this I wonder," he said under his breath. He pushed on the discolored section, and it slipped silently in upon itself.

A soft click sounded, and a door opened beside the mismatched portion of the wall, revealing a passageway that disappeared into the heart of the building's interior.

Tiger cautiously entered the darkness, his hand instinctively grasping the handle of his sword that hung across his back. The door closed behind him, leaving him in the pitch-black hallway. His elven eyes allowed him to see enough to walk unhindered, but they did not give him any kind of advantage if someone sprang out ahead of him. The passageway ended, and a small door appeared before him. Light seeped from under the door, illuminating it in an eerie, foreboding glow.

The faint sounds of chatter could be heard, and what sounded like the clinking of metal. Tiger arched an eyebrow. He reached for a handout and gave the door a push, but nothing happened. He felt around for a handle, but could not feel anything, nor could he see well enough to discern any kind of latch.

He was about to knock boldly on the door when it opened, flooding his eyes with the bright glow of candle and firelight.

"What the?!" a surprised man yelped seeing Tiger standing before him.

Taking the surprise as an invitation, Tiger pushed the man aside and rolled into the room, while drawing his sword in one fluid movement. As he did, he realized his current course of action might not have been the smartest move. He landed in a defensive posture on one knee, his eyes adjusted to the light in time to see dozens of daggers, swords, and a spear or two pointing at him.

"Uh... hi?" Tiger said. Looking around quickly, he could tell he had stumbled upon something he probably should not have.

"You followed me?" a young woman's voice called, dumbstruck behind the wall of angry faces glaring at him.

"Yes," Tiger said honestly, slowly sheathing his sword as he stood. His hands raised in surrender.

He realized that the drawn weapons currently being pointed at him hadn't moved yet because the orders to kill him were being delayed. He hoped this was because they were too surprised at his appearance. Because he certainly hadn't foreseen this turn of events.

"Who are you?" the woman asked, forcing her way through the throng of weapons to stand before him.

Tiger's mouth dropped open, and he gaped at her. It was the Atticatten woman he was chasing. Her face, which he had not seen until now, was soft-featured and beautiful, despite the current look of perplexed anger.

"Uhm... T-Tiger. Tiger Darqlaw." he stammered before closing his mouth and regaining his poise.

"You are persistent; I'll give you that much," she spat. "Why did you follow me?"

Tiger opened his mouth to reply and then shut it again, failing to come up with a suitable response. The truth was, he wanted to see her.

Look at her, examine her, and ask her questions about her kind. Everything that was currently passing through his mind seemed insufficient to explain his determination to chase her. He reasoned this answer would probably not help his current situation and decided to just stare at her, dumbfounded.

"Well, now that you've found the Anarchs, you do realize I could make you disappear forever?" she growled as frustration began to boil in her eyes.

"Of course," he replied honestly. He began to regain common sense, and it was telling him that he was treading on very dangerous grounds.

She narrowed her dark green eyes at him, "What do you want?"

He'd heard stories of a thieves' guild operating in the darkness of Xonthian City. He never really believed the tales, however. The truth of it, which Hon'shu had pointed out to him, was that no one could actually find the guild or capture any thief committing a crime. Tiger's argument to his father was that it did not mean the guild did not exist. It just meant they were good at what they did.

"I want to know your name," he said, smiling charmingly at her.

The Atticatten woman's eyes widened in surprise. She burst into laughter, which was echoed by the mass of thieves around him, "You've got guts, young one, I'll give you that. Storming in here, just to know my name?"

Tiger shrugged shyly, his eyes sparkling in the fire-lit room.

The woman chuckled, "Put your weapons away and get back to work. I'll handle this one," she said, waving a dismissive hand around. "Back to work!"

The weapons slowly faded into sheaths as the mob that surrounded him dispersed, giving him his first real look around the room, which was large and square in design. Two fireplaces flanked it, with tables of all sizes scattered around between them. There was a staircase in the middle of the room, disappearing through the floor above them, and another set descending to the cellar. Aside from those features, the room was bare of any designs or artwork. Piles of gold and silver littered the tables surrounding the stairs, with books, quills, and ink sitting on another table beside them.

"Yatáki," the woman said, snapping Tiger's attention back to her.

"Huh?"

"You wanted to know my name," she replied, crossing her arms under her supple breasts.

"Oh. Uhm, yeah. Thanks," he replied shyly.

"So, what are we going to do with you?" she asked, though he suspected the answer was not so simple.

"I don't mean you and your organization any harm," he said, waving a hand around the room.

She chuckled, "The Anarchs are far from being afraid of a half-breed like you."

Tiger ignored the racial slur. Instead, he returned her gaze and watched her closely. He had to be careful and was well aware that she was in control here.

"You've put me in a tight spot. I have no desire to kill anyone without proper cause. Unfortunately for you, you not only foiled my attempt at robbing that store clerk, but you also followed me and found our hideout," she pointed out gravely, "Thus giving me plenty of cause to slit your throat and call it a day."

Tiger nodded, trying to keep the blood from rushing from his face. He was already sweating, and keeping his cool was becoming difficult.

"I tell you what," Tiger began, the tone in his voice smooth and even, "Let's discuss this over a pint, and maybe we can come to a mutual agreement."

Yatáki cackled heartily. "You sure do have balls, kid." She wiped a tear of mirth from the corner of her eye and continued, "I like your spunk. I agree to your parlay, so let's see what you have to say."

Tiger sat across from Yatáki at an ale and food-encrusted table. She explained that the tavern they sat in was operated by the Anarchs. Its owner, Robert Betler, who also ran the seedy establishment, was a tall, gangly man. He watched every movement the patrons made from behind the counter, like an emperor surveying his subjects. It was run mostly as a front to give some of the Anarchs' collected wealth back to the streets. The common room was just as dirty and stained as the table. The fireplace sat empty except for a small mouse that scavenged for food in the corner. The windows were coated heavily with smoke and dirt, which made it impossible to see through.

"So, you think we should just let you go?" Yatáki asked pointedly, taking a sip from her mug.

"Yes, of course," Tiger replied, "In fact, I think we should join forces."

Yatáki choked on her ale. "What?"

"I plan on going to Fort Pointe sometime in the near future. I could use all the help I can get, and I suspect you're pretty good in a fight," he replied, shrugging slightly to adjust his shirt.

"I have no love for the Fire Isle Mages, but I certainly do not have a death wish either. You're crazier than I thought if you think you can make a dent in this war," Yatáki scoffed, shaking her head in dismay. "Do you even have experience in fighting? Have you ever killed anyone?"

Tiger ignored the question. "Don't you want to live in peace?" he asked. "Besides, having an organization like the Anarchs fighting in the war… Well, wouldn't that be better than stealing?"

"Hon, the world will always be chaotic; it's how people evolve. Besides, the Anarchs live well thanks to the war. Putting their lives on the line for the causes of magi's and clerics isn't exactly profitable."

"Then why do you steal and give it to the common folk?"

"Because, despite what you might think, it's the everyday people that make this city hum. Not the snobs on Highborn hill, in their mansions and walled off fountains," Yatáki said. "The Anarchs have been around longer than anyone can remember. We're not blood thirsty like the Mercs, and we keep to ourselves. What's in it for us when all those bodies get buried or burned in pyres? Nothing."

Tiger thought for a moment, then replied, "Very well. Let me go then, knowing that I may not live to see my next birthday. I won't rat you out, I have no reason to, and it wouldn't serve either one of us if I did."

"You may be right on both accounts, but why should I take the risk of letting you leave, when others have met their end?" Yatáki asked, fixing him with cold, calculating eyes.

"Because I would rather gain your trust as a friend than betray you for no reason," Tiger stated, returning her piercing stare.

A heavy silence fell between them as the tension became nearly palpable. Finally, Yatáki nodded in agreement and took a deep swig of ale.

"There's something about you, so I will agree to let you go. Under one condition," she added.

"What is that?"

"You leave the Anarchs alone and don't ever return to the slums unless invited."

"Fine," Tiger said, flashing her an honest smile. He stood and bowed his head slightly before turning toward the door.

Yatáki watched the half-elf young man walk out the door and disappear into the crowd outside.

"That one's dangerous," Robert said, coming over to retrieve the used mugs.

"Yeah, but I believed him. I don't think we've seen the last of him. Or I haven't. He doesn't strike me as one to give up to easily."

"Bah, lies. He wanted to save his balls from your grip. Face it, he was scared to death," the balding tavern keeper spat, grabbing his own crotch in illustration.

Chapter 10 – Life Lessons

Tiger hurried into the drill yard just as the bell reverberated through the compound. Men were lining up, which Tiger fell into. He was getting used to the early mornings and quick, intense training of the morning drills.

At lunch, however, he was called into Commander Sworren's office once again.

"Tiger, sit down," the commander ordered a little more gruffly than previous invitations.

"Yes, Sir," Tiger replied and took the offered seat.

"What's this I hear of you using magic to fend off a fiend of the night?" the commander asked, assuming his natural pose at his desk.

Tiger tried to keep the shock and mirth from his eyes, but before he could hide it, Sworren had seen it.

"So, it's true?" the commander asked with raised eyebrows.

Tiger opened his mouth to answer. Shut it. Then opened it again, but said nothing. He didn't know what to say. If he said he could use Magic, then the Paladins would get involved. If he told the truth, he'd expose Bree, and again the Paladins would get involved.

"Well?" the commander said irritably.

Tiger sighed. "Sir. It was all staged. There was no fiend, no vile creature of the night. A friend of mine was helping me play a trick on Aldrani. I needed some way to get past his attitude toward me. And there was certainly no magic," Tiger said finally, not entirely a lie. But not the truth either.

Commander Sworren peered at Tiger for a few moments, then asked, "A trick, huh?"

Tiger only nodded, "Please don't correct him. As you said, I need to find a way into the unit. This was the only thing I could come up with."

"But it's based on a lie." Commander Sworren said, then added, "The truth will come out eventually."

Tiger nodded. "I'm aware."

Sworren shook his head. "I don't like it. But I'll allow it to play out. Don't do it again."

Tiger stood and bowed, "Of course, sir, it won't."

"Dismissed," Sworren said with a derisive wave of his hand.

Tiger left the commander's office, his heart pounding loudly in his ears, well aware that the interaction could have gone far worse. He returned to the unit where men were pairing up to begin sparring, his heart returning to a normal rhythm, leaving his limbs shaky from the spike of adrenaline.

"Tiger, get in line with a sparring sword!" the drill sergeant barked, "Aldrani, pair up with Tiger! If you two so much as twitch without my say, you'll be pushing those boulders for the rest of your miserable lives!"

Tiger did as instructed and collected his gear and faced off with Aldrani. The man had lost his usual glower and toughness.

His once-hateful brown eyes were replaced with respect and admiration.

Tiger sighed. *"Built on lies,"* he thought, his mind echoing Commander Sworren's words.

He had no way out now; he had to continue forward. They sparred as instructed for several hours, then, as a team, they took turns pushing the boulder around the compound.

By the end of the day, Tiger was tired and drained and longed for his bed.

"Hey, Tiger," Gim, the soldier he'd met pushing the rock, called, "Some of the guys and I are headed down to the Stone Flame for some drinks. You interested?" he asked.

Tiger looked at him and the men beside him, and slowly nodded. Aldrani said nothing from behind the group, only fixing Tiger with a stare. "I would like that," he replied.

The group patted themselves on the back and headed to the tavern on the other end of town. As they walked, men joked with one another about their mothers. Tiger was lost in his thoughts. The rage and anger he had felt only a few days ago was starting to melt away. Now, it was replaced with fear. What would happen now? Was he going to fight in the war once he completed the Swords of Justice academy? More importantly, would Cav, the tavern owner, be at the Stone Flame, and would he remember him?

As they entered the tavern, Tiger quickly looked around for Carv. He didn't see him. He breathed a sigh of relief as the first round of drinks was ordered. He wasn't sure what Carv would remember about being healed, and he didn't want to find out.

The weight he had been carrying since his father's death was lifting slightly, and with each drink, more and more of the fear slipped away into memory, as he watched the soldiers around him laugh and talk aimlessly. He realized he wasn't alone, just as Bree had said.

"Tiger, you keep putting those back, we'll have to carry you!" Gim said between swigs.

Tiger raised a brow and turned his attention to the reddening faces around him. He burst into laughter. They looked like drunken fools. "I admit it, it's nice to be out here, drowning our cares away. Right, Aldrani?"

The quiet, angry man Tiger had seen when he first joined the Sword of Justice peered at him. He only snorted and returned to his ale.

"Bah, ignore the fool. He'd sell his own mother for a pint!" Gim said.

Tiger took a sip of his drink. "Would he?"

Aldrani turned away with a huff and downed his ale. The table of men around them burst into laughter. Although Tiger wasn't sure they even knew or cared, what they were laughing at.

The rest of the night went by uneventfully. Tiger didn't stay long. The Stone Flame still held an air of impending doom, despite the tavern owner's absence. Tiger slipped out and returned to the apartment. The sound of jubilation echoing down the nearly empty street of the city as he opened the door.

When he arrived home, he sat down and started to pull off his boots before climbing into bed. Bree appeared from the balcony.

"You know, we have a door," Tiger said, checking his feet for blisters.

She made a dismissive sound and tossed her cloak on the bed.

"We're going to eventually have to confess to Aldrani that it was just a prank. He's been spreading rumors around that I can use magic and summon you," Tiger said with a resigned sigh.

Bree snickered, "We?"

Tiger chuckled softly. He stared at his foot a moment and then looked up at her. "I want to say I'm sorry," he said.

Bree looked down at him. "Why? For what?" she asked.

"For the… anger, being mean to you. You were right," he replied.

She shrugged in response.

"I'm not alone, just misguided," Tiger said solemnly, "I'm glad you followed me and found me on the road. I was in so much despair, anger, fear, hurt… pain."

Bree sat down on her bed and watched him carefully. "You deserve to be, and it's not that you need to ignore it," she said.

"It's that I need to use it to become better, and grow, and learn from it," Tiger whispered.

"Exactly," she replied.

He nodded. "Thank you."

"You're welcome," she whispered.

Days and then weeks drifted by. His free time was balanced between training and growing his companionship with the Swords of Justice. Tiger ascended the stairs to their apartment and expected to find it empty. Bree was sitting on the edge of her bed, peering at him as he entered.

"I figured you'd be out, hunting… Is that what you'd call it?"

"It is," Bree replied.

"Why are you still here?"

"I want you to come with me tonight," Bree said as she stood up.

Tiger shot her a perplexed look.

"Come on," she said, stepping to the door.

Tiger followed, and they walked out into the night.

"When your father died, did you see him get killed?" Bree asked after a few blocks.

The city was quiet except for the crickets, a few people, and the occasional trash cart that wandered the city. Lamp posts illuminated their way as they went and bathed them in dull, orange light as they approached the entrance to the slums. A side street ran south toward the city walls, hidden in the shadows of the stone work that surrounded the city, and the taller, mid-level homes.

"No. I guess I didn't," Tiger replied finally, her blunt question taking him by surprise.

"Have you ever killed anyone, Tiger?" Bree asked.

"No," he whispered in response. That question seemed to come up more often lately, he thought to himself.

"It's not easy to take another person's life," Bree said, glancing sideways at him.

Tiger did not say anything, only staring straight ahead as they walked.

"Have you ever seen someone else take another's life?" Bree asked patiently.

"No. I almost did."

"How do you mean, 'almost?'"

"A few months ago, before my father was killed, I saw the tavern owner Carv get beaten in the streets. He nearly died. But I healed him, I think," Tiger confessed. It felt strange saying it aloud, like a secret had finally gotten out and become real.

"That was noble of you, but do you realize that by doing that, you may have caused more pain?" Bree asked.

"How?"

"Consider for a moment what may have occurred afterward: Whoever attacked Carv probably received his punishment and then was released, free to hurt more people. Carv himself, however, would be forever changed by the incident. He may never trust people again. I would go so far as to guess he is no longer the owner of the tavern," Bree explained as they walked.

"But I saved him, I gave him a second chance at life," Tiger said.

"Aye, but in doing so, you altered his fate," Bree pointed out. "Think of what would have happened if you hadn't healed Carv, the tavern owner. His attacker, Bo, was it? He would have been hanged, and anyone else who could have been hurt or beaten would have been spared."

"I don't understand," Tiger said with a furrowed brow.

"What I'm trying to say is that by sacrificing one person, you can save many more," Bree said.

"Then there is no hope for anyone if that many sacrifices are needed," Tiger replied.

"You must be careful with hope, Tiger; it is a very powerful emotion. Take, for instance, the scenario I just gave you; by giving Carv hope for a new life, you may have given him too much."

"How?" he asked.

"When you healed the tavern owner, you gave him hope in the future; he was able to continue his life. But what kind of life did you leave him in?" Bree replied.

Tiger pursed his lips in thought.

They heard a scream nearby. Tiger and Bree sprinted in the direction of the sound, only to find a dark-cloaked man pulling a dagger from the chest of another man.

Tiger started for the attacker, but Bree put a hand on his shoulder, keeping him from moving.

"No," she hissed, "Watch them; learn from the darkness that drives people. Do you see the loss of hope they have? If you run to save the victim now, you would give him hope, and while you do, the attacker will slip away into the shadows."

"Then I'll stop him," Tiger said, growling low in his throat.

"And let the victim die?" Bree said, raising an eyebrow, "Every choice you make, every time you meddle in the destiny of others, you affect more than just one person."

"You sound like my father," Tiger replied.

The attacker finished stabbing the man to death and rose from the blood-stained road to wipe his blade off and collect the gold pouch from his victim.

"Now watch. And don't interfere," Bree said, glancing at him.

She glided effortlessly toward the attacker and descended on him from the shadows that surrounded the gruesome crime. Within a heartbeat, she had pounced on the man, his screams echoing in Tiger's ears. It dissipated as Bree sank her fangs into the man's neck. Blood began to flow from his flesh, melding with his victim's essence. The flow of crimson slowed, and she tossed the body to the ground in a heap. She looked over to Tiger; her eyes humorless and tempered with humility.

"I thought you said you were different?" Tiger asked.

She sighed and stood before him, her face a mask of sorrow. "I still need to feed. I still bear the curse of the vampire. Just because I can survive in the daylight doesn't mean I don't have needs."

"Is that the lesson you wanted to show me? That I shouldn't ever trust anyone?"

"I wanted to show you that, there are killers in the world. I wanted to show you that there are consequences for our actions. Do you think I enjoyed that?" Bree said, waving a hand to the gruesome scene a few feet away.

"How should I know if you enjoyed it?"

"I wouldn't hold it against you, if you did, or if you thought me a monster."

Tiger studied her. "No, I don't think you enjoyed it."

"Because I didn't. I have to live with the consequences of my actions." She ran a hand along her lips, trying to wipe away the stain of blood. "Thank you for not lying to me."

Tiger arched a brow at her. "What do you mean?"

"You didn't say I wasn't a monster."

Tiger watched as she turned and disappeared down the street back toward their apartment. He wanted to hate her, but he couldn't. Was he scared of her? Yes, that much he could admit. In the end, however, she was teaching him that taking the life of someone was not easy to do. Those actions had consequences, and everyone had a role to play in the world. He couldn't save all of them. He wondered if the day would ever come when he would deal out death. Would he hesitate or leap fearlessly from chaos and into the open arms of the abyss? He wasn't so sure he would be ready or strong enough.

Tiger walked up to the Stone Flame, the tavern and inn set in the heart of the city. He feared that the GateHar Paladins were waiting here for him to return, the spot where his healing powers first manifested. The previous night's events with Bree still fresh in his mind, he was even more nervous and anxious to be seen around the city center.

The sun was bright overhead, illuminating the city's gray outer facade with warm light, though it also cast dense shadows in the recesses of alleyways and side avenues. The splash of the large fountain that sat in the center of the square echoed through the streets, mixing with the cacophony of voices and dialects that flowed through the air.

He opened the door and entered the tavern. He was too preoccupied with being spotted the last time he was here to actually see the interior of the Stone Flame. It was a well-furnished tavern in good condition. Being in the city's main square, it was one of the city's most prestigious taverns. Merchants and statesmen from all over Xonthian stayed here whenever they came to visit. Thick wooden tables and chairs dotted the clean stone floor while a large wooden and rock fireplace burned lazily in one corner. Candle chandeliers hung above him, casting warm, inviting light down upon the well-polished bar. The smell of something cooking mixed with the pungent odor of stale beer and tobacco smoke.

Tiger walked to the bar and took a seat, the afternoon crowd had thinned, and most of them had returned to work, leaving the tavern to hum quietly before the evening crowd showed up with the setting sun. His eyes scanned the nearly empty tavern for Carv. Not immediately seeing the aging tavern owner made him wonder if he was in the kitchen.

"What can I get you, sweetie?" The woman behind the counter said.

"Mead, please," he replied.

"Alright," she smiled in response.

The woman twisted around to the shelf behind her and poured Tiger a mug of mead, then turned back and handed it to him.

"Thank you," he said, setting a silver piece on the counter.

"Aye," she said as she turned to go, but Tiger stopped her.

"Wait. Is Carv here? Or his wife, Krystal?" Tiger asked.

"No, dear," she replied, her face becoming visibly saddened.

"Where are they?" Tiger's face felt as if it were draining of color. His heart leapt as fear grew in his throat, his mouth suddenly becoming dry.

"He committed suicide shortly after that Hon'shu fellow was assassinated, poor Carv thought he had been resurrected by the vampire that killed Hon'shu."

Tiger's heart exploded in his chest as the pebble of fear that grew there dropped with a heavy thud into his stomach.

"You ok?" the barmaid asked.

"W-what happened to Bo?" he asked.

"Well, I believe he was executed a few days ago. Shortly after Carv killed himself, Bo caught Krystal alone and killed her," the barmaid whispered, her eyes cast down in sorrow. "He then went home and beat his pregnant wife to death. Guards found him pounding her into a pulp. Her family didn't even recognize her.

Tiger tried to push out of his chair and only succeeded in falling over. He scrambled to his feet and stumbled from the tavern. As he reached the side of the building, his stomach wrenched, sending breakfast to the cobblestone road.

"Every choice you make, every time you meddle in the destiny of others, you affect more than just one person." Bree's words echoed in his ears, as if solidifying themselves in his consciousness.

Iro kneeled down to flip the cover off the corpse. "You didn't move them?"

"No, sir," the city guard said, standing behind him. "They were foun' jus like that."

"Any witnesses?" Iro asked.

"The man in the home there, said he woke in the middle of the night to a scuffle outside. When he got up to check, he saw two people talking over the two dead bodies," the city guard said, jabbing a thumb toward the home behind him.

"Alright, bring him out here, I want to talk to him," Iro said. He pushed the dead man's head to the side and saw two puncture marks on his neck. His skin was pale and looked dry, as if he had been left in the sun too long. He covered the body and then studied the other. This one had several stab wounds in his chest and several defensive marks. A coin purse lay between them on the cobblestone road. Blood pooled around it, like an island in an oasis of crimson. He covered the man up and stood as the city guard returned with the witness.

"This is Hobbs, Sir," the city guard said.

Iro nodded and greeted the man. "Tell me, Hobbs, what did you see?"

"I woke to some shouts, and when I looked out the window, I saw these two kids standin' a few feet away talkin'. Just like I told the city guard."

"Kids?" Iro said with a raised brow.

"Well, they are younger than me at least," Hobbs said with a nervous chuckle. "If ya get my meaning."

"Anything else about them?"

"Well, one was blond, the other darker-haired. Both had long hair, though the boy, I assume it was a boy anyway, had his hair tied up." Hobs plopped a fist on top of his head in illustration. "About all I could make out."

"You've been helpful, thank you," Iro said.

"Were they mages? They infiltrate the city?" the elder man asked.

Iro glanced over his shoulder and shook his head. "No, you're safe. Looks like this was just a territory dispute." Iro lied.

Hobbs nodded, accepting the answer before heading back to his home and disappearing inside.

Iro looked down at the two bodies. It looked as if the vampire waited until after the murder of the first man occurred. He furrowed his brow. Impossible. He clenched his jaw. "Kids?" he said to no one.

"Excuse me, sir?" the city guard asked.

"Nothing, get these bodies off the streets," Iro said before heading down the street, questions buzzing around his head like flies eating away at the corpses.

Chapter II – Dispatch

Tiger lowered his sword beside him and watched the soldier in front of him with an appraising eye. His mind, however, was drifting— he was unfocused.

Weeks flowed into months as his time with the Swords of Justice continued. Hon'shu had taught him a great deal about combat. Now that the Swords had accepted him, he was able to focus those skills and sharpen them to a keen edge. Tiger grew in confidence, learned new skills, and became agile. His time with Bree also grew more frequent. Her direct methods of showing him human nature caused sleepless nights, her grotesque teachings illustrated human nature like he had never seen. She expanded on the lessons he'd learned about Carv and the consequences of his actions, and how to watch the world around them with grave understanding. His time with the Swords of Justice was almost meditative next to Bree's dour, horrific education.

Tiger twisted just in time to allow the spear to pass by harmlessly. The sword he wielded came back and caught the soldier he was sparring with in the chest, causing the man to stumble back. Their armor during training was made from studded leather patches and inlaid steel rings in vital areas around their chest. Even though their weapons were blunted, the spear could have done severe damage to Tiger's throat.

"You're a fast bugger!" Gim said.

"Thanks," Tiger grinned, bringing his sword to Gim's neck before the soldier could counter. Tiger was well aware of how lucky he had been. His body had taken over, despite his mind's preoccupation.

Orders and corrections were barked through the drill yard where fighters were scattered about, their practice weapons clanging together randomly. The sun above was secluded by clouds, a reminder that rain was not far behind.

"Damn!" Gim grunted. "For a kid, you sure do know your sword."

"I had a wonderful teacher," Tiger said solemnly as he set the practice sword down on the rack. "And I'm not a kid."

"Sure, kid," Gim retorted with a grin.

"Alright, you maggots, that's enough for now. Line up!" the drill sergeant yelled.

The men around Tiger snapped to attention, each one coming together like a well-choreographed dance.

The group, including Tiger, lined up to await their inspection. He saw the king's new military advisor, Adalrico Lothar, march into the yard, with Commander Sworren, who was talking heatedly with a man Tiger knew as Oskar Salomo. Both men were visiting from the castle. They were there with a small detachment of the Xonthian Army, in preparation for what Tiger assumed was deployment to the front lines.

Advisor Lothar was short, balding, and plump from over-indulgence at the hands of his privileged life. His robes bulged around his belly, giving the impression that he was hiding a basket of food under them. He had dark blond hair with gray streaks like sun-bleached wood.

General Oskar Salomo was the advisor's exact opposite. He was lean, strong-muscled, and carried himself with an air of dignity. He had long black hair and sharp blue eyes that watched the assembly of soldiers with an appraising glare.

They walked past Tiger's unit to a more seasoned unit nearby. They began to review those men, who were, by Tiger's estimates, at least a year or more into their training.

"After the untimely assassination of our great military leader Hon'shu, the king and his advisors have decided that now would be a good time to go on the offensive, to quell any momentum the Evil Army has received from the death," Advisor Lothar said grimly to the unit opposite Tiger's own.

"You have been chosen for an important mission. The finest warriors the king has to offer will be sent to North Kelsa to disrupt the Evil Army stationed there. You are to report back any new intelligence and show them no mercy. If necessary, we want the entire village razed. I want nothing left standing!" General Salomo said.

"You will accompany the Xonthian Army, and infiltrate further into the enemy's territory than anyone has in a long time," Lothar said, grinning mischievously.

"We will take a ship west around the Xonthian Mountains and land just on the other side of the Cliffs of Irga. We will set up a base camp there and march west to North Kelsa," General Salomo shouted, "Report to the docks immediately, we leave tonight!"

Commander Sworren shouted his confirmation and turned to the veteran unit, ordering them to move out.

His unit was dismissed, and everyone went about their duties.

Tiger walked to where the three men were talking and bowed respectively.

"Yes?" General Salomo said, arching a brow at the young half-elf, "Tiger Darqlaw, is it? Your father was an honorable man; he'll be missed."

"Yes, my lord," Tiger said, fixing the general with a determined look, "Thank you. I wish to accompany you to North Kelsa."

General Salomo looked at him as if appraising his worth, then nodded, "Very well. As long as Commander Sworren agrees, and you understand, you won't likely return. Alive. This isn't exactly a market run, kid."

Commander Sworren looked at Tiger. "You realize that if you leave with them, you can't come back, right?" He asked. "You will be going on your own, and not as a soldier of the Swords of Justice. You have not earned the right for that title."

Tiger thought for a moment, then nodded, "I understand."

Sworren narrowed his eyes. "You put hard-earned sweat, blood, and tears into getting here, now you're abandoning everything— for what? This isn't some kid's game you play 'war' in. This is real," Commander Sworren said. "Besides, what kind of leader would I be if I let the child of one of this country's greatest generals wander off to war? Your father instilled so much knowledge. It'd be a waste if we lost you."

"I've learned there is more to this war than title and the son of some diplomat," Tiger said before continuing. "I will not grow as a leader, as a warrior, without knowing my limits. I won't learn in a drill yard what the battlefield can teach me. My father was right, the Swords of Justice wasn't my destiny, my path. It was, however, my bedrock. It was and is the foundation of everything my father instilled in me. I have deep respect and admiration for the Sword of Justice, but I will always be an outsider. No amount of training will change that. No drill will alter it. If you give me this chance, I know it will be what I need to grow."

"You will die," Sworren said.

"I might, sir," Tiger replied.

"What do you say, General Salomo?" the commander asked.

"I think you speak the truth. Both of you. And as I said, whatever you choose, I will agree with," General Salomo said, then continued.

"However, I do think it is unwise, for exactly the same reasons you have stated."

The silence between the three of them grew until suddenly, Commander Sworren turned and pulled a sword from the rack and tossed it to Tiger. "Spar me. If you win, I'll let you go. If not, you stay."

Tiger bit the inside of his lip as his jaw suddenly clenched with a jolt of adrenaline. Commander Sworren was not joking. "Sir, how-"

Tiger began, but was cut short as the commander lunged forward, his sword slicing through the air in an overhead strike.

Tiger twisted aside just in time, the blade whistling past his shoulder and embedding into the wooden edge of a nearby rack with a splintering crack. He gripped his own sword tighter and retreated a step to create distance. Sworren yanked his weapon free and turned to continue his attack.

"You're too polite for the battlefield, boy," Sworren growled, advancing again with a series of swift thrusts that forced Tiger to parry frantically. Metal clanged against metal, echoing through the training yard. General Salomo watched from the sidelines, his expression unreadable. Soldiers, many of them who had been lined up, broke ranks to get a better view of the match.

Tiger blocked a low sweep aimed at his legs. Sworren was relentless, his style a blend of raw power and cunning efficiency. Every strike was meant to overwhelm Tiger's defenses. But Tiger had anticipated this. He had spent enough time sparring with his father as a child growing up to know how to parry an attack from someone bigger and stronger.

They circled, boots scraping on the stone floor littered with stray bits of straw and dust. Sworren pressed forward, driving Tiger back toward the wall shields behind them. Tiger feigned a stumble, letting his guard drop, as if to catch himself. Sworren took the bait, swinging wide for an arc aimed at Tiger's neck.

Instead of blocking, Tiger ducked low and rolled to the side, coming up behind a stand of spears. He toppled it over with a shove, and spears clattered across the dirt. Sworren cursed. Tiger had successfully broken the commander's momentum.

Tiger didn't waste a chance. He darted forward and aimed not for a direct hit but for Sworren's hilt. His blade hooked the commander's crossguard in a twisting disarm, a move drilled into him endlessly by his father. Sworren's sword flew from his grasp, skittering across the stones.

The commander roared. He charged bare-handed, tackling Tiger with the force of a battering ram. They slammed into the ground, grappling in a frenzy of elbows and fists. Tiger couldn't breathe. He began to panic. Sworren's weight pinned him. The commander's hands clamped around Tiger's throat. "Yield!" Sworren shouted.

Tiger's vision blurred at the edges. No, he thought, not like this. He couldn't fail. He bucked his hips, using Sworren's own weight against him. They rolled toward the wall. Sworren's head cracked against the base of a shield mount, stunning him for a split second.

That was enough. Tiger twisted free, scrambling to his feet. He scooped up a sword and pressed it to Sworren's chest. "Yield, sir," Tiger said between gasps of breath.

Sworren stared up at him. He let out a short laugh, almost as if he were coughing to hide it. He rubbed the back of his head. "I yield."

General Salomo stepped forward. "Well, Commander? Does he go?"

"Fine with me," Commander Sworren replied.

"You'll be expected to hold your own. You won't be pampered where we're going," General Salomo said with a sharp edge to his voice.

"Of course, General Salomo," Tiger bowed again, "Thank you, sir."

He turned and took his leave; and as he did, the answer to his father's question hit him like a bolt of lightning from the heavens. He would never be better than his father. They were always learning, pushing each other. There would be no end to learning the arts of war and battle. As soon as he cleared the drill yard, he broke into a sprint, eager to find Bree and fill her in on what had transpired. He hoped she would come with him.

"You agreed to do what?" Bree raised her eyebrows in surprise/ "You've been training a lot, I understand. Invading the enemy's territory is no place to test yourself."

Tiger paced the small room they shared; his arms crossed in concentration.

"Look, I understand you are eager to die, but trust me, it's a painful and lonely road," Bree added bitterly.

"Don't you want to go? It was your hometown, right? Don't you want to rid the Fire Isle Mages from your home?"

Bree narrowed her eyes at him. "Don't think for a minute that cleansing my home of the vile undead hasn't already crossed my mind. But there are some things that even I am unwilling to face."

Tiger stopped and looked at her. Her crimson eyes shone bright with anger and something he thought resembled fear and pain. He studied her for a minute before she finally turned away.

"Go, if you are so eager to die. But I will not," Bree said.

"I'll help you," he said.

"You'll what?!" she snapped. Turning on her heels, she glared at him incredulously.

He watched her calmly and shrugged the tension from his shoulders. "You said vengeance is a lonely road. You won't be alone, I'll be with you, I'll help you face whatever you are unwilling to face alone."

"This isn't about—"

"It is about you, it's about us, it's about all of us," Tiger interrupted. "You're right, though, I would do it for the anger in my heart, but there's something more here than just you and me at stake. I want to go, to help Xonthian, but more importantly, I want to see what happened there. I need to see it with my own eyes. I need to see the scars the world suffered at the hands of the Fire Isle Mages."

Bree glared at him coldly, calculating her words carefully before responding. "You would travel to a place that could very well hold your grave, just to understand what is happening outside of Xonthian City?"

"Yes."

"Would you be so brave, knowing that what you may see there could break you; tear your soul from your chest? The horror of battle is not something anyone should be subject to, let alone a highborn as yourself," Bree said coldly.

"I was brought up on Highborn Hill, but make no mistake, my feet are planted firmly on the ground we walk upon. I would gladly die if it meant leaving this life a better place for all," Tiger replied evenly. "Eventually I will have to prove to myself, to you, to whomever, that I can…" He trailed off as if the words were too hard to speak.

"Kill? You have never taken a life before, now, you want to march into battle where all there will be is death," Bree snickered and turned around to look at the setting sun, "Very well, I'll go with you, if only to make sure you don't throw your life away or make a fool of yourself."

"Thank you," Tiger said, standing beside her.

They stood there, looking out over the city, and the gold light bathing the rooftops like a blanket of warmth.

"Why are you so stubborn?" Bree whispered.

Tiger glanced at her sidelong, a look of confusion playing across his face.

"Never mind," she added. "I'd better feed before we leave, as food is going to be scarce on the ship."

She leapt out the window and disappeared into the shadows of the city, leaving Tiger to stand alone in the small room. The sound of vermin clawing on the floor was his only companion. Dread crept into his mind, unbidden and sharp, causing his heart to pace with a growing amount of second-guessing.

General Salomo was standing on the deck of the HMS Frost Bane as Tiger approached. Bree trailed close behind, wrapped in her form-fitting robes and black cloak. Strands of golden hair were partly visible in the depths of her cowl, like veins of precious metal hiding in the depths of the abyss. Tiger was armored in a light chain mail shirt and leather jerkin, while thick leather breeches covered his legs, and worn leather boots protected his feet. The TigerClaw was strapped to his back, and a dark gray cloak over that completed the only armor he could piece together on such short notice.

"Who is this?" the general said, pointing to Bree with his v-shaped chin.

"This is my friend, Bree. She's accompanying me; I hope there's no problem."

"What business is that of mine? We agreed to let you tag along, you made no mention of a…. woman."

Tiger peered sidelong at Bree. She was hiding the anger well that he knew must be bubbling up inside her. He started to reply, but it was Bree who spoke.

"I have family in North Kelsa. I'd like to make sure they're okay."

The General ran his eyes up and down Bree's black leather-clad body. "You look like a spy."

Tiger stepped in front of Bree and set his shoulders at General Salomo, more to keep Bree from lunging at the man than anything. "She speaks the truth. She's been fighting the Fire Isle Mages for a long while. She's tired and wants to get home. She's been trying for a while."

"Uh-huh."

"By the Goddess's ire," Tiger said, raising a hand to his heart.

The General shook his head. "It's more than that. We can't protect her. You say she's been fighting the Mages? Prove it."

Before Tiger knew what was happening, he felt the dagger at his back pulled from its sheath. Bree suddenly appeared behind the general with the blade pressed into his ribs. "Is this proof enough?"

"By the gods, woman!"

Bree backed away and tossed Tiger his dagger.

"Any other concerns?" Tiger asked, sliding the blade back in place on his belt.

"Fine, but she eats your rations."

"Good," Tiger replied.

"As soon as our order to set sail comes, we will be leaving," General Salomo said as the two approached the gangway. "You will be bunking with the rest of the men."

Tiger and Bree hurried up the walkway and disappeared into the depths of the hull. The ship was a large frigate with massive guns hidden out of sight in portholes on either side.

From his conversations with Cord growing up, he knew the cannons were enchanted with explosive energy. Every time fire was applied to the wick atop the iron barrels, they would shoot whatever projectile was loaded. Cord had told Tiger stories of how his ships were saved many times over because of such cannons aboard his father's frigates. These weapons were only a few of the Cleric sanctioned artifacts in use by both military and private ventures. There were other exceptions to the Clerics' far-reaching influence on the use of magic. Tiger had heard of people, such as high-ranking officials within both kingdoms who could use powerful magic. It was rumored that Cettera's princess and princes were attuned to the magic arts. The Atticatten, Dwarves, and Elves, known as the elder races, were exempt from the Paladin's rules and regulations and used magic freely in their kingdoms.

The HMS Frost Bane was unremarkable in looks aside from the gun ports. It was a normal, military frigate with two masts and a bridge at the aft. Xonthian colors flew proudly above the crow's nest high in the mainmast.

Tiger inspected the cramped crew quarters. Men were stacked one above another in hammocks that swung with the gentle lapping of the water outside. Arms and armor packed every other free space from floor to ceiling. There was an electric buzz in the room, alive with eagerness and compressed tension.

"This is going to be fun," Bree muttered, sarcasm dripping from her fangs like blood.

Iro walked through the gates of the compound. The sound of men training in the yard around him echoed through the walled complex. He approached a man doing pushups and peered down at him.

"Excuse me, soldier?" Iro asked. "Do you have a minute?"

The man growled and stood. He was angry-looking, lanky with narrow brown eyes. He peered at the Paladin with contempt.

"What do you want?"

"What's your name, son?" Iro asked, flipping his collar over to show the insignia of GateHar.

The soldier snorted. "A Paladin? I don't have anything to say to you."

Iro knew he was lying. The man's eyes suddenly darted from side to side as if looking for an escape.

"Of course not, what's your name? Just want to have a friendly conversation between two men. Name's Iro—and you?" Iro said, holding a hand out expectantly.

"Aldrani," the soldier said. He spat at the Paladin's feet and started doing sit-ups.

"You seen anything strange around here?" Iro said, dropping his hand to his side. "I heard rumors that one of you had run across a vampire."

Aldrani's grunts grew louder as the number of crunches grew. Each repetition strained the man's body.

Iro knelt beside the soldier and whispered. "Didn't happen to see anything like that, did you?"

"No," Aldrani growled. "Thirty, thirty-one, thirty-two."

Iro pursed his lips. "Maybe your C.O. might know more about it. Maybe I should call on him."

"Thirty-nine, forty," Aldrani said, then stopped to glare at Iro, "He wouldn't know anything."

"Oh, and why is that?" Iro asked.

"Because, whatever it is you think happened, didn't," Aldrani said, before standing.

Iro stood and peered at the soldier. He was lying again. A smile tugged at the corner of Iro's lip.

"Well, maybe you're right," Iro said.

"Of course I am, now if you'll excuse me," Aldrani said as he picked up a boulder the size of his head.

Iro watched him before turning and disappearing out of the gates

he had walked through moments ago. Things were starting to make sense.

Chapter 12 – Home is Where the Sword is

The plains of northwest Xonthian were bare and strewn with rocks. Their base camp was perched precariously on a mesa overlooking the Straits of Irga to the north, the vast grasslands west, and dense forest south. The HMS Frost Bane, anchored just offshore, bobbed in the waves that crashed against the rocky beach. The camp was set up quickly, and scouts were sent on ahead in search of patrols. Tiger and Bree set up a tent just west of the camp that overlooked the rippling ocean. The wind whipped at the canvas, making it hard to get any sleep.

"Burrrr, that wind is bone-chilling!" Tiger said, crawling into the tent with Bree.

"I wouldn't know," Bree replied with a shrug.

"You okay?" he asked, feeling as if she was detached from the things around her.

"I have not eaten in days. Every minute I don't feed, I risk losing control," she replied, glancing at him with glazed-over eyes.

Tiger drew his cloak up around him and watched her. He didn't know what to say or how to comfort her. She'd said very little throughout the trip, and even now, she barely spoke.

"I thought staying below deck and out of the sun was supposed to help?" Tiger asked.

"It did," Bree whispered, barely audible above the wind. "Four days stuck on that boat, without anything to eat, and now having to move in the daylight as we march west."

"I will need to be careful in the next few days. Attacking the Mages will bring out my wrath and the hunger as well. Feeding in front of one of the soldiers will complicate matters," Bree muttered as she wrapped her arms around her knees.

Tiger nodded. Life would become much more difficult for them both. She would be hunted by the Paladins of GateHar, and Tiger would be prosecuted for being associated with her. His secret of healing the barkeeper would also likely come out and be tied to his death, as well, suicide or not. He remembered with a start that Iro, the Paladin he met after his father's death, was already suspicious of him. He forced the lump that had suddenly formed down.

As dawn approached, the scouts returned and reported no sign of Fire Isle Mage patrolling the area. With the knowledge of their invasion having gone so far unnoticed, they set out from their camp to the outlying farmlands of North Kelsa.

Tiger and Bree followed along behind the formation of a hundred soldiers, who talked about their trip and the lack of a welcoming committee. The group ahead of them joked that the Evil Army had left overnight, and the war was in fact over. General Salomo, who rode his warhorse beside them, didn't think it amusing and scowled at them for their behavior.

Hours before sunset, they reached the first farmhouse. The crop that had once been painstakingly cared for now lay wilted and abandoned in the dirt. Orders were barked, and the soldiers began to spread out, weapons drawn in preparation for their advance toward the heart of the village.

"Move, cover that barn. Flanks, move back, protect the center wedge," General Salomo yelled from atop his horse.

Tiger and Bree went ahead with the lead group of twenty men. They were the spearhead that drove toward the main house of the farm, quick and disciplined. As they approached the house, several mages, dressed in black and red robes with fire emblems embroidered on their shoulder, stumbled out of the house with swords drawn. A few of them blinked, as if fighting off the remnants of slumber. Before they could counter with any sort of offensive magic, the first few men ahead of them slammed into the Mages, driving swords and axes through their bodies like a ship cutting through the waves.

Tiger and Bree burst through the back door with a half dozen soldiers securing their rear. Four Mages barreled down the staircase in time to see their explosive entrance. They each wielded fierce swords; their edges appeared charred, almost as if they had been burned. Bree leapt at them, taking two of them down to the ground before they could react. She was heedless of what the soldiers might think of her savage and bloody attack. Everyone was too preoccupied, and the vicious attack went unnoticed. Tiger was right behind her. He drew his sword and came up to meet the third mage on the staircase, who had enchanted his blade with fire as Tiger assumed an offensive stance. The TigerClaw clashed against the long sword of the Fire Isle Mage, sending showers of sparks across the kitchen. A mage to his rear began to whisper an incantation. Before he finished, the air in his lungs had caught fire, sending a burst of flame up his throat.

Bree, who was standing over the bodies of her first two victims, grinned evilly. "Mess with Fire and you'll get burned," she growled.

The group of soldiers behind her filtered into the downstairs area and began to secure the rest of the house.

Tiger backed down the stairs, allowing the Mage to think he had the upper hand against the smaller, boyish-looking half-elf. Tiger grinned as his foot reached solid ground, and before the Mage knew what happened, he found the TigerClaw thrust up through his belly and into his lungs. He fell lifeless into the pool of blood left behind, as Tiger jerked the blade from the Mage in a swift, angry motion.

"Easy there, save the anger for a more equal adversary," Bree said, laying a soothing hand on the young warrior's shoulder.

Tiger looked over his shoulder at her and nodded as the bloodlust he felt began to fade.

She looked at him with concern but said nothing.

"W-was it supposed to be that easy?" Tiger whispered.

Bree shook her head. "It was for me, but I'm the exception. We'll have to contemplate that later," she said.

"All clear," the soldiers called from the interior of the house.

Tiger looked down at the body. His father was right; he did feel a piece of his soul wither away at his actions. The weight of it finally hit him; He wanted to tell Bree. But before he could, they were back outside regrouping with General Salomo. The other soldiers were still fanned out and began to move westwards again.

"Let's move out!" General Salomo called as he turned his horse around.

The Fire Isle Mages were not the group of monsters that Tiger had expected. They were men and women, like any other. What had caused them to grow into such anger and hate that they would invade and wipe out nearly all of Western Xonthian? He knew they wanted to use magic without restraint, and to him at least, after seeing them fight, that seemed like a bad idea. Their rage caused their spells to grow in intensity. His father had told him how, during his time in the front lines, they'd killed and maimed everything in their path. They commanded Liches and vampire assassins like weapons. It was even rumored that they could summon demons. He turned his attention toward advancing.

Small skirmishes broke out along the march west until they came to the village. The buildings, many of which were burnt-out husks of their former selves, lay abandoned and forgotten. A windmill in front of them turned slowly in the dusk-fueled breeze, lazily pushing the air through large propellers.

Bree looked around and whispered under her breath. "So dead." Her words were so quiet that even Tiger could barely hear them.

The village was spread out with a few dry silos dotting the northern parts of the town. An encampment of Mages, still unaware of their presence, communed at the center, near open-air tents and a fire pit.

"They're oblivious to our presence," Tiger whispered to General Salomo over Bree's shoulder.

"Shhhh," he replied and then motioned for the flanks to move north and south. He spurred his horse forward and led the rest of the men straight toward the Mages.

As Tiger drew closer, he saw about eighty to ninety men, along with a dozen or so Orcs. The lack of undead in the vicinity was a good sign. They would not have to worry about Liches or the dead returning to life.

Before they could get within bow range, an alarm went off in the camp, sending Mages and Orcs scattering for weapons.

"Charge!" General Salomo yelled as he kicked his horse into a gallop.

Tiger and Bree ran toward the flutter of activity in the camp. As they got within the firelight's red glow, they were met by several Orcs wielding spears. Bree crashed through the first one, sending its body hurtling through the air and crashing into the ruins of a house. The second one tried to run her through, but was blocked by Tiger's sword as he parried it aside. Using his forward motion and the upward arc of his sword, he twisted around and drove it through the creature's side.

Tiger then darted for the next nearest Orc. A blur of silver came down on the monster's head, cleaving it in two with a loud 'thunk'. He howled in triumph.

Bree lunged at a mage and sank her fangs deeply into its throat, hoping there were no soldiers of theirs around to witness her savage feeding. She heard Tiger's rage and felt the air crackle with feral strength. She felt empowered by his sudden display of primal rage. The soldiers around him felt it too as they began to rip into the Mages and Orcs, suppressing any attempt at a counter-offensive.

Tiger ran through the center of camp, where several Orcs and a Mage tried to attack him, their swords and spears grazing his skin, barely drawing blood. As he turned on them, one of the Orc's swords came down across his chest, splitting the chain and leather he wore in two. The path left a gash in his torso, causing him to stumble and gasp in pain. With the realization of his mortality came the fear of dying. His bloodlust snapped like a cold winter storm, sending him tumbling back to reality.

He grunted in pain and turned in time to parry another blow that was aimed at his head.

An Orc's spear came down, intent on knocking the young warrior out. But he was able to roll away and counter the Orc that had drawn blood. His chest felt as if it were on fire, blood mingled with sweat and dirt. His weak counter-attack glanced off the creature's thick hide, and he cursed at his weakness.

Tiger stepped off balance and came down at an angle with the TigerClaw, slicing the Orc's leg and severing an artery. The monster howled in pain and dropped to the ground in anguish. The Fire Isle Mage that was watching the blundering attempts of Tiger's actions began to whisper an incantation. Realizing the danger he was in, Tiger jumped over the corpse of the Orc and drove the tip of his sword down into the Mage's chest. The impending magic spell was silenced with a wet intake of air.

The sound of battle raged around him. He grasped his chest and tried to catch his breath. As he pulled his sword from the Mage, he barely avoided an Orc from severing his arm. Tiger fell backward into the blood-drenched dirt, unsure how he managed to keep from losing the appendage. Mud splattered his face as he landed, causing him to close his eyes in reaction. As he cleared what he could from his eye sockets, he opened them again in time to see the Orc looming over him, the tip of his sword poised to strike downward. But as the Orc was about to deal Tiger his final blow, it suddenly flew backward, like a doll being tossed across the room.

Bree walked over to where Tiger lay in the mud and offered him her hand. "Get up, we're not done yet," she commanded.

Tiger stood and grimaced at the pain the movement caused. Adrenaline was flowing in his body, and he knew that was all that kept him going. He felt detached, like he was seeing things from a distance. The sounds he heard were muted and drowned out by the beating of his heart as it pumped blood from the wound in his chest in a slow, steady stream.

"Come on, the northern flank hasn't closed in yet; we're going to investigate," Bree explained, pulling Tiger along.

He stumbled and noticed offhandedly that his hand ached. He looked down at the offending limb and realized he had a death grip on his sword. His knuckles were white from the strain.

They passed by the general store north of the camp. The sun had come to a final rest below the horizon, leaving them with a cold, bitter breeze generated from the ocean further west of them.

Tiger's eyes adjusted to the dim light, and as they rounded the silos, they both froze. Standing in front of them were about forty well-armored zombies. The remnants of their northern flank moaned at their approach. Leading them was a Lich. His skeletal frame and deeply sunken eyes radiated power as they glared intensely at Tiger and Bree.

Liches were like a puppet master pulling the strings of the undead. Powerful necromancers who could raise and control various creatures of the grave. They were once Fire Mages who, through the course of studies, had turned to the darker arts and sacrificed their life energy for that of the tomb.

Beside the Lich were a man and woman wearing tattered and torn garments, simple, older-style farm clothes that had seen better times. Their flesh had long since rotted away, leaving behind ligaments and bone.

"Mom. Dad?" Bree whispered.

Tiger shot a wide-eyed glance at her and saw she was oblivious to the army behind her parents. She was frozen in terror and confusion. He felt her trembling slightly in his hand, which she still gripped.

"Bree?" he whispered carefully, afraid she would shatter.

She didn't reply.

Bree dropped Tiger's hand and crept toward the advancing undead. She looked defeated and hopeless.

Tiger ran to her and put a hand on her shoulder, trying to keep her from getting any closer. "Bree, look at me," he whispered, the pain in his chest nearly forgotten, "They are not your parents anymore. They died long ago; let them go. Bree, I know what you must feel. Confusion, renewed pain. But now isn't the time—if we don't warn the others or do something soon, we'll be joining your parents in the afterlife," Tiger said.

"I saw their bodies. They were dead when I left them, weren't they?"

"They were brought back to life by a Lich; let them go," Tiger said. Forcing her to turn and face him. He looked into her tear-filled eyes.

She appeared as innocent as she must have been before being changed into the creature she was now. Her already youthful appearance had lost its hostile countenance, and once again it reverted to being a young adult. Bree stared at him; their eyes met one another with combined understanding and acknowledgment.

"Let them go," Tiger said again. "They wouldn't want to be remembered this way."

Bree turned from Tiger and strode toward the undead. He froze in place, unsure what she meant to do. The rage and anger he had always known from her began to rebuild the crumbling wall around her heart.

"I—" she began while removing her gloves. "I'm sorry!" she yelled as she pushed out toward the advancing undead with her hands.

As she did, the air around her and out toward the horde of undead began to crackle with energy. With a crack that sounded like thunder splintering a tree, everything from Bree's outstretched hands to several yards behind the army burst into flames. The Lich exploded, and every zombie within the fire's grasp suddenly fell lifelessly to the ground, burning in a huge pyre.

Tiger instinctively ducked at the sound of fire exploding outward. He glanced at Bree, a look of shock on his already horrified visage, washing over him. He quickly replaced his mask of compassion. The charred remains of the vampire on the study floor beside his father, back in Xonthian City, flashed through his mind. That made sense now. He felt as if a piece of something fell into place. For a moment, he felt… guilty? He wasn't sure why.

Tiger walked over to Bree, her chest heaving with exertion.

He grasped her outstretched arm gently, "It's over," he whispered.

She looked at him, water streaming down her face. "I'm sorry, Mom, Dad. Forgive me," she said before dropping to her knees in tears.

Tiger knelt beside her and pulled her close, his heartbreaking beside hers. They had both lost parents to the horrible war and the vile creatures of the Evil Army. Tonight emphasized their pain.

He held Bree close as she cried while the sounds of battle slowly receded behind them.

"What happened here?" General Salomo asked as he approached the two on the ground. "You two okay?"

Bree didn't answer. Her face was buried in Tiger's blood-stained and muddy shoulder.

"Yes, we're fine. We were able to use the campfire to ignite the grass and burn the Lich and the undead. It had taken control of our northern flank," Tiger said without further explanation.

General Salomo nodded and looked at the burning field of undead creatures. "Campfire, huh?" he said. He peered down at the two on the ground before pulling on the horses' reins and leading them away.

Tiger caressed Bree's matted hair as her sobbing grew shorter. "I promise you and the world," he said. "We will end this war. One way or another, it will end. We will both have our vengeance."

He had been so callous toward her, and all the while, she was in as much pain as he had been. Bree had hidden it better than he had, under her façade of anger and spite. Unlike Tiger, however, she had never received closure. Not until now.

Chapter 13 – A Path Chosen

The last few days had been a blur. After securing North Kelsa, they had spent the night in its ashes before trekking back toward the ship. Now, she sat in their tent, watching as Tiger clutched his bedroll tightly. His knuckles were white from his grip. Light from the setting sun filtered through the thick canvas tent. Despite the warm radiance, the tent was cold. Even Bree could feel it. She wiped away beads of sweat from his face and forehead in a vain attempt to comfort him.

"Please, Bree. Don't turn me," Tiger said, his eyes closed tightly in pain.

Bree looked down at Tiger. "I wouldn't dare," she replied.

She wasn't sure he could hear her. By the time they got back to base camp, Tiger's wound had become so painful that he nearly fell off General Salomo's horse. The wounded had been brought back to the camp following the battle at North Kelsa. Although Tiger had attempted to hide his injury, the blood he left behind as he walked made it impossible.

Bree took a damp cloth and wiped Tiger's face. She saw the pain in his features.

The deep gash across Tiger's chest had not fully clotted by the time they returned. The medics washed it, bandaged it, and told him he had an equal chance of dying from his wound or living. It was up to the Goddess of Life now.

"Bree, don't leave me," Tiger said, tossing his head to the side.

Bree frowned. "Why would you think I would do that?"

He didn't respond.

"Bree?" General Salomo's voice called from outside their tent.

"I'll be right back," Bree whispered to Tiger.

She stood and ducked past the tent's flap to see General Salomo standing there.

"What can I do for you?" Bree asked.

"How's the boy?" he said, though his eyes told her he didn't seem that interested.

"He's fighting the infection. The wound was deep; he's lucky to have made it this long," she said, looking over her shoulder to the tent.

General Salomo nodded. "We're getting ready to move the wounded. Can he make it aboard? Or do I need to send some men to carry him?" he asked.

Bree knew she could move Tiger by herself. But, if she did, it would lead to questions she didn't want to answer. "Yes, please send some men to carry him," she replied.

He turned to leave but stopped, and turned back to her as she started to duck back under the flap of the tent.

"I want to thank you. If you two hadn't stopped those undead from flanking our position, there would have been far more casualties. I admit I was not happy to have someone as young as you two along. But you've both fought bravely. I hope Tiger makes it back okay. You two deserve more than I can give you," he pursed his lips with finality, then walked off.

Bree watched him march up the hill toward the rest of the camp. If Tiger wasn't dying, she might have felt some pride. Bittersweet as it may have been.

General Salomo ordered two men to carry Tiger on a stretcher aboard the ship, along with a handful of other wounded men and a medic tasked with keeping all fifteen men alive.

Bree didn't envy the medic. Some of the men were worse off than Tiger was. All of them were in throes of pain and anguish, and a handful were missing limbs.

The ship was minimally staffed on their return trip, and Bree didn't dare feed. It hadn't been that long since the battle, so she wasn't hungry enough to risk it. She was assured the trip back would be quicker.

Tiger swung in rhythm with the waves of the ship. His body was wrapped in blankets, like a cocoon.

"Here, make him drink this," the medic said, handing Bree a bowl of foul-smelling liquid.

Bree's temper with the medic was getting short. Each time he came by, the medic would glower at her and treat her like a chambermaid.

"He needs water to drink and to keep him cool," she growled as the man handed her the bowl.

"You know where it's at, he doesn't need his hand held," the medic said. He walked off, oblivious to the fire growing in her eyes.

Bree stood, disappearing up the hatch to retrieve a bucket of cold seawater and a jug of water from the ship's supply.

When she returned, Tiger was moaning. His face was deathly pale. He was attempting to vomit but was having a hard time. She ran over to him and pulled him to one side. He spat out a small amount of water and then settled back down.

"You better not die, you hear me?" she said, placing a hand on his forehead; he was burning up.

She took the water from the jug and poured it into a mug. "You have to drink this," she said.

Bree lifted Tiger's head up and dribbled some of the cool water into his mouth. "I am not giving you whatever shit that medic has cooked up. It smells worse than death does," she said.

She sprinkled more water into his mouth, giving him time between drips to swallow. "Come on, that was pretty funny. You could at least give me a smile."

She didn't know why she was talking to him like a patient or a child. "Damnit, Bree, what is your problem? Not like you haven't seen how this will end," she muttered to herself.

She knew. She knew all too well.

Tiger moaned slightly, and she set him back down in the hammock to sleep.

"Tiger, you die on me, so help me…" she said, getting the rag wet in the cold seawater before setting it on his forehead.

The ship's hull groaned with every wave. Bree kept close to Tiger, watching the rise and fall of his chest. Each breath was a question, held in suspense.

His fever climbed through the day, and now his skin burned under her touch. Sweat soaked the blanket. The smell of salt, blood, and sickness hung thick in the air.

Tiger stirred, a low sound escaping his throat. His hand twitched, reaching for something unseen. Bree caught it, holding it down gently. "Easy," she whispered. "You're safe."

He wasn't. She could see that now. His lips were cracked, his pulse fluttering wildly in her hands. She leaned close, listening for the breath she could barely hear.

The medic passed by once, muttered something about letting the fever run its course, and disappeared again. Bree didn't watch him go. She only kept her eyes on Tiger, seconds between breaths.

When his body went still, her heart froze with his. She pressed her ear to his chest, but there was nothing. Then, faintly, a thud. Another. Weak, but there. Relief washed over her.

She sat back and resumed watching his chest lift and fall.

"You know, back in North Kelsa, the winters were rough sometimes," she began, her voice a soft murmur against the creak of timber. "Snow would pile against the door. I'd wake to frost on the window. I'd draw on them with my fingertip, nothing good, mind you. But it entertained me."

She dipped the rag in the bucket again, wringing it out with a twist, and pressed it to his neck. "One morning, I slipped out before dawn, boots crunching over the fresh layer outside. The village lay quiet, smoke curling from chimneys like lazy wisps. I followed a trail into the fields, and the stocks of abandoned crops were frozen in place. Like icicle trees, their cold bite soaked into my clothing. I didn't care."

Tiger's chest rose and fell in a shallow rhythm. "There was a frozen stream on the other side, I'd play in it during the summer months, but during the winter it was frozen solid like a mirror reflecting the heavens. I'd skim a pebble across it, watching cracks spiderweb out from the impact. The sound, like whips cracking, caused laughter to bubble up from my throat. Such a childish thing. Wasn't it? Even in war, I found the peace to just be a child."

She poured a trickle of water over his lips, letting it seep in slowly. "My parents searched for hours that day. When they found me, my cheeks were red and my fingers numb. They were so mad. They wrapped me in wool blankets by the hearth. I watched the fire sparks fly upward. I remember thinking I was never as cold as I was when I was thawing out beside the fire. Enthralled by the wonder of it all."

Bree straightened, her gaze fixed on his unmoving face. "Those woods taught me to listen to the silence. To feel things, to live..." She fell quiet at that. She peered at Tiger. "To live."

Bree spent her days and nights at Tiger's side. Time narrowed to a crawl. His fever finally broke on the fifth night. The medic came in to check on him and smiled at his handiwork. Unaware that his medication had been tossed out along with the bile, Tiger would spew up every so often.

"He's doing well," he said, feeling Tiger's head with the back of his hand. "I wish all my patients were faring as well."

Bree thought that if he was competent, they might fare better.

The medic left Tiger and Bree to sit in the dim shadow of a single candle that sat on a small table nearby.

"Bree?" Tiger whispered through mucus-sealed lips.

"Tiger!" she said, pulling her stool closer. "You're awake, thank the Goddess."

He opened his eyes slowly. "Water," he said weakly.

"Oh, yes, of course!" Bree poured a mug full and handed it to him.

He took it and started drinking heavily. She could see his body shivering uncontrollably.

"Wait, slow down," she said, grabbing the mug from tipping back further. "You'll get sick and toss it up again."

He stopped and handed it back to her. "You make a pretty good medic," he said.

Bree chuckled. "Well, I'm not sure about that." She took her cloak and laid it over him and watched as he pulled it to his chin.

"Where are we?" he asked.

"On the ship, headed home. We'll be there in a few hours."

He nodded slowly. "Good. Wake me when we get home."

She laughed out loud, mirth sparkling in her eyes. She was glad his eyes were closed. He did not see her wipe a tear away.

Tiger staggered down the gangway to the dock with Bree following close behind, carrying their gear. He was barely able to walk without stumbling, she gave him support up the ladder, but he refused it any further. She insisted on carrying all their gear, and he did not argue.

His chest still ached, but it was cleaned, bandaged, and was starting to scab over. The movement of climbing the steps, however, reopened the wound, causing blood to soak into the wrapping. He walked across the dock with Bree beside him. The familiar sounds of Xonthian City greeted them. There were shouts from nearby vendors hawking their wares, while the cries of gulls circling above punctuated the cacophony. Bree pulled her cloak tightly around herself, shielding herself from the hungry light of the early morning sun. The TigerClaw was wrapped and stuffed into Tiger's pack.

"Sir?" a messenger said from the end of the dock. "The king would like a word with you."

Tiger arched a brow. "Now? We just got back," he said. He was sure they had kept both his and Bree's secret hidden from the soldiers. Or at least from his perspective, they had. During battle, he was more focused on staying alive than hiding their abilities.

Bree mumbled curses under her breath.

"Fine," Tiger said, clearly in pain.

"See you at home?"

"You can't go alone; you can barely walk."

Tiger thought for a moment. "Are you sure? You'll be walking into unknown territory."

She shrugged. "Long as I keep my head down and let you do the talking."

"Alright."

Tiger and Bree followed the messenger to the castle and were led to the audience chamber, where the king and queen were both waiting. They were dressed in normal, royal purple, and appeared to have just returned from a walk outside. The queen held a handful of freshly picked flowers and was attentively stroking the petals.

"Good day, Lord Tiger," the king said jovially.

Tiger bowed his head slightly and grimaced at the pain the movement caused in his chest. "Allow me to introduce Bree," he said with a motion toward his companion.

"Welcome, dear," the king said, eyeing the shadowy figure beside Tiger. "I received a report just this morning on what had happened. I'm glad to see you are alive and mending."

"Thank you, your highness," Tiger replied.

"Did you see what you needed to see?" the king asked.

"Yes, your majesty," Tiger replied.

"Was it worse than you expected?"

Tiger nodded.

"War is an ugly place. People die. There are casualties; there are victims much like your father," he said, leaning forward to look at Tiger directly. "I cannot pretend to know how you must feel, but I can see how much you've changed since your father's death."

"Your majesty, there are people dying around the world, and both kingdoms can only maintain their own borders, never able to aid one another enough to push the threat back. You send men, hopelessly outnumbered, to the northwestern shores of Xonthian in a desperate measure to subdue the Fire Isle Mages. And yet you sit here and presume to tell me about victims and casualties?" Tiger snapped, his vision suddenly narrowing as anger boiled under his skin.

The King sat back with his mouth agape. "You dare raise your voice to me?" the king replied, his anger flaring in response.

"Hon..." the queen said, laying a soothing hand on her husband's. "Let Tiger speak his mind; you would have listened to his father."

"I mean no disrespect, your majesty. It has been a long and emotional journey for both Bree and I—I am in pain as you can see," Tiger said, moving his arm aside to show his bandaged chest.

"You will remember your manners in my presence, Lord Tiger," the King said venomously.

"You wanted to see me. If you have questions about the assault, then ask. Or let us take our leave so we can tend our wounds and regain our strength," Tiger replied. "We are both weary of this war and want to see an end."

The king nodded. "I am open to suggestions. I didn't mean to make it seem like I was ungrateful for your involvement. Your father was a valuable resource. Losing him has cast a shadow on our campaign."

"Bree and I are tired, wounded, and in need of rest. But aside from this, we have proven ourselves capable. We are self-contained and able to infiltrate the mage territory," Tiger explained. "We can blend in with the locals far easier than a large army."

"What do you mean?

Bree glanced sidelong at Tiger but said nothing, her caution clearly visible in her pale features.

"We don't stand out. We could go places soldiers might not get to."

"Go on," the king said.

"Your grace, if you want to win this war, my father believed it'd take unconventional means. But he never really knew what that would look like. What if it took something like a small team of warriors, who could travel freely, and disrupt the mages in ways an army couldn't?"

The king nodded as if taking in Tiger's words. "Like you two? But what makes you two so special?"

His heart leapt into his throat. He had to be extremely careful about what he said. "As I said, we're self-sufficient. I believe we have proven ourselves in North Kelsa, you've seen the reports?"

"I have."

"Then let us do what we can, where we can."

The king thought a moment and then nodded. "I'll tell you what. I would like to provide you with a small stipend. Use it as you see fit against the Mages," the king said.

"We don't need your charity," Tiger replied.

"Tiger, it may seem like too much for you, right now, but having a kingdom's support behind you could add credibility later on," the queen added.

"Please don't take this wrong. But I don't want your money. I don't want to be the puppets of any government body," Tiger said, looking between the king and queen.

"Nor do we ask you to be a 'puppet'. You wish to fight the Mages on their ground and in doing so, risk your life. That is far more dedication than anyone has ever shown," Queen Arabelle added.

"Take the funds, Tiger, think of it as an investment in your future. We don't want to see you toss your life needlessly to the wind. And I ask for nothing in return, this I swear," the king said sincerely, raising a hand.

Tiger had known the King long enough to take his word seriously. He was not one to go back on anything he promised, despite being a political figure. It often put him at odds with other factions or city officials.

"Very well," Tiger said, bowing his head again slightly.

"Tiger, be careful when you do decide to fight the Mages. What you saw in North Kelsa was only the beginning. There are worse things out there than the atrocities you've seen so far," the king said, motioning to his advisor, "See that Tiger and his friend are given. Hmmm. Three hundred silver a week."

Tiger's eyes widened in surprise. That amount of silver was nearly as much as his father got paid for services to the king.

"I don't want any money. Not from any crown. I've had everything all my life, my father provided. And yet, we lived modestly. I would not dishonor that by taking so much from the people of this city."

The king set Tiger with a thoughtful expression before nodding. "Fine, one hundred fifty."

"And see that a Cleric tends to their wounds," The Queen added.

"I am fine," Bree snapped. She wanted nothing to do with the holy order.

"And I'll heal. We don't need a cleric," Tiger quickly added. "I didn't want any silver, remember? We will be fine with one hundred silver coins a week. I would ask that while I am mending, I am given access to the royal gardens, to help Master Yordsith while I am healing."

"Of course, you may, Lord Tiger," Queen Arabelle said warmly. "Can I ask why?"

Tiger bowed his head slightly to hide the shadow of pain and sorrow. "It reminds me of my father: who loved tending to the gardens back at the estate. And I need to focus my mind."

"Of course. You're welcome anytime," Queen Arabelle said.

King Si'anne looked at her, then back at Tiger and smiled, "Fine, one hundred silver a month, and you shall have access to the gardens."

"Thank you, your grace," Tiger replied.

"Thank you," Bree whispered.

"May the gods favor you, Lord Tiger. And thank you for your services at North Kelsa," the king said.

Tiger and Bree were escorted from the castle by the messenger who had brought them. They left him at the gate and headed toward the small apartment.

The city seemed different to him somehow. Darker, like it was drained of all life, all its glory. He felt heavy. Each step was a labor that took every ounce of his will. The smells, the sounds he was accustomed to, were muted and barely noticeable. Pain shot through his chest, and he caught himself on Bree's shoulder, the only thing near to him. She glanced at him, the silent concern she had clearly visible on her face.

"I'll be okay," Tiger said as he started up the stairs.

Bree was close behind. As they came to the landing, he noticed she had stopped mid-way up the stairs.

"What is it?" he asked.

"Thank you," Bree said.

"What?"

"I haven't had a chance since North Kelsa. Thank you for being there for me. For lying for me, for covering up my… my curse."

"Of course," Tiger said with a smile.

"It's been so long since I've had someone to share a life with. I've grown cold and distant," Bree explained as she climbed the stairs, "Thank you for being there and not judging me for what I am."

Tiger arched a brow. "What are you?" he asked.

"A monster," she replied.

"I don't think that at all," he said.

Bree opened the door to their room and stepped inside, "I am the same type of creature that murdered your father, I am the same type of monster that killed my family and turned me into what we both hate most," Bree explained as she dropped their packs on the floor next to the door.

"You're not a monster; I don't believe that as much as I once did. Besides, I should be the one thanking you. You saved my life," Tiger said.

Bree glanced at him, noticing how the youthful luster in his eyes had faded away, leaving behind a harder, young man's eyes in their place. "I don't deserve such generosity, but thank you anyway," she said.

"You're welcome," Tiger replied.

Tiger nodded with finality and smiled at her. She forced a smile, and they both lay down in their respective cots. He kicked off his boots and folded his arms across his chest protectively.

They fell asleep within moments of lying their heads upon the pillows. The bed seemed to sway and shift as if they were still on the ship. The weight of the world was selflessly burdened upon their shoulders; the overwhelming pressure of it caused the pain in his chest to throb as he drifted into slumber. His only comfort was the strange, warm feeling he felt growing in his heart. Alien and foreign, it warmed his skin to the tips of his toes.

Chapter 14 – Roses of Xonthian

The darkness around the city felt somehow comforting to Tiger as they stood in the shadows of an alleyway. Very few people passed by. Those who did walked with their heads down, as if dragging themselves home after a day working in the fields.

"If the king is paying us to hunt Mages, shouldn't we be doing that?" Tiger asked.

"You're not ready," Bree said.

Tiger shot her a glance. "Why?"

"Because you're avoiding a very important topic. Even if you were, we need a plan. Do you have one?"

"No."

Bree nodded. "Thought so."

"Him?" Tiger said, watching as a shady-looking man walked by.

"No," Bree said, shaking her head under the cowl of the cloak. "Are you sure you want to be out here with me?"

"Why wouldn't I?" Tiger said, rubbing at this chest.

She looked at him levelly. "You're finally able to move around without opening those wounds. Stop scratching them, you're going to bleed. It's only been a few weeks since we got back."

Tiger muttered under his breath.

"I don't care if it itches," Bree replied with a scoff.

"I'll be fine. I won't scratch, how's that?" Tiger said. "I'm tired of being cooped up at the apartment."

Bree rolled her eyes back toward the people passing by. "As for why not, there's the horror of seeing my hunt and feeding on some poor soul," Bree said, more seriously.

"Why not animals?" he asked, his face hardening at the topic.

"Why don't I drink animal blood? I do and will. I don't like doing this, Tiger, if I could, I wouldn't."

He pursed his lips. "Did the vampire who killed my father do it for sustenance or pleasure?" he asked.

Bree looked at him sullenly. "I don't know. I'm not like other vampires. I don't do it under someone else's orders. I don't do it for sport or fun. All I can speak to is my own actions," she said.

"I know you're not like other vampires. I didn't mean it that way," Tiger said.

"And if we were out in the wild, I could feed more off animals. Any animal around here will be domesticated; dead animals in the city tend to raise alarms," Bree said, more irritably. "If you don't like it, then leave."

"And dead humans don't raise alarms?" Tiger sighed. "No, I said I'd come with you."

The two stood in the shadows, watching people pass by anonymously. Tiger rubbed his chest absently and then stopped, eyeing Bree from the corner of his eye. She wasn't paying attention.

"Dead humans are, sadly, a common occurrence. Which brings me to the topic you've been avoiding," Bree said.

"What's that?" Tiger asked with a raised eyebrow.

"You haven't talked about the farm or the battle afterward," Bree replied, looking at him.

"I—I don't know what to say," Tiger said, casting his eyes down the road they were watching.

"How about how it made you feel?" she replied.

Tiger closed his eyes as he relived the death he'd dealt in North Kelsa. His hand clenched in a fist at his breast, as if remembering the burning of the wound as his flesh was split open.

"Tiger?" Bree asked.

He felt unshed tears around the edges of his eyes as he opened them. Fear, anger, and resentment fought in his chest for control. "I felt nothing," Tiger said.

"Do you still feel nothing?" she prodded.

Tiger shook his head. "No, I feel pain. Like, my soul became tainted by the act."

"Good, then you'll be okay," she said with a reassuring smile before moving down the street from their hiding spot.

"What do you mean?"

She peered sidelong at him. "If you had enjoyed it, or didn't find it anything other than an act of evil, I'd be worried."

Tiger followed quietly behind her. The two watched as a man followed another man into a dark alley. "Do you?"

"Do I what?"

"Do you find what you do an act of evil?"

She froze in her tracks and fixed him with a level look. "Every time I feed, I hate myself. I hate the act, the taste, the pleasure it gives me as I feel the warm life of someone slide down my throat and warm my cold belly. Yes, I find it evil."

He opened his mouth to say something, anything to comfort her. But he couldn't, so he closed his mouth and nodded. She turned her attention back to the man they were hunting. A few seconds later, there was a crash. Bree walked into the dark corridor between two overhanging buildings.

The first man held a dagger, dripping with blood. The second man clutched his throat as blood poured out.

"Oi, you! Get outta 'ere!" The man said.

Tiger couldn't see the smile spread across Bree's face. She walked over to the murderer and caressed his cheek, "Oi?" she mocked.

Tiger turned away as Bree bit into the man's neck, his scream suddenly and forever silenced. Tiger sighed inwardly. He wished he could take her hunger away. He wanted to share the burden of her pain and guilt.

Tiger looked out at the gently churning waves. The dark blue water rose and fell with a hypnotizing rhythm. The smell of salt and fish hung in the air. The sun was high overhead, warming the sand and rocks that made up the beach of the city.

He turned his attention to the road and his quest to find food. The market he was currently walking along sat on the northern edge of the city, nestled against the nearly white sands of the beach.

Tiger stopped at a fishmonger and bought a few steaks of tuna. He paid the man and turned to leave when a voice called out.

"Well, look what we have here," Yatáki purred as she walked up to him, her Atticatten tail flicking back and forth.

Tiger felt cold steel press against his throat. He didn't even dare to swallow. "Going to slit my throat right here in front of everyone?"

"Bah, no," she said as she dropped the knife away.

"Not profitable either, was it?"

"Nope," she said before looking him up and down.

He chuckled.

"You've changed, lil' Tiglet."

"Yatáki, good to see you again," Tiger said with a genuine smile

"Those for me?" she asked, tracing a finger along the fish Tiger just bought.

"No. They're my lunch. Although I suppose I could get you one if you're interested?" he said.

She chuckled. "Inviting me on a date?"

Tiger blushed, causing her to erupt in giggles.

"Fine, I'll join you. I'm interested to hear how you got that," Yatáki said, pulling Tiger's collar down enough to see the tip of the scar on his chest.

Tiger turned around and bought another steak from the vendor.

"Come on, I know a great place that will cook these up perfectly," Tiger said, leading her down the street.

The two walked to a small, detached building just before the northeastern gate of the city. It was a cozy place with several large trees that draped green leaves down around a patio. Several tables and chairs sat at the center.

"Wow, you take all the girls to this place? You must be rich," she said.

Tiger chuckled. "No, you're the first. It's close to the Swords of Justice. I eat here on occasion when I need good food and a quiet place to relax. My father and I came here a lot when-" he said, the mirth draining from his eyes.

"It's a beautiful place," Yatáki said with a smile. She took a seat at an empty table.

Tiger followed her but said nothing. He thought the memories of this place were warm and inviting. It remained untainted by his father's passing. It was one of the few sanctuaries in the city he could come to and escape those memories.

"Ah, Tiger!" a woman said from the door to the restaurant, "It's good to see you."

"Hello, Marria. Good afternoon," Tiger said, waving a jovial hand at her.

"And you bring a lady friend this time? Ooooh, your father would be proud," she said with a wink. "What can I get you two, today?"

Tiger blushed again, then handed her the paper-wrapped tuna steaks. "Can you cook these up, please?" he asked.

"You know I can," Marria beamed. "Anything to drink?"

"Ale, please," Yatáki said, bubbly with amusement.

Tiger's face went even redder. He noticed Yatáki was enjoying this far too much. "Er… mead, please," he said.

"Alright. I'll get these cooked and back out to you shortly," Marria said, taking the fish from Tiger. She disappeared into the restaurant.

Yatáki giggled. "You sure do have a way with people. Do you make friends with everyone you meet?"

Tiger thought a moment. "I didn't realize we were friends," he said finally.

It was Yatáki's turn to look at Tiger. "Well, I mean… I haven't buried you yet," she grinned.

"Yet."

"You know, Tiglet, I think I was right about you."

"About what?" he asked with an arched brow.

"You're destined for something greater. That scar hasn't marred your personality. You're still undeterred by the horrors of the world," Yatáki said evenly.

"Thank you?"

She smiled at him. "I like you, Tiglet. You have life, it flows out of you, and it's infectious."

Marria returned with a goblet for Tiger and a mug for Yatáki. She gave Tiger a wink as she set his goblet down, and he thanked her.

"See?" Yatáki giggled.

Tiger shrugged. "I guess," he replied.

"Well, in either case…" She pursed her lips in thought. "You know what, why don't you come by later and train with the Anarchs?"

Tiger gaped at her in surprise. "What? Why? I thought you were mad at me for the whole, you know, finding your hideout?" he said with a flourish of hand movement.

"Oh, you're still on my shit list for that," she grinned. "And I'm sure there will be more than a few questions from the rest of the Anarchs. Robert will probably blow a cork."

"Then why?" Tiger asked.

"I don't want to see your pretty face scarred," She grinned.

He didn't blush. He knew she was stalling.

"Fine," she said with a pout, "Because you've kept your word, you haven't said anything. I heard what happened at North Kelsa and how you were injured. I don't know if I could ever live with the knowledge if I didn't do something to help you. I can't join you on whatever fool crusade you're on, but I can teach you all I can. The Anarchs deal in more than coin. Information can be just as valuable."

"And you think I'll give you intel on what exactly?"

She shrugged. "There are smugglers in the city who work for the Fire Isle Mages. I'd love to see them put out of business. If someone close to the king could tell me where I might find them…" she let the implication linger in the air between them.

"Alright, that's fair," Tiger said. "As long as it doesn't put innocent people or the guards at risk."

"Of course," Yatáki said. "Beside, I need to make sure you don't rat us out. Keeping you close, on a leash, will keep the other Anarchs from sticking you like a stuffed pig."

Tiger snorted with amusement. "Right."

Marria returned with two plates and set them down in front of Tiger and Yatáki. "Enjoy," she said with a smile.

The plates of blackened tuna smelled of fire-roasted herbs and spices. Steam billowed from a mound of rice set between the fish and a few pieces of vegetables. The two companions ate quietly, each one lost in thought. When they finished, Tiger paid and left a generous tip.

"I'll come by tomorrow. Want me to meet you at the Tavern, or the Hideout?" Tiger asked.

"Come by the Hideout. Don't think it would be a good idea to see Robert for a few days after I tell him about this," Yatáki chuckled.

"And you'll tell me about this, 'Tiglet', name you're calling me?" Tiger asked with a grin.

She giggled and took a sip of ale to avoid answering him.

Tiger opened the door to the apartment and stepped in. He looked over to Bree's bed and saw it was empty. His heart sank. He set his sword down and started to take his cloak off when he heard soft footfalls on the balcony next to the window. He looked up to see Bree stepping down into the room.

"I missed you," Tiger said as Bree came in from the cool night air outside.

"What?" Bree asked, perplexed.

"I thought we were going out together tonight?" he added quickly.

Bree raised an eyebrow.

"I mean. Uhm... Are we going to go out still, right? I thought I missed you," Tiger said, feeling his cheeks suddenly flush.

"We are. I do have womanly needs, you know," Bree replied.

Tiger's cheeks flared even further, causing Bree to turn and snicker quietly to herself.

"Oh, well," Tiger said as he coughed and turned to hide his embarrassment.

"Come on, let's go," she said.

Tiger nodded and followed her outside.

She looked up at him, and he quickly glanced away, unsure what else to say.

"Uh, nice night," Tiger said.

She arched a brow. "Aye, it is," she said.

"I'm glad we're here together. Tonight. It's nice out, I like being here." He turned away, embarrassed at his ramblings.

"I'm glad you're here," she said softly.

The two stood in uncomfortable silence before she turned and followed someone who had caught her attention. Tiger watched her a moment, then followed behind.

"What a dolt," he told himself, shaking his head.

Tiger knelt to pull some weeds from the dirt and tossed them in a pail he was carrying. The gardens were as large as the training grounds and full of different types of flora and fauna. It was inside the castle walls, in-between the two wings of the castle, where it saw very little of the setting sun. Currently, however, the sun was high overhead, illuminating the garden in full bright radiance, giving the grounds around him a warm, earthy smell. A large copse of fruit trees circled the outer section of the garden before it ended up against the castle's outer wall to the west.

"Is this where you spend all your time nowadays?" a sultry voice asked from the tree grove.

"Huh?" Tiger looked up to see Yatáki leap down from the tall trees.

"You—How'd you get in here?"

Yatáki giggled. "I'm a thief, hon, I can get in anywhere I want... mostly," she said with a grin.

Tiger arched a brow and looked over his shoulder to the castle. "Better not let a guard see you. It would be kind of hard to explain how you got in here," he warned.

Yatáki shrugged.

"When I'm not training, I'm here. The gardener doesn't mind, and I get time to relax and center myself," he said casually, as he trimmed a dead branch from a rose bush with a dagger. "What are you doing here?"

"I was bored and thought I'd come to see you for a change," Yatáki said, plopping down in front of him to play with a flower. "What do you mean, 'center yourself'?"

"Just something my father taught me. You have to take care of your mind and body. This," Tiger waved a hand around the garden in illustration, "helps with my mind. Calms it down."

"Very poetic," Yatáki giggled.

Tiger chuckled. "How's the guild?" he asked.

"As good as any day, I suppose."

"Any interesting gossip?"

"It's been pretty quiet. Unusually so."

Tiger caressed the rose petal and leaned over to inhale its sweet scent.

"How's your chest?" she asked offhandedly.

"It's fine," He pulled the collar of his jerkin down enough so she could see the pale scar that disappeared down his chest.

"Looks like it healed all the way."

Tiger smiled. "It's healed up nicely. It's better, it's been, what, two months?" he said.

"Aye, true. That's good. How are you doing otherwise?"

"Okay, I guess. Why?" he replied, looking at her quizzically.

"I only ask because you seem preoccupied lately. You're easily distracted when we spar," she smiled knowingly.

Tiger looked up at her from the rose bush he was trimming and arched a brow. "You sure are perceptive," he said flatly.

"It's a gift," she giggled as she inhaled a blue lilac beside her.

"Why does my chest hurt? Not from this injury. But when Bree isn't at our apartment? Why does it feel so light when she is?" he asked, clipping a fresh red rose from its stem and setting it beside him in a small bushel.

Yatáki burst into fits of giggles. "It's called being in love, hon," she said, wiping tears of laughter from her green eyes.

Tiger glared at her and blushed, nearly matching the red of the flowers around him. "Why is that so funny?"

"I never thought I'd have this kind of conversation with anyone," Yatáki replied, her voice filled with bubbles of mirth.

Tiger muttered under his breath.

"Look, hon. I can't even begin to explain things to you. But if you feel that way about her, why not tell her?"

"Because of what we are. How could it ever work?" he admitted with a shrug of his shoulder.

"What you two are makes little difference. It's who you are that defines you. You two both have hearts, and from what I understand, though hers may not be beating in her breast, she still feels emotions, right?" Yatáki replied sympathetically.

"I think so," Tiger said. Sitting back on his heels. He studied Yatáki. "Why would I feel this way about her? Why not you?"

Yatáki laughed. "Tiglet, why does the sun rise in the east and set in the west? Why is anything the way it is? I couldn't answer that, even if I knew," she replied.

Tiger smiled at the somewhat rhetorical question. He began to feel a strong friendship with Yatáki, the more time they spent together, but it was Bree that his heart had fallen for.

"If you have feelings for her, then tell her," Yatáki repeated as she forced the giddiness from her words.

"What if she—" Tiger began, but was cut off by Yatáki waving a dismissive hand.

"Don't even begin to question things, do it and see what happens. Think of it like going into battle, except that you won't die; you may feel like you'll want to. In either case, take the plunge into uncertainty."

Tiger pursed his lips and nodded. "I think I understand," he said.

"Good. You've grown up, hon, welcome to the world of adults," Yatáki said with a smile as she reached over to ruffle the young man's hair.

"Ha!" Tiger replied, playfully swatting her hand away.

Tiger kept two of the roses he was trimming and carried them home carefully in his sweaty hands. His heart was pounding loudly in his chest.

"Like going into battle..." he repeated, "Think I'd rather be facing a hundred Orcs right about now."

The sun was setting, and he knew Bree would be getting up soon to make her nightly rounds. He ran nimbly up the stairs to their room and stood at the door. He took a deep breath and walked inside.

Bree was still lying asleep in her bed. She stirred awake as he entered and turned to look up at him.

"Morning," he whispered.

She stretched, causing every muscle in her body to tighten, a moan of ecstasy escaping her lips. She reminded him of a cat stretching out in the sun.

"Yup," she replied.

Tiger walked over to her bedside and knelt, handing her the roses. He could barely hear anything over the beating of his heart while his mouth suddenly relieved itself of any moisture.

"Huh?" Bree said, puzzled. She looked at them, taking them carefully, "For me?"

"Yes," Tiger croaked. He cleared his throat and smiled. "Aye, for you."

She smiled warmly and inhaled the fragrant smell. "Thank you."

"You're welcome," he said, grinning foolishly.

She giggled. "You are cute, that's for sure," she said.

"Thank you?"

She laughed and sat up on the bed beside him. "I'm starving. Let me run and grab someone to eat, then I'll hurry back, and we can talk."

Tiger smiled and nodded. "I will await your return."

"I know you will," she replied. Setting the flowers in a goblet they had. She poured some of the water from the basin into the makeshift vase and set them next to her bed.

Tiger watched her move about the room and felt somehow lighter. It felt good.

Bree disappeared out the window and through the alley beside their building, leaving Tiger alone in the dimming light of their quarters.

He sighed heavily as she left and then stood up. Lighting a few candles, he turned and lay on his bed to await her return. He folded his arms behind his head and allowed his consciousness to drift between random topics that started with Bree and moved to Yatáki and then his father.

"Love, son. It's a complicated emotion," he remembered his father saying. "One day, a woman will enter your life and change it so completely that you'll never know that it happens."

"How will I know when I'm in love?" Tiger had asked.

Tiger remembered his father had thought for a moment and then frowned when he failed to think of a reasonable answer. "There are no words for the way it feels; you will simply know," Hon'shu had said.

Tiger blinked the memory away and looked up at the water-stained ceiling. He recalled the conversation he'd had with Yatáki earlier in the day.

"Why does my chest hurt? Not from the injury, but when Bree isn't at our apartment? Why does it feel so light when she is?" he had asked.

"It's called being in love, hon," Yatáki had said.

Tiger's mind clouded over as his body relaxed on his bed, as his eyes grew heavy and fluttered in and out of slumber. Time stood still, and the world around him evaporated. His senses began to shut down as he drifted further into unconsciousness. As he did, he dreamt of a lake.

He was standing on its shores, the cool water lapping gently against his bare feet. Hidden in the mist at the center of the lake was a large, gray castle, its impenetrable walls looming out of the depths like a stone giant. He looked over his shoulder to see Bree walking up beside him.

She grasped Tiger's shoulder and turned his body toward hers, then grasped his face gently in her soft, small hands. Her lips pressed against his; they were cold and tasted of blood.

Somewhere in the depths of Tiger's subconscious, he was awoken by the realization that the dream was of real flesh touching him. Bree's lips were lightly touching his. He opened his eyes to see her closed ones inches from his face, fingers touching his cheek lightly.

The tang of blood seeped into his mouth, but he had little mind for it. He was more aware and concerned with the feelings his body was going through. He closed his eyes and reached a tentative hand up to caress her long blonde hair that fell like curtains of silk around his face. Warmth crept through his body, and his heart raced in his chest.

She pulled back slightly and opened her eyes. The deep crimson orbs that watched him were bare to his probing gaze. He saw her soul burn with a fiery light inside, where it reflected the passion he felt for her.

"We can't do this right now, Tiger," she said, swallowing hard. "When we are ready, however, we will make it well worth the wait."

Tiger caressed a stray hair from her face and smiled up at her. "I understand," he replied, short of breath.

She crawled beside him and lay down, resting a hand on his heaving chest.

"When did you begin to see through me?" Bree asked after several long heartbeats.

"What do you mean?" Tiger asked, laying a hand on her shoulder protectively.

"When did you see me for more than just a monster—why did you?"

Tiger didn't have to think long; he knew exactly when it was. "When you were forced to kill the husks that were your parents," Tiger replied gently.

He felt, more than saw, Bree close her eyes. "I was weak then," she said.

"Crying isn't weak," Tiger whispered soothingly.

"I'm sorry," she said.

"For what?"

She swallowed again before responding. "For falling apart like that. I don't know what came over me," she said.

Tiger shrugged his free shoulder slightly and said, "I don't think you have anything to apologize for. You are... human."

Bree looked sideways at him, her eyes glassed over with moisture, causing her features to revert to a more youthful appearance like she had in North Kelsa.

"I'm sorry, I didn't mean—" he began, but was stopped when she placed a slender finger on his lips.

"No, you don't need to apologize, it's just that- it's been so long since I've been called human."

"You have your soul, do you not? That makes you human in my book," he said.

They lay beside one another, the tension slowly draining from their limbs while their breathing became steady once again.

"Bree?" he asked tentatively.

"Yes?"

"I love you."

"I know," she smiled at him, "I am glad you do. And I hope I can return those feelings. But it's been so long since I have loved anyone."

"I understand. I'm not going anywhere, I'll wait," Tiger replied.

"I'm glad. Good night," she whispered.

"Good night," Tiger said, though he had no illusions of falling asleep. He was wide awake now. He did not mind. He was smiling from ear to ear.

He had taken a leap of faith and landed on his feet. He made a mental note to thank Yatáki the next time he saw her.

Chapter 15 - In Light of Secrets

Iro stood at the landing, a tentative hand placed on the handle. He turned it gently, but it was locked. He peered over his shoulder to the acolytes behind him, dressed in heavy armor and brandishing swords. He turned his attention back to the flimsy apartment door and, with a grunt of exertion, kicked it in and nearly off its hinges.

A blond woman leapt to her feet as he bolted toward him. He tackled her, clasping a cloth over her mouth. It was dripping with a substance that caused anything that tried to inhale it to pass out, including the undead. She struggled, but it was too late. The substance was doing its job.

The young man who was lying in the same bed was on his feet beside her as the other soldiers filtered into the room. He started to pull Iro off the woman, but was blocked by the rush of men into the room.

"On your knees!" they yelled, holding swords to Tiger's throat.

Tiger did as instructed, his green eyes wide with panic. "What's going on! Let her go!"

Iro threw Bree to the floor and chained her hands with manacles made of silver, enchanted to keep the essence of magic from being manipulated. Something he used with regular occurrences on mages. "Tiger, Bree, you are under arrest for the use of magic, as well as harboring a creature of the undead, and murder."

Tiger's hands were bound with the same magic muting chains and he was dragged to his feet. Iro did the same with Bree.

"I've finally got you two," Iro said with a sly grin.

A soldier hit Tiger with the pummel of his sword, causing stars to jump across his vision, as if the night sky had engulfed him.

Tiger woke with a start; his hands were still bound behind him. The stench of decay, mold, and other darker smells assaulted his nose. His eyes cleared enough to see he was lying in a cell. The darkness around him was held at bay by a flickering torch somewhere on the other side of a slotted door.

"Bree?" he croaked, then swallowed the lump in his throat, and tried again. There was no response.

His skull throbbed in time with his heart, causing waves of nausea and pain to wash over him. He stood shakily, using the wall as support. It was cold. The image of a tomb came to his mind. He fought the surge of panic down and stumbled toward the door of his cell.

He tried to look down the hallway, but all he could make out was the torch that gave him the little light he had, and another cell beside his.

"Bree?"

Again, there was no response.

A metal bolt clanked open, followed by the thundering of boots echoing down the stone corridor. Tiger backed away from the door and saw the Paladin he had met at his father's house.

"You're awake, good," Iro said. He took a set of keys from his pocket and opened Tiger's cell. "Come on, move it."

Tiger was led down the hall to a room, and his heart dropping to his feet. He suddenly felt cold fear draining what resolve he had left. The entire room was awash in fiery light from torches, candles, and a flaming brazier in the center with various implements protruding from it. The stench of blood and excrement was heavy in the thick air, adding to the already nauseous mixture of the cell. He was pushed into a stained chair. His chains were held in place with a single plank that also doubled as the chair back.

"Now then, I have a few questions," Iro said, fixing Tiger with a glare. "Answer them truthfully, and this will all go well. If not, well." Iro ran his hands along the handles of the metal spikes sticking in the embers of the brazier.

"Where's Bree?" Tiger asked.

"The vampire you were snuggling with?" Iro said with a disgusted snarl. "She's being prepared for her last rites."

"You can't do that!" Tiger said.

"I can, and we will!" Iro said.

"The king will hear about this."

Iro chuckled. "Unfortunately for you, the king doesn't know you're here. The church does not answer to any king. We answer to the Goddess."

Tiger stared at Iro, fear crawled up his spine.

"Now then, I know it was her that killed your father, Hon'shu," Iro said, pacing around the cauldron of fire and embers. "So, who was the pile of ash?"

Tiger furrowed his brow. "The pile of ash? That was the vampire that killed my father!"

"You expect me to believe Bree saved your life? Why would she? Who are you to her?"

"No one, I don't think," Tiger said, biting his tongue. He suddenly felt like he was being manipulated. His eyes darted around the room as if looking for a lifeline. Seeing none, he returned his defiant stare toward Iro. "I awoke to screams. I ran downstairs, and my father was dead, and a vampire was looking over the corpse. He and I fought, I was knocked unconscious, and when I awoke, I was back in my bed."

"Don't lie to me!"

Iro lunged at Tiger, planting his hands on the chair's arms. His face inches from Tiger's. "It's true!"

"We became aware of your vampire whore shortly after your father's death, we got suspicious reports about a fight in Fort Pointe, involving a blond woman and a vampire. Riled up those poor folk down there with something good. Your girl caused a lot of panic down there. Stringin' that poor sap up in the butcher's shop."

"No."

"What?" Iro said, brow furrowed, and returned to pacing.

"No, she wouldn't do that."

Iro laughed hollowly. "She's got you by the short hairs, does she?" Iro studied him then snorted. "In any case, we know you two have been working together since then. Of that I'm certain." He walked over to a table and held up a cloth-wrapped sword. Tiger knew immediately whose it was.

"It's amazing to be holding this weapon after so long," Iro said as he studied the sword. "Clerics have tried and failed countless times to remove it from the soil. Even with magically imbued cloth, no one could touch it. Yet here it is. I can feel its power, even through the sheath. It's electric in my hands."

"How?" Tiger said.

"The weapon is still a mystery, isn't it? For decades, this sword was buried near the Dark Forest. How did you come by it?"

Tiger knew he had no answer. "I-I was found by it, by a friend," Tiger said finally.

"Found? See, I think you know a lot more than you're letting on, about who you are, why you're here. But allow me to enlighten you on what I do know," Iro said, as he ran a hand along the sword's sheath. "You somehow saved Carv, whether by healing magic or necromancy, I don't know. No way for me to learn that, considering the poor tavern owner is now dead and buried. That gave you your first taste of power. I think your girl killed your father, then you burned a pile of… house steward, maybe? To make it look like there was a third person there. You and she collected the sword and then proceeded to kill your way around Xonthian City. A cutpurse here, a murderer there. But it was your time in North Kelsa that was your undoing. You see, I have contacts in the military. They told me some interesting facts about you and your vampire whore."

Despite being cold, Tiger felt the sweat trickling down his back. They had been so careful, and it was for nothing. He had inadvertently condemned them both.

Iro peered down at him, a sly smile plastered on his face. "They found bodies consistent with vampire attacks. And then there was the entire company of undead that, for some unexplainable reason, had become engulfed in flames. That must have been your doing."

Tiger opened his mouth to try to explain, but closed it again. The futility of his situation hit him. Iro was going to bury them both, and there was nothing he could say or do to prove otherwise.

Iro strolled to the table and set the sword back down, then returned to stare menacingly at Tiger. "You are a filthy magi, and as such, you'll be exiled to the Fire Isles," Iro said before lifting him up.

"I'm not a mage!"

Iro dragged Tiger back to his cell, tossing him in before slamming the door shut. Tiger hit the hard stone floor with a shoulder and cracked his head against the wall. The world spun, and he could no longer hold his stomach back. He threw up before passing out. Iro's laugh echoed down the hallway as he left.

Tiger woke to the sound of footsteps and voices. He tried to sit up, but he had no energy, no desire to face Iro again so soon. He was in pain from the chains biting his wrists, from being flung into the cell, and from having placed Bree in such a horrible situation. He didn't know how to escape their current predicament.

"Open the door," he heard a voice say.

"I still think you're being manipulated," Iro said with a growl.

"I'll make that determination," the second voice said as the door opened.

Tiger felt a hand help him to sit. It was an elderly man with clear blue eyes who peering at him from under a bushy brow.

"Tiger?" the man asked.

Tiger only nodded.

"My name is Kendrick."

Tiger knew who he was, though until that moment, the man's identity had been obscured by pain and nausea. He had presided over his father's funeral. He was also the king's spiritual advisor and a trusted cleric of GateHar. He was slightly hunched over from age and had a scar that ran down his wrinkled cheek.

"Why are you doing this? Let me talk to the king," Tiger said.

Kendrick shook his head. "The king has nothing to do with this. This is a church matter. It's our charge to keep the people of Xonthian safe from the magic arts that have corrupted this land. As such, it falls onto me to decide what must be done."

"If we could discuss this with the k—"

Iro stepped forward as if to slap Tiger, but was held fast by Kendrick. "Tell me what happened, boy, and be truthful," Kendrick said without further preamble.

Tiger told him, just like he had told Iro, everything that had transpired from his father's death to meeting Bree. He left out the parts about Bree killing mages and criminals, as well as much of the campaign in North Kelsa.

Kendrick studied him, sitting back on his heels. He nodded and stood with a groan.

"There is no deception here," Kendrick said, though it wasn't clear if he was speaking to Iro or Tiger. "Although he is holding information back. That much is apparent. Still… he's not a mage, in any case."

"Sir?" Iro said, clearly irritated.

"You say you brought the vampire here during the day?" Kendrick said, peering sidelong at the Paladin beside him.

Iro only nodded.

"Very interesting," Kendrick said. "Have the Fire Isle Mages figured out a way to keep vampires alive in the sun, or is this something else? Are you Hon'shu's son?" Kendrick asked, peering down his nose at Tiger.

"Yes," Tiger said, then quickly added, "Wait, no. He was my adopted father. I-I was found abandoned near the Dark Forest."

"Where were you found?"

Tiger shifted, trying to take the pressure off his shoulder. "I was found near the sword."

Kendrick raised a brow and turned to look at Iro. "That is interesting."

Tiger sat against the stone wall and watched Kendrick closely. He could tell the cleric was contemplating the situation and events. After several heartbeats, the cleric turned and led Iro out of the cell, the door locking behind them.

Time melted away. There was no sense of night or day in his cell. Rats scurried in and out of holes in the wall, waking him from a fragile sleep as they nibbled on him. He wiggled up into a sitting position, leaned against the cold, hard wall, and stared at the door. Desperation settled over him, and he had the stomach-churning realization that Bree must be dead. They would have tossed her in a pyre by now, or quartered her body, and buried her in pieces in some gods knew what kind of hole.

The images that his imagination conjured unbidden sickened him. He wanted it to end. All of it. He couldn't live with himself knowing that he had caused her death. She had only ever shown him a willingness to help him live with his father's passing and understand his place in the world. She had lost so much already, her own family.

A door nearby opened, followed by boots echoing along the corridor, breaking him out of his self-loathing. He glanced up to see Iro standing at the door.

"To your feet, magi," he spat, before opening the cell.

Tiger got to one knee before being pulled unceremoniously up to his feet and dragged from the cage.

"Move," the Paladin growled, shoving him down the hallway.

"Where are you taking me?" Tiger asked, stumbling forward through the door to the stairs that wound upward like a serpent.

Iro didn't answer.

The two emerged into the main building of the GateHar Cathedral. He had seen the inside on several occasions and knew it anywhere. The temple sat at the center of Xonthian City, just west of the main square. Its imposing architecture was usually a marvel to behold. But like all things recently, it was drab and muted in appearance. Neglected by the ongoing war. Even the colorful stained glass that ran the length of the main hall felt lifeless and flat, matching his melancholy. The Goddess GateHar rose majestically over the asp at the other end, her crown of stars encircling her head as she watched Iro escort Tiger toward an unknown future.

Tiger was pushed along the side aisle toward the front of the building that led out to the main avenue. Once outside, the sun assaulted his senses, causing him to flinch from the bright light as it rose over the eastern horizon.

Sitting in the street was a carriage with a coffin, causing his heart to sink. "Bree?"

"Get in," Iro said, pushing Tiger forward and up into the back of the cart.

Tiger scurried to the coffin and whispered, "Bree, I'm here, I'm sorry." He turned to Iro and Kendrick, eyes narrowed in anger. "What have you done?"

"She is subdued at the moment. A concoction of herbs, in addition to being wrapped in silk bandages. She's quite docile and incapable of movement," Iro grinned maliciously.

"She's awake?"

"More than likely, yes."

"How does she breathe?" Tiger asked.

Kendrick looked at him quizzically. "She can't. She doesn't even breathe like you, and I do. She has no need for it."

Tiger felt his face flush. He'd felt her chest against his when they'd lain together. He was sure he could feel it move in concert with his own.

Iro laughed uproariously. "Her body remembers how to breathe; that's why she still appears to breathe. But she's dead, she doesn't need the air to live, as we do." He chuckled and shook his head.

"Right, well. All set?" Kendrick asked.

Tiger peered up to see the elderly cleric climbing into the driver's seat with Iro. "What have you done?"

Kendrick peered over his shoulder at Tiger. "Nothing yet. That's why we're here. We're going to Angelic Island, the Lord and Lady of the Gate. They will determine your fate."

"Still don't understand why," Iro spat. "We can just kill them both and be done with it."

"I am not so sure Tiger is a mage. And his sword—those are elven runes on the blade, at least some sort of elven rune. Then there's the vampire—"

"Bree," Tiger interrupted. "She has a name."

"Yes, the vampire is a day walker. This must be studied," Kendrick continued. "As well as Tiger's unique sword and his connection to it."

"Doesn't mean I agree with it," Iro said, snapping the reins.

The wagon jolted forward. Tiger sat against the coffin and watched while the city melted away as they progressed along the road.

Chapter 16 – Road of Reflection

Tiger wedged himself against the coffin and rail of the wagon, using it to rest his head as they rolled ever south. The eastern edge of the Dark Forest loomed over them as the road skirted around it. The smell of pine, mixed with damp earth, hung in the air, a sign that a storm had passed by not long ago.

"We're only a day out, I can see the forest," Tiger said, focusing his voice on the crack between the lid and base of the coffin. If Bree could hear him, maybe that would help. "I always thought the reason it was called the Dark Forest was because of the shade the trees cast. I learned one day, during a camping trip with my father that it was because the spirits of previous warriors roam there." He chuckled. "Though he would always end that tale with a hardy laugh. Like he was teasing me. You don't suppose it's true, do you?"

There was no answer from the coffin. He hadn't really expected any.

"What are you talking about back there? Keep quiet," Iro growled.

Tiger ignored him. "My father and I would hike through the woods and camp on the shores of the ocean to the north. We'd go fishing, and if we were lucky, have a hearty meal of salmon," Tiger whispered. "One time, I was hiking through the forest, and a panther followed me home. Can you imagine a child coming home with one of those in tow?"

Hours melted away, and soon the sun set beyond the western sky. Tiger would tell the coffin what he saw: people who passed them by, the sights, the sounds. Anything he could think of to keep the connection between them alive. Eventually, the carriage was drawn to a halt near the edge of the Dark Forest, and Iro and Kendrick dismounted. They began to set up camp, one getting a fire going while the other prepared bedrolls.

"I… I need to relieve myself," Tiger said.

Iro peered at him, and then Kendrick nodded.

"Fine, come on," Iro said. "You run, and I'll lob your bits, balls, and all, right off."

Iro uncuffed one hand and held the manacles while Tiger did his business. When he was done, his wrists were rebounded before being escorted back to the cart.

The two men of GateHar made dinner and only gave Tiger the rabbit carcass to pick over, as if he were a savage. There wasn't much to eat, and with his hands bound behind him, he ate it off the floor of the cart. Kendrick gave Tiger a sip of water from a skin. He replaced the stopper and leaned against the wagon's side, peering down at Tiger.

"You must be asking yourself, why here, why you. You're a half-blood, of course, you can use magic," Kendrick said, glancing over his shoulder toward Iro. "Do you know how I became counselor of faith to the king?"

"No," Tiger replied.

"The queen is a devout woman. During her time on Angelic Island, in the seminary before becoming a lady in waiting, she was climbing the ranks of being a priestess. Not a lick of magical prowess, but then, one doesn't need that to be a cleric," Kendrick sat against the wheel with a groan. "That's where I met her. I was one of her teachers. Anyway, the king came into the picture and swept her off her feet, carried her away. All that's, as the scribes say, history. When they married, she insisted I be chosen to fill the role. So I moved into the position with humble acceptance."

"What has that got to do with Bree and I?"

Kendrick seemed to ignore the question and continued telling his story. "The Clerics of GateHar are tasked to find the balance between the divine and magic. We believe that it was the gods who gave us this power to wield magic, while the mages only seemed to defile its use, through destruction and the perversion of the dead." Kendrick stood and turned to fix Tiger with an indifferent stare. "We could have let you go, being a half-blood. It makes sense that you have a natural talent for using magic. Bree, on the other hand. Well, even I don't know what to do with her, and so I must ask a higher power."

Kendrick returned to the fire, setting the water skin down beside him as he did.

Tiger watched the flame from his position on the wagon. Kendrick's words echoing in his mind, churning. Shadows of the past flickered to life, as if they passed through the distance of time to appear before him. He drifted off into a trance as embers deep in the pit snapped and ascended upwards into the sky, to add their luminescence to the heavens above. Ghosts of the past taunted him. His father's voice echoed from the abyss. "What happened? Why are you here?"

"I—I don't know. I wanted to avenge you," Tiger told the ghosts he saw in the flames. "I wanted to fight in the war. I wanted to prove myself."

"Then why are you here?"

Tiger felt the answer before he spoke it. "I was afraid. Bree, she…" Tiger glanced sidelong at the coffin. "She showed me that there was more to life than rage. Now, we're prisoners. And it's my fault."

"How is this your fault?" the ghostly voice of his father asked.

"It was I who pushed us to go to North Kelsa. I let my guard down. I-I should have stopped her from hunting."

"Can you change a leopard's spots? How can you keep her from feeding?"

"She was only there because of me. If I had left her, maybe she'd not be here now."

"Would you have left her? Why are you lying to me?" the voice asked.

Tiger sighed. "No, I wouldn't have left her."

"Then how is this your fault?"

"If I had gone to the war, I would have avenged you, and she would not be here." Tiger lay his head on the coffin. "I'm sorry, Bree. This is all my fault. I just wanted to fight in the war, like my father. No, that's not it. No, I wanted to end the war. It must end."

The days folded from one into another. The routine of stopping, little food, escorted breaks, and sips of water continued. After a week of a painful journey, Tiger finally saw the outskirts of Fort Pointe. He propped himself up against the coffin and peered up over the rail.

The high walls of the city towered above them as they drove the wagon through the eastern gate. The stench of decay hung heavy in the air, mixed with mud, smoke from fireplaces, and animal dung.

"I've never been here before," Tiger whispered to the coffin. "It's… it's depressing." Tiger described everything he saw to her as they rode through the main avenue.

Residents passed them, fixing Tiger with a dispassionate stare as they did. Mothers pulled children close as they walked by. Men, most of them wearing some type of armor, patrolled the streets. The sound of military drills echoed down from the courtyard of the fortress on the western edge of town, a sign that the war that had raged for a century was at their gates. From talking with his father, Tiger knew that Fort Pointe was the last bastion in the battle against the Fire Isle Mages. If the Wall of Ages, which was about a day's travel west, ever fell, Fort Pointe was the last hurdle the evil army would have to overcome. Seeing the town, held together by prayers and dirt, brought little comfort to him. Had he journeyed here, alone, angry, vengeful, he knew he would have died.

Kendrick and Iro lashed the horses to a post outside of a store and disappeared inside. Within a moment, they returned with very little in the way of provisions to help carry them the rest of the way to Port Orlynns. Another reminder of just how bad things were on the front lines of the war. After a brief stop to let the horses rest and drink from a trough, they were once again on the road south. High grass replaced shorter bracken as the walls to the city disappeared in the distance behind them.

"I wish you could see this with me," Tiger whispered to Bree. "The grasslands are beautiful. You can see the wind brushing the tops of their stalks, as if the gods were running a hand along fur."

He peered down at the casket and sighed inwardly. I'm sorry, no longer seemed suitable for how she must be feeling, and for the amount of guilt he felt.

As the sun sank into the west, below the Xonthian Mountains, a deep chill crept up his spine. He began to shiver.

"Can I have my cloak, please?" Tiger said, peering up over the rail to Kendrick and Iro, who were setting up camp for the evening.

Kendrick nodded to Iro, who stood with a grunt of annoyance. He walked to the driver's chair and produced the cloak that was wrapped around the TigerClaw and tossed it into the back of the wagon.

"Thank you," Tiger said. He wormed his way under the wool cloak, and the shivering began to subside. He lay down against the coffin and fell fitfully asleep.

The lowlands around Fort Pointe melted away into dense underbrush and trees that surrounded Port Orlynns.

Tiger spent his time drawn close to the casket, continuing to whisper the things he saw to Bree. His heart ached every time he thought of her tied up inside, alone in the dark. He knew she must be hungry and hoped she'd either survive this trip or pass with no fear. At least that's what he told himself as he spoke one-sided to her.

The smell of pine mixed with the fresh ocean breeze that blew in from the southeast. The sounds of the bustling port city washed over him as they drove along the main thoroughfare, before stopping at the gates of a GateHar temple. The weather matched Tiger's mood. Grey clouds threatened to drop cold rain on the already damp earth.

The cathedral sat along Half Moon Bay, like a white and grey deity, perched along a sandy shore. Iro brought the carriage to a halt, and he and Kendrick dropped down to open the gate that barred them.

Tiger was eager to be done with the journey. He smelled worse than the fish stench that wafted his way from the nearby pier. A week or more in the back of the wagon had caused so much pain, and he hadn't slept very much at all. His entire body felt ready to give up, and even though the aches were real, they felt somehow dull and inconsequential next to what Bree must be enduring.

The pair of clerics pulled the wagon into the yard around the temple and unloaded their gear. When it was completed, they walked around to the back and pulled Tiger unceremoniously out, tossing him into the mud like a sack of grain.

"Get up," Iro said, yanking on his bound arm like a puppeteer's string that controlled him. "I said, stand!"

Tiger scrambled to his feet. He was unbalanced, and the damp earth made it harder to gain traction. When he was once again standing, he was marched through the door of the temple and down a flight of stairs to a barren and damp cell. Mold clung to the walls while rats scurried along the edges of the room, disappearing into the walls as the door slammed closed.

Tiger sat against the cold stone wall and shivered. Now he was wet, with no cloak. He watched as the light Iro had been carrying faded away into the darkness, the last spark of hope fading away into the abyss. He bowed his head. "This is all my fault," he said. The door at the end of the hallway slammed shut as if in punctuation.

Chapter 17 – Under a Moonless Sky

A loud thud woke Tiger from a restless sleep. He jerked awake, causing the rats nibbling on him to scurry away.

Iro stood at his cell door. "Time to go," he said with a growl.

Tiger worked his way to his feet and stumbled toward him. When he got within arm's reach, he was yanked along the corridor and up the stairs that led back to the courtyard.

He was taken to the docks that ran along the cathedral. The private docks were the temple's defining feature. Unlike the GateHar building in Xonthian City, it was built with the protective bay in mind. The third largest fleet in the world was stationed there, behind Cettera and the

Merchants Guild. The guild made up the remaining traffic in and out of the harbor. The Half Moon Bay was home to the Xonthian's navy. GateHar had a few vessels it used for missionary, shipping, and other humanitarian needs.

The smell of rotten fish hung heavy in the air as their boots reverberated along the wooden pier, breaking Tiger from his reflection of history. He glanced up to see a frigate moored to the dock. Thick hemp rope wrapped around large wooden cleats attached to the dock. Two massive masts towered above them, various lines and rigging spiderwebbed across the entire ship. Seeing it caused Tiger's heart to sink. Would he ever see Xonthian again?

Iro pulled him along and up the gangway before leading him to the brig below. He locked the cage closed and disappeared back up the stairs.

Where the cells in the temple were empty, hard floor with a scattering of hay to sleep on, the brig had a wooden bench, a bucket, and a porthole that thankfully let in fresh air. The stench that hung in the cathedral's basement had been rancid, but now the only thing that assaulted his nose was his own putrid musk.

Commands from the above deck floated down to him through the open portal. They would be underway soon. He sat on the bench and bowed his head. He wished he were home with his father. What had he gotten himself into?

Tiger sat in the corner of his cell, the ghosts of thoughts whispering to him of the failures over the past several months. Meeting Bree, the battle at North Kelsa, and being arrested for the murders of violent criminals. All of it bore on his soul.

The porthole had been closed at the start of the voyage, sealing him off from even the slightest hint of the outside world. He could no longer see the moonlight dancing on the waves or feel the sea breeze against his skin. The sense of isolation gnawed at him, a relentless predator feasting on his mind.

The ship's timbers creaked and groaned, a mournful symphony that echoed Tiger's inner unrest. He listened to the rhythmic complaints of the wood, each groan resonating with the ache in his heart. He imagined the ship as a living creature, struggling against the weight of its burdens, much like himself.

Suddenly, the stillness was shattered by the sound of alarm bells ringing out across the ship, their urgent clamor slicing through the night. Tiger sprang to his feet, straining to hear through the thick wooden planks that made up the ceiling of his cell. The ship lurched violently, throwing him against the wall.

"Pirates!" someone shouted from above deck, followed by a chorus of terrified voices.

Tiger's pulse quickened. He clenched his fists, feeling the familiar surge of adrenaline course through his veins. Despite his imprisonment, the instinct to fight, to survive, had not been dulled.

The door to the brig burst open, and Kendrick stumbled in, his face pale and eyes wide with fear. Kendrick, once a figure of authority and discipline, now looked desperate. A stark contrast to his usual composure.

"Tiger!" Kendrick gasped, fumbling with the keys at his belt. "We need your help. The ship is under attack, and we're outnumbered."

Tiger narrowed his eyes. "Why should I help you?"

Kendrick's hands trembled as he unlocked the cell door. "Because if we don't fight back, we'll all be dead before dawn. You help us, and I'll make sure you're awarded some freedom. You have my word. Give me your wrists."

Tiger hesitated, weighing his options. Then, with a grim nod, he stepped out of the cell. "Fine. I'd rather die with a sword in my hand." He held his wrists up, and Kendrick unlocked the chains.

Kendrick nodded. "Follow me."

They hurried up the narrow staircase, where chaos washed over the deck. The ship was ablaze with activity as crew members fought off the invading pirates. The night sky was filled with the clash of steel, the crack of cannons, and the screams of the wounded.

Tiger's eyes quickly adjusted to the dim light, and he took in the scene. The pirates were a motley bunch, their faces twisted with savage glee as they swung from ropes and clambered over the ship's railings. The crew of the ship, outnumbered and outmatched, fought valiantly but were being driven back.

Iro held his position at the rail, pushing men off in wild rage, but even he was becoming overrun.

"My sword?" Tiger said, glancing at Kendrick.

"Here!" a man said, pushing a bundle into Tiger's arms.

Tiger grabbed TigerClaw. It felt warm. He would have studied the feeling further, but was attacked by several pirates. He leapt into the fray. His movements were swift and precise, a deadly dance of silver and blood. He fought with a ferocity born of desperation and pent-up frustration.

Kendrick fought by his side, his own blade flashing in the moonlight. Together, they carved a path through the melee, rallying the crew around them. The tide of battle began to turn as the crew, inspired by the surge, fought with renewed vigor.

Tiger found himself face to face with a hulking pirate, the man's face a mask of scars and cruelty. The pirate swung a massive axe, but Tiger dodged the blow and drove his sword into the man's side. The pirate let out a roar of pain and fury, but Tiger was relentless, pressing his advantage until the pirate fell to the deck, lifeless.

Around them, the battle raged on. Tiger saw the determination in the eyes of the crew, their fear replaced by a grim resolve.

Suddenly, an explosion rocked the ship, throwing Tiger off balance. The deck tilted beneath his feet as if a giant wave had slammed into it.

"We're taking on water!" someone shouted.

"They fired an entire broadside into the port side!" another voice cried out.

Tiger's eyes widened. "Bree!"

He ran to the stairs that led down into the hold but it was too late; It was flooded.

"Bree!!" Tiger dove into the cold water, dropping his sword on the deck of the ship as he did.

He swam forward into the hold, but it was too late. Water was flooding the lower decks and rising rapidly.

"Bree!!" he yelled, his voice muffled by the water.

The bow of the ship tilted down, shifting the water and floating debris, pushing Tiger back toward the stairs. He scrambled up and grabbed his sword as it slid along the deck.

"Forget it! Abandon ship!" he heard the captain yell over the roar of battle.

A pirate flung himself at Tiger as he reached the deck, and he barely managed to parry the pirate's sword aside. As he did, Tiger pressed the attack, countering with his own blow that shattered the pirate's blade, sending shrapnel into the man's chest. The TigerClaw sang into the man's shoulder. Tiger set a foot on the man's chest and kicked him free. The pirate's body flew backward into the hold and down the stairs. He heard the man's body splash into the water.

Another explosion sent the mast flying through the air, forcing Tiger to cover his face in shock. As his vision cleared, he saw Bree floating above the waves as they crashed over the sinking hull of the ship. She dropped the body of the pirate that Tiger had tossed down the hold. Blood ran down her face and neck, mixing with the water in gory ribbons.

She tossed the husk of the man to the deck. Her bare feet glided effortlessly along the water as she stalked toward the pirate's vessel. Her tattered silk bandages were singed and soaked with blood and soot. They wrapped themselves around her body, protecting her like gossamer threads. She looked like a floating wisp of smoke, drifting toward their attacker's ship. But it was the unmistakable wrath of vengeance on her face that scared him. The pain, the hatred; it writhed on her usually pleasant features.

"Oh no," Tiger said aloud to no one, suddenly fearful of what she might do. "No. No, Bree! Don't sink their ship! We need it!"

He prayed she heard him through the defying roar of her rage.

"By the goddess!" Kendrick said, coming up beside him. "Goddess, save us!"

Tiger snickered. "I don't think the Goddess is the one who's going to save us."

Bree, with an animalistic roar, launched herself at the first pirate to cross her path. She sank her teeth into his neck and ripped it out, bathing her body in crimson. She howled in both pleasure and pain.

The crew on the deck of the pirate ship suddenly shifted its focus from the clerics of GateHar to the vampiress feasting on them.

"Stop her!" Iro commanded as he ran up to Tiger and Kendrick. "This is madness! Unholy!"

"You want to stop her?" Tiger asked, waving a hand toward her. "By all means."

Iro drew his sword back as if making to strike Tiger down.

Tiger held his sword out, just as Iro lunged forward. Tiger twisted aside, barely able to deflect the blow.

"You two are a disgrace to the Goddess!" Iro yelled.

Tiger swallowed the lump in his throat. "How can I convince you, we're not?"

"You can die."

"Enough, Iro!" Kendrick said, stepping between the two fighters. "Focus on getting everything we can ready to bring aboard the pirate ship. Gather what men we have and make a stand on our ship. Their vessel is our only chance of getting out of here."

Iro growled and spat at Tiger's feet before disappearing into the crowd of men standing dumbstruck at the helm.

"Will she stop?" Kendrick asked.

Tiger only shrugged.

"Pray she does," Kendrick said before following behind Iro.

Tiger picked up his discarded sheath from the deck and walked toward the slanted rail. He sheathed his weapon and threw the strap over his head before climbing the ladder that led up to the sturdy deck above.

A body flew over the rail, narrowly missing him, and splashing into the water. He peered up to see Bree drinking deeply from a pirate before discarding him like a husk of some exotic fruit. She was bathed in blood. The once-white bandage that flowed around her body now stained dark red.

"Bree!" Tiger called out, his voice a mix of shock and urgency.

Bree turned, her eyes glinting with a predatory hunger that sent a shiver down Tiger's spine. For a moment, he saw a flicker of recognition in her eyes, a brief glimpse of the woman he knew beneath the bloodlust.

"Tiger," she whispered, her voice barely audible over the sounds of battle.

She turned her attention to the next pirate, who ran a spear used for whaling through her chest. She pulled the man toward her, pushing the weapon through her chest like a painless splinter.

"Gods, no! Plea—"

Bree bit into the man's flesh, breaking his fearful plea short.

When the last remaining pirate had leapt into the water or lay dead on the deck of the ship, Bree stumbled toward Tiger. Her feet left bloody footprints along the teak wood as she stood before him. A look of pain, anguish, and horror flooded her eyes.

"Bree?" Tiger whispered.

"I'm a monster," she said and fell to her knees.

Tiger's mouth gaped open. After being locked in a coffin for almost a month, the only thing he could think of was that *she* was the monster? He was the one who had got her locked up; he didn't deserve any mercy. He looked down and slid down to kneel before her, taking her into his arms. "I'm the monster, I should have listened to you. I'm sorry."

She pushed him away and glared at him. "You are not the monster. Look at what I did!" she waved an arm around the deck full of bodies.

Tiger opened his mouth to reply, but no words came to him. He closed it again and set her with saddened eyes.

"Stand, vile creature!" a voice said behind them.

Tiger stood and faced Iro. "You'll not touch her again. Not while there is breath in my lungs."

Iro leveled his sword at Tiger.

Tiger glared at the man, contempt plastered on his grimy face. "Go on, do it. Bree will rip your throat out before my last breath."

"Enough, you two," Kendrick said, helping a wounded sailor to the deck. "Help me get the wounded on board, and the supplies we can recover."

They worked quickly, moving the wounded to the pirate ship and gathering supplies. The remaining crew members, though weary and battered, followed Kendrick's orders without hesitation.

As the sun began to rise, casting a pale light over the bloodstained decks, the crew finally managed to secure the pirate ship. Kendrick stood at the helm, surveying the scene with a grim satisfaction.

"We did it," he said quietly, turning to Tiger. "Thanks to you and... her."

Tiger glanced at Bree, who was sitting against the rail, knees drawn up.

"Anyway, let's get this ship moving," Kendrick said, nodding to the captain who was taking his station at the wheel. "We need to put as much distance between us and any reinforcements."

"Yes, sir!" the captain said.

Tiger approached Bree cautiously and kneeled next to her. "Are you alright?" he asked softly.

Bree opened her eyes and met his gaze. "I will be," she said.

Tiger nodded, relieved. "We're not out of this yet, but we've got a fighting chance now."

"I should have gone down with the ship, at least then you might have had a chance. But as long as we fight together, you'll never be free," Bree muttered.

Tiger's face softened with a mixture of sadness and guilt. "Don't say that, Bree. You're not a burden. You have nothing to apologize for. Without you, we wouldn't have made it."

Bree looked away; her eyes distant. "I-I didn't want to control it back there, but somehow, it, Tiger. The bloodlust... it's overwhelming. I'm afraid of what I might do. What I might do to you."

Tiger placed a hand on her shoulder, his grip firm but gentle. "We'll figure it out. You're not alone in this, Bree. We'll face whatever comes together."

Bree closed her eyes, taking a deep breath.

"You two, stand!" Iro commanded as he approached. Kendrick came up beside him as well.

Tiger stood and squared off against Iro, standing in front of Bree.

"Enough," Kendrick said, stepping between the two warriors. "Tiger, the men, we are indebted to you and… Bree. But, if you two don't mind, will you please stay below until we arrive?"

Tiger looked between Kendrick and Iro, his jaw clenched in repressed anger. He felt Bree stand and put a hand on his arm.

"It's okay, Tiger, anything is better than that box," she said.

"I'm afraid we'll need your sword back as well," Kendrick said, holding up a thick burlap sack.

Tiger removed the sheathed weapon from his back and slid it into the bag, which was tightly wrapped and secured.

"If you'll follow me," Kendrick said, waving a hand toward the stairs.

Tiger nodded and followed the two clerics downstairs, where they were led back to the brig. They were given a blanket and some hay, and the door was left unlocked. Tiger turned to Bree, who curled into a ball against the wall of the ship. He wanted to comfort her but had no idea how. He sighed and sat on the bench that sat in the corner. He was happy she was alive, but wondered what it had cost her. And would she forgive him?

Chapter 18 – Angelic Island

Tiger felt the shift in the current through the hull of the pirate ship, a subtle but constant reminder of their imprisonment. The wooden vessel creaked and groaned as it cut through the dark waters, its timbers whispering secrets of past misdeeds and long-forgotten voyages. Three days had passed since the battle against the pirates, and the weight of those hours hung heavy in the air of the brig.

The brig was dimly lit by a single lantern hanging from a rusted hook in the ceiling, casting flickering shadows across the walls. The air was thick with the scent of salt and decay, a blend that turned the stomach and made every breath feel like a struggle. Tiger and Bree sat together on the cold, damp floor, their backs against the rough-hewn wood of their cell.

As they sat in silence, the creak of footsteps echoed down the narrow staircase that led to the brig. The sound was familiar, a rhythm they had come to recognize over the past three days. Kendrick was coming to visit.

The aging cleric pulled a stool from the corner of the cell's door and sat down with a groan. "These old bones haven't seen a fight like that in some time." He chuckled, then added. "I guess I don't bounce back like I once did."

Tiger snorted derisively.

Kendrick glanced between the two sitting on the floor. "At any rate, I've managed to calm Iro for the time being. Though I'm not sure for how long. While I am not convinced you two should just be let go, you showed us great mercy in not killing us all."

"What are you going to do with us then?" Tiger asked.

"We'll take you to see the lord and lady of GateHar. As planned," Kendrick said. "They'll know what to do with you. Iro is brash, stuck in the old ways. Kill first, ask questions after. But, since I'm in the employment of the king, I have other obligations. I've known you and your father for a very long time, and I'm more forgiving."

"Then why are we prisoners?" Tiger said, narrowing his blazing green eyes at the cleric.

"I'm still a Cleric of GateHar. I still have my duties and sacraments," Kendrick said with a shrug, as if his vestments were growing heavy. "I admit, you two have put me in a predicament. Part of me wants to side with Iro, the other is fascinated at the mere fact that she hasn't slaughtered us all."

Bree's crimson eyes slowly looked up to fix the cleric with a glare. The older man shivered.

"We'd both have every right to fight tooth and nail for our freedom, after your treatment of us in Xonthian City," Tiger said.

Kendrick nodded. "Indeed." He stood and pushed the stool back to the corner. "We'll be arriving soon. I'll come get you two, and we'll head out. Don't give me a reason to set Iro on you, and you'll remain uncuffed."

Tiger watched as the cleric disappeared up the stairs.

The afternoon sun dipped toward the horizon, casting long shadows over the rugged terrain. The air was thick with the scent of salt and seaweed, mingling with the faint aroma of woodsmoke from the town they were leaving behind. Tiger's horse, a sturdy chestnut mare named Tempest, moved with an easy grace, its hooves clattering rhythmically on the cobblestone path.

Tiger glanced over his shoulder at the harbor, the masts of the ship swaying gently in the breeze. He could still hear the distant shouts of sailors and the creaking of timber as the vessels rocked in their moorings.

The town of Ascent, with its narrow streets and closely packed buildings, seemed almost peaceful in the fading light, but Tiger knew better. He felt the tension in the air, a palpable sense of unease that had settled over them like a shroud. The clerics who watched them from darkened windows and doorways glared accusatorily at them. Yet, they didn't even know who they were. The mere fact that they were strangers on the island was enough to warrant suspicion.

Kendrick and Iro rode in silence behind them, their eyes boring holes in their backs, prodding them along the path and keeping a wary eye on the two prisoners. He felt the heat of anger penetrating the back of his head, coming from Iro's piercing gaze.

Tiger bristled but held his tongue. Now was not the time for a confrontation, though the desire to lash out burned within him. They were on a remote island, weeks away from the mainland. There were very few options of escape. Provoking the Paladin would do no good.

As they continued their journey, the landscape began to change. The rocky lowlands gave way to dense thickets of shrubs and twisted trees, their branches creating a lattice of shadows on the ground. The path narrowed, forcing them to ride single file. Tiger's eyes darted toward every movement in the underbrush, every shift in the shadows, as he strained to catch any unusual sounds. Would the clerics ambush them?

Kendrick slowed his horse, raising a hand to signal a halt. "We rest here," he announced, dismounting and tying his horse to a nearby tree. "We will continue when the sun begins to rise."

Tiger and Bree exchanged a wary glance but followed suit. Iro remained on guard, his eyes never leaving Tiger and Bree.

Tiger stretched his legs, feeling the tension ease slightly from his muscles. He moved closer to Bree, his voice barely a whisper.

"I need to cover my skin," she said.

Tiger raised a brow at her. They had no clothes, and she was wearing very little actual clothing. Her bandages, torn and tattered from the fight on the ship, were held together by sheer luck. Strands of long ribbons, tied together around her appendages and chest, were all that held their remains in place. His heart ached for her. He didn't have anything to offer her, no cloak, no blanket, or bedroll. They had lost everything when their ship was attacked.

"If I don't," she said, breaking his thoughts. "The hunger will come back sooner."

"I know," he whispered.

"What are you two plotting?" Iro growled, shoving Tiger toward the campfire Kendrick was setting up. "Sit down!"

Tiger stumbled but caught himself, glaring at Iro. He knew better than to provoke him, but the constant hostility was wearing thin. As the fire crackled to life, casting flickering shadows on their faces, Kendrick handed out small portions of dried beef and water. The fire's warmth was very little comfort against the chill of the evening.

After they finished eating, Kendrick rose, his expression unreadable. "Rest. We move at dawn." He glanced at Iro, who nodded and took up a position a few paces away, his sword resting on his lap.

Tiger and Bree settled down, but the cold, hard ground made sleeping nearly impossible. Tiger lay close to Bree, her body a shield against the night's chill breeze. He whispered, "We'll find a way out of this, Bree. We have to."

She nodded, her eyes meeting his with a flicker of hope. "Will we?"

Tiger watched her, his mind racing. She could easily kill them all and leave the island without so much as a second thought. Why was she so reserved? Had her time in the coffin done more damage to her than he realized? It must have, he couldn't even fathom being wrapped up and sleeplessly aware of being imprisoned.

Dawn came too quickly, the sky lightening to a dull gray. Kendrick was already up, packing their minimal supplies while Iro stood watch, his eyes never straying far from Tiger and Bree.

"Get up," Kendrick ordered. "We have a long day ahead."

Tiger helped Bree to her feet, their movements slow and stiff. They mounted their horses, the animals sensing their riders' unease as they kicked the earth irritably.

Unable to withstand the silence for a second day, Tiger drew his horse close to Kendrick. "Tell me about Angelic Island. There is a lot of wildlife here. They don't seem to be afraid of us."

"Why should they? There are no natural predators here," Kendrick said with an ironic smile toward Bree.

Tiger glanced around, noting the peaceful demeanor of the animals they passed by. "How did this happen?"

Kendrick's smile faded. "The GateHar Clerics have maintained a careful balance here for centuries. We protect the island and its inhabitants, ensuring that no harm comes to them. It's part of our duty."

Tiger's curiosity deepened. "And the clerics? How do they fit into all of this?"

Kendrick's eyes darkened. "The GateHar Clerics have always believed in maintaining balance and order, both in nature and within their ranks. They see themselves as stewards of the island, protectors of its unique environment. But their methods... can be harsh."

Tiger felt a chill. "Harsh? Like capturing and imprisoning people?"

He nodded. "Our actions are often misunderstood. We have a purpose, a greater good we strive for. Sometimes that means making difficult decisions."

Tiger's frustration bubbled to the surface. "And what purpose do Bree and I serve in this grand scheme of yours?"

Kendrick's gaze shifted to Bree, who was riding silently beside them. "You and Bree are different. You possess abilities that the GateHar Clerics may be interested in. Something to be studied."

"Me? Why me, though?" Tiger said, though the question seemed far harsher toward Bree than he meant. He shot her a look as if to say I'm sorry, but she didn't respond. He saw she was curious as well.

"Well, your ability to handle that sword of yours," Kendrick said, glancing at the wrapped bundle strapped to the back of Iro's horse. "That is a very unique weapon. That sword is not just a weapon. It holds ancient power, something the GateHar Clerics will want to understand. Your skill with it, your connection to it, makes you invaluable."

Tiger's hand instinctively moved to where his sword should have been. The weapon had always felt like an extension of himself, but he had never considered it might be more. "And Bree?" he asked, trying to steer the focus away from himself.

Kendrick hesitated, then sighed. "Bree's abilities are... less tangible but no less important. Her resilience against the sun, her strength in the face of hunger. I believe that studying her could unlock secrets that benefit us in the war against the Fire Isle Mages. Against her kind and the undead hordes."

Bree's eyes narrowed, her voice low and controlled. "You want to study us like we're animals?"

Kendrick shrugged. "That's not up to me."

Tiger felt a wave of anger and protectiveness. "And what if we don't want to be your experiments?"

Iro, who had been silently listening, interjected with a cold smile. "You don't have much of a choice. Refusal isn't an option."

Kendrick held up a hand to silence Iro. "Please, let's not resort to threats. It's a valid question. Again, it's not up to me. However, that said, if it helps us end the war, wouldn't that be worth the sacrifice?"

"You talk about sacrifice as if it's something we owe you. We didn't choose this," Tiger said with a growl. "And you, Iro—who are you to tell me what choice I have? You know nothing of me, you never even stopped to ask."

Iro's eyes narrowed. "Sacrifice? I have led battalions of men into battle against the Fire Isle Mages. Flesh melted away from bone. Those who were thought to be gone rised from the grave and renew their attack. The filthy magi only destroy. You've lost your father. You of all people should know that loss. But I have lost family, loved ones, men, and women under my command. There is no amount of suffering to quantify the sacrifices I have made and seen."

Kendrick's expression softened, as he spoke, showing a rare glimpse of empathy. "I understand your anger, Tiger. But the stakes are high. The Fire Isle Mages are a threat not just to us, but to the entire realm. If we don't find a way to stop them, many more will suffer. Do you not want to end the war? Your father once thought he could. What if you held the keys to ending it?"

Tiger wanted to argue, but he couldn't form a convincing counter. He did want to end the war. Sacrificing himself or Bree had never crossed his mind. However, if he were honest with himself, he knew eventually it may come down to that.

As his thoughts bore down on his shoulders, the landscape around them began to change. The dense shrubs and low trees gave way to rocky highlands. The path they followed wound upwards, the incline growing steeper with each step. The air grew cooler, the scent of pine and earth filling their nostrils.

Tiger looked up, his eyes scanning the terrain. The highlands were rugged and unforgiving, a stark contrast to the serene lower lands they had passed earlier. The path was narrow, bordered by sheer drops on one side and jagged rock faces on the other. It was a place where any misstep could be fatal.

As they ascended, the wind picked up, whipping through their clothes and chilling them to the bone. The horses struggled on the rocky path, their hooves slipping on loose stones. Every step was a battle.

The conversation from earlier hung heavy in the air, unresolved and tense. Tiger glanced at Bree, seeing the restraint in her eyes. They would endure this together, whatever the cost.

Hours passed in a relentless climb. The path leveled out at last, opening into a plateau that offered a breathtaking view of the island below.

Kendrick halted, allowing them a moment to catch their breath. "We're close now. Just beyond this ridge lies the heart of Angelic Island. The Great Cathedral of the Goddess."

As they reached the plateau, the wind's biting cold was momentarily forgotten in the awe-inspiring sight that unfolded before them. The cathedral stood majestically in the distance, its white marble facade glowing eerily in the pale light of the late afternoon. The structure was imposing, its grandeur accentuated by soaring flying buttresses that arched gracefully outward, giving the cathedral an ethereal quality.

The cathedral was the centerpiece of a sprawling complex. Surrounding it was a monastery, a collection of stone buildings with terraced gardens and neatly arranged farm plots. Sheep grazed contentedly in the fields, their soft bleating mingling with the wind's whisper. The farms, with their neat rows of crops, were a testament to the island's careful stewardship, a stark contrast to the rugged landscape they had traversed.

"The monastery and the surrounding lands," Kendrick continued, "house the clerics who aid in maintaining the island's defenses and performing the rituals necessary to keep the balance. The sheep and farms you see are part of the self-sustaining system we've created here. The land is cared for, the people are protected, and the island remains in harmony."

Bree took in the sight with a mixture of fascination and wariness. "And what are we supposed to do here?"

"You and Tiger will be taken to the inner sanctum of the cathedral, where the clerics have prepared a place for you. We'll have to discuss what to do next with the Lord and Lady."

As they approached the cathedral, the grandeur of the structure became even more apparent. The marble glistened in the fading light, its surface smooth and polished. The cathedral's entrance was flanked by massive columns, each carved with intricate symbols and patterns. The heavy wooden doors, adorned with golden fittings, beckoned them into the heart of the sanctuary.

The surrounding monastery was a hive of activity. Clerics in flowing robes hurried among the gardens and fields, focused with dedication and duty. The sight of them working harmoniously with the land added a layer of normalcy to the otherwise imposing atmosphere. A large statue of the Goddess GateHar stood in the center of town, as if watching over the monks below. Blue and gold banners with a crown of stars fluttered in the breeze.

One of those being watched over by the goddess greeted them as they passed through the gate to the cathedral. He bowed slightly as they approached before shooting Bree a vile glare.

"Welcome, Kendrick, we've been told to expect you," the young man said, reaching a handout to grasp the horse's bridle.

Tiger jumped down as Kendrick dismounted, followed by Bree and Iro.

"Will you be okay here?" Tiger said, leaning toward Bree to whisper.

"I'm fine," she replied.

"Doesn't hallowed ground—" Tiger started, but she cut him off.

"I said, I'm fine."

He looked at her and nodded.

Each of the riders handed the monk their horse's reins. After relieving their mounts of their gear, they followed Kendrick toward the main portal to the cathedral with Iro bringing up the rear. As they entered, two Paladins stood watch, dressed in bright plate mail, polished and gleaming in the early dusk. Their helmets were basic, split-visor helms painted white, with the symbol of GateHar on either side. Their breastplates were similarly adorned in color and decoration. A highly decorated sword that looked just as formidable dangled at their sides. Each one held a spear and shield, the GateHar symbol of a crown and of stars proudly depicted at its center.

Kendrick led them through a series of wide, arched doorways into the cathedral. The interior was equally magnificent, with high vaulted ceilings and stained-glass windows that cast a colorful glow across the marble floors. The air was thick with the scent of incense, mingling with the cool, fresh breeze that flowed through the open windows.

Inside, the cathedral's vast nave stretched out before them, lined with rows of pews and adorned with ornate chandeliers that hung like clusters of stars from the ceiling. At the far end of the nave, the altar stood in solemn splendor, bathed in a soft, golden light. A mural of the Goddess was painted along the wall that made up a portion of the apse beyond the altar.

Kendrick guided them toward a set of stairs leading to a private chamber above the nave. The walls of the chamber were adorned with more intricate carvings, and a large window provided a view of the island's sweeping landscape below.

"This will be your temporary quarters," Kendrick said, opening the door to a modest room. "We don't have a dungeon on the island. This is a prayer room. Clerics are locked here during the fast, to cleanse their souls before… Well, I'm sure you don't care."

Tiger snorted and stepped inside, followed by Bree. The door clicked shut and locked behind them. Bree began to pace the small chamber. He wanted to comfort her, but he didn't know how. He stood in the center of the room and watched her with empathetic eyes. This was all his fault.

Chapter 19 – Hollowed Earth

After Kendrick had left them in the room, a pair of clerics arrived with their first meal: a basic fare of bread, cheese, and water. The food was bland but sufficient, meant more for sustenance than enjoyment. They were also given plain robes to wear. Simple garments that replaced their tattered clothes from the ship.

The robes were practical, made from rough-spun fabric in muted colors, and although they were not particularly comfortable, they provided modesty and warmth. The clerics who delivered the meals spoke very little, their faces hidden behind the hoods of their own robes. They would leave the food on a table near the door and retreat quickly, leaving Tiger and Bree alone.

The room was small, with only a few pieces of furniture: a low bed with a thin mattress, a simple wooden table, and a couple of chairs. The window provided a view of the vast landscape, but the comfort it offered was only a reminder of their isolation.

Bree spent much of the day pacing and muttering to herself. Tiger remained seated on the edge of the bed, trying to process their situation. They spoke little, their conversations terse and focused on practical matters. The silence between them was heavy, filled with unspoken fears and doubts.

The second day mirrored the first, with the addition of a growing sense of routine. The clerics brought their meals at regular intervals, maintaining an almost mechanical precision. They brought no news, only the bare necessities of food and drink.

Finally, on the third day, Tiger couldn't take it anymore. "I'm sorry, Bree." Tiger started, peering sidelong at her. "I haven't had time to apologize, for… for you being captured. I can't take this any longer. I can't even imagine the horror of not being able to move, dark, cramped."

"It's not your fault."

"It was. My leap of faith landed us here."

"This was always going to be the outcome of associating with a monster like me."

"You're not a monster."

"You keep saying that, but do you believe it?" She stared at him a moment, then turned away.

"I do," he replied. "You know I do."

She shook her head as if in disbelief. "Do you think they will let a monster like me just leave?" Bree asked, her voice tinged with frustration. "Or let us leave? No, of course not.

Tiger leaned back in his chair, his gaze fixed on the flickering light. "I doubt it. Why are you not mad at me?"

Bree had finally stopped pacing. She sat on the edge of the bed, her eyes fixed on the lantern's light. Tiger, seated at the small table, watched her growing agitation with concern.

"I used to think I had everything figured out," Bree said suddenly, her voice barely above a whisper. "Before all this, I was so sure of my place in the world. I had plans, goals... now, it's like everything has been pulled out from under me."

Tiger looked up, his expression softening. "I'm sorry."

"Stop saying that, this is not your fault!"

He clenched his jaw. He wanted to argue. But he needed to hear her voice; he deserved her anger. He took a breath and let it out slowly. "I understand what you mean, though. It's like the ground beneath us is constantly shifting. But you're not alone in this. You haven't been for some time now."

Bree's shoulders sagged, her frustration giving way to a deeper sense of vulnerability. "I don't know how to handle this. I feel so powerless. All this anger and frustration, it's like a storm inside me that I fight to control. Every day is a struggle."

"I'm here with you. Let me share the burden."

"How?!" she said, turning on him, eyes blazing with fury.

Tiger flinched at the intensity of Bree's outburst but remained calm, his eyes steady as he met her gaze. The raw emotion in her voice and face was rarely shared. It shook him to see her bare herself. She always kept it bottled and hidden away.

"I know it's not easy," Tiger said. "I don't have all the answers. I can't magically fix everything. But I'm here, and that means something. I know this is all my fault. I'm so—" He cut himself off.

"Sorry?" she growled. "I'm the monster! It's because of me we're here. I am the one who murdered those men in Xonthian City. If it wasn't for that, Iro might not have found us! We wouldn't be locked up in this tower like… like."

"Monsters?"

Bree's eyes flared with a mix of defiance and pain. "Yes! Monsters. That's what I feel like. I've always tried to do what's right, but everything I touch seems to end in death. I never wanted this. I never wanted to hurt anyone. And now you're paying the price for it."

Tiger moved closer, his expression a mixture of empathy and love. "Bree, I keep telling you, you're not a monster. Monsters don't feel remorse. They don't keep an angry, vengeful kid like me from running off to war. What matters is that we're here together. If I could take the pain off yor shoulders, or you could share it. I would gladly take that burden."

Bree's anger began to wane, replaced by a more profound sadness. "I wish things were different. I wish we could go back and change everything."

"Me too," Tiger said, then added. "I'd have fought Iro to keep him away from you."

Bree peered at him. "This is not your fault."

"And you're not a monster. So, I guess we owe each other an apology."

The room fell into a contemplative silence. They had more pressing matters than lamenting over changes that couldn't be made, not when their survival took precedence. The flickering lantern cast soft, warm shadows on the walls, a small but significant comfort in their isolated world.

On the fourth day, their routine continued, but the confinement began to take its toll. The isolation was wearing on both of them, and the lack of information about their fate or purpose was beginning to wear on their patience.

During one of their meals, the clerics arrived with an additional note from Kendrick. The note was brief and written in elegant script:

Your cooperation is appreciated. We are in discussion with the Lord and Lady of GateHar on how to best proceed. Please be patient.

The note provided no comfort, but it was a sign that Kendrick had not forgotten them entirely. The promise of further answers, however vague, offered a glimmer of hope.

As the day wore on, Bree's pacing slowed, and she sat beside Tiger on the bed, their conversation lingered like a weight between them.

The door to their room creaked open, and Kendrick stood in the doorway, his expression unreadable. "It's time," he said curtly. "Master Davin wishes to speak with you."

Tiger and Bree exchanged a glance. Bree's eyes were filled with a mix of apprehension and defiance, while Tiger's expression was one of determination, he wanted this all to end, one way or another. They rose from their seats, and with a final, reassuring nod to each other, they followed Kendrick down the winding stone corridors of the cathedral.

The hallways were dimly lit, the cold marble floors echoing their footsteps. The walls were adorned with intricate tapestries depicting scenes of battle and divine intervention, a reminder of the clerics' ancient traditions and their sacred duty. As they walked, the air seemed to grow colder, the atmosphere charged with an unspoken tension. Iro joined them and followed close behind.

Kendrick led them to a heavy wooden door with iron fittings, engraved with ornate symbols that Tiger recognized as sigils of protection, intricate swirls, almost like rope intertwined, with no end to them. He had seen them at the castle, back in Xonthian City. Kendrick knocked three times before pushing the door open.

Inside, the room was surprisingly warm and inviting. Rich tapestries hung from the walls, and the furniture was plush and well-crafted. A large oak desk dominated the center of the room, behind which sat Master Davin. The man was middle-aged, with a sharp gaze and a demeanor that commanded respect. His robes were of finer quality than those worn by Kendrick, signifying his higher rank.

Master Davin looked up from a stack of papers. His piercing eyes settled on Tiger and Bree, his face darkening at their arrival. Iro entered after them, closing the door. The guards flanking them only heightened their sense of confinement. Tiger noticed Bree's clenched jaw, her anger palpable as she struggled to keep her fear and hunger at bay. It had been a week since she last fed, since the skirmish with the pirates, and her patience was wearing thin.

"Thank you, Master Davin," Kendrick said, offering a slight bow before sinking into a plush chair.

Master Davin Kristoff was a short, bald man whose deep-set wrinkles spoke of years of hard-fought battles or hidden sorrows. Tiger couldn't distinguish the difference. His dark grey eyes, peering through the thick lenses of his spectacles, scrutinized the newcomers with a practiced intensity. After a brief assessment of Tiger and Bree, he turned his attention back to Kendrick.

"I'm glad to see you made it back alive. Filthy pirates." Davin said, his tone brisk as he navigated the obligatory courtesies.

"Indeed, your grace," Kendrick replied with a forced smile.

"And I assume these are the individuals mentioned in our conversations with the Lord and Lady?"

"Yes. I've prayed each night since learning of them, hoping the goddess would offer guidance. Alas, her silence is as profound as it is disheartening," Kendrick admitted, his bitterness cutting through the air.

"Lady Acacia and Lord Eros are currently in prayer. They have entrusted me with holding final judgment and with carrying out the Order's course of action," Davin said, his gaze shifting past Kendrick to fixate on Tiger and Bree.

Tiger shifted uneasily under Davin's scrutiny.

"Personally, I agree with Iro, we should just end their miserable lives here and now," Davin explained, looking narrowly at Bree. "But the lord and lady wish a different course of action. If you two can survive through the Passage of Revelation with your lives, we will bow to the

Goddess of Life's wishes. If you live, we'll take you before their lordships, who will decide your fate from there."

"Who are Lady Acacia and Lord Eros?" Tiger asked.

"They are Lord Clerics, holy czars of a sort," Kendrick explained shortly. "They oversee the island as well as the entire order."

"What is this trial you want us to undertake?" Tiger asked nervously.

"The Passage of Revelation is a rip in the earth that descends into a nightmare," Davin explained. "The kind of nightmares that you wake from to find yourself drenched in a cold sweat. Aside from that, I cannot say. The experience is different for each person, and no one who has returned speaks of their trials. Kendrick, take them to the Passage and wait three days for them to return. If they don't return, consider them dead and return to me for further instructions. I'll see that Iro here brings you food and drink."

"Yes, your grace," Kendrick said, bowing slightly.

Iro bowed respectfully as well, though his eyes never left Bree.

Kendrick turned and opened the door between the two guards, leading Tiger and Bree back into the main chamber, Iro following close behind. There, he led them further into the temple, where they descended down an intricate set of stairs to a chamber below the main cathedral.

"I thought you didn't have a dungeon?" Tiger asked.

"The temple sits against the mountains you saw when we arrived," Kendrick said, his voice reverberating in the hollow chamber. "The Pillar, as we call the mountain range, was found to have very unique properties. Beneath it lies a kind of focal point of magic that acts in unpredictable ways. Clerics, once they have fasted and cleansed their souls, are brought down here to the passage and will pray for several more days. Without food or water."

"Some come back with the blessings of the Goddess," Iro said, and then added, more brightly, "others, however, simply go mad and kill themselves." He grinned at Bree. "Her mercy will be swift, and painful for you."

Kendrick cleared his throat and stood before large double doors that he pushed open. They creaked ever so slightly but gave way to another, smaller chamber. On the other side from where they stood were two expertly detailed statues standing on either side of a cave entrance that descended further down into the darkness. Braziers lit a path forward, which ended at a dais with water. Several chandeliers hung above them, like stars against an earthen sky.

"Enter and exit through here. I'll wait three days if you are not out by then; we will assume you have failed or died. If that is the Goddess's will," Kendrick said without preamble. "May she be with you."

Bree muttered under her breath, then stepped up to the crack in the wall. Tiger made to follow behind her, then stopped.

"I recognize GateHar, but who is this other statue of?" Tiger asked, pointing to the unidentified statue beside him.

"Kia, the God of Death."

Tiger swallowed hard and turned to Bree, who arched a brow at him.

"Ready?" she asked.

"Let's do it," Tiger replied.

The pair entered the cold darkness of the cavern, leaving behind the dancing flames of the torchlight for the pitch-black darkness beyond.

As they descended into the shadows, their eyes slowly adjusted to the inky blackness. Both could see in very little light, so navigating through it was slow but steady. They could make out sharp rocks on both sides and a winding floor that dove down into the heart of the earth.

The path leveled off and then twisted to the left, requiring them to walk single file through the darkness. Soon, the rocky wall that followed them down disappeared and was replaced by an open pit on both sides that dropped off into the bowels of the earth. The wind they had felt entering the passage bit cold against their backs, their robes whipping angrily around, like a vengeful wraith.

They didn't dare talk for fear of losing their concentration on the rocky walkway. Before they could worry about how much longer they had to balance across the windy void, it ended, dumping them onto a wide ledge that narrowed at one end.

"That was fun," Bree mumbled, fruitlessly pushing her hair back behind her ears.

"Oh, yeah," Tiger replied, rolling his eyes.

Tiger walked over to the narrow passage and saw that it opened into a large chamber. Bree followed behind him and looked around the room. From its vague outlines, they saw it was round and devoid of any natural cavern features. The walls were smooth and polished and appeared man-made. Set in the middle was a pedestal with the two statues they had seen above, back-to-back, facing the walls.

They approached the statues to get a better look. As they did, a blinding white light exploded around them, followed by a loud boom. The reverberations sent them flying back from the pedestal, landing a few feet away, their breath knocked from their lungs.

They lay motionless in the returning darkness, unaware of the spectral beings floating toward them, their ghastly faces twisted in satisfaction as Tiger and Bree slipped into unconsciousness.

Tiger shifted and sat up. His head was pounding in between his ears, and it sounded as if bells were ringing loudly nearby. White specks of light danced around his vision, causing his senses to whirl in a dizzying array of confusion. What had happened? How long had he been out?

He looked around the room and saw it was empty. He began to panic and stood up quickly to look around. Bree was nowhere to be seen.

"Bree!?" Tiger called into the darkness.

"She's not here," came a cold, bitter reply from behind him.

He whirled around and drew the TigerClaw, which was strapped to his back. His mind only briefly lingered on how he had gotten the weapon. The Clerics of GateHar hadn't given it back. Or had they? Tiger and Bree were sent into the cave without anything except the robes that adorned them. He peered around in confusion—no one was there. The statues sat idly on their pedestal; the shadows unwavering around them. Light emanated from nowhere, yet it was everywhere. He could see the room clearly. There was no source of the illuminating mechanism.

"Who are you?!?" he asked, his voice reverberating through the empty room.

"I am whoever you want me to be," the disembodied voice echoed.

Tiger glanced around but saw no one. As he turned back to the statues, the outline of a body slowly became visible. Like heat rising from a rock, it shifted and molded into his father.

"F-father?" Tiger stammered, taking a step forward.

"Yes, my son. I have been waiting for you," Hon'shu replied. His features were pale, and Tiger saw black patches of blood on his neck.

Tiger froze and watched the ghostly figure of his father float toward him. "Stop! You're dead!" Tiger said.

"Am I? I feel alive enough... I'm hungry as well," Hon'shu replied, drawing closer to his adopted son.

Tiger stepped back again and leveled his sword at his father. "No. You died. You're dead. This isn't real. Don't come any closer." Fear cracked his voice as tears began to sting his eyes.

"You DARE raise a sword against me. You ungrateful bastard! I raised you. You owe me your life, boy!" Hon'shu hissed. "I hunger for flesh!"

Tiger saw Hon'shu's mouth open, revealing long, pointy vampiric fangs. He gasped and stumbled backward. "No!"

Hon'shu lunged at his son, fingers trying desperately to grasp his leather tunic. "You live with one of my kind. You will only fall to her, if not her, then me! Let me be the one to taste your blood!" Hon'shu said.

Tiger's eyes widened in horror as his father pulled him closer, licking his lips mockingly.

"N-no. Bree wouldn't—No!" Tiger pushed back from his father. He wheeled around, his sword clumsily missing his father's neck.

"You will succumb to her in time. Why not instead, fall to me. You love me, don't you?" Hon'shu pleaded, drawing closer to Tiger as he backed up toward the pedestal.

"My father is dead. You are not him!"

"I AM YOUR FATHER!" Hon'shu howled.

Tiger sidestepped his father's advance and brought his sword up Hon'shu's side. The apparition was too fast. Hon'shu turned and came around behind Tiger, a ghostly white sword suddenly in his hands, pressing against his son's throat.

"You will feed my hunger. It is your destiny to betray those you love. Bree has already fallen to hunger. She has gone crazy with bloodlust. Should you pass from this hall, you will continue to fail those you love. Those loved ones, those close to you, will fall before you, a hopeless victim to your meaningless promises and vows," Hon'shu growled in Tiger's ear. "Vows of protecting them, even though you have no power or right to do so, will cause only pain and needless death and suffering."

"Please, stop, this isn't real, you are dead," Tiger said, pushing his father back, if only temporarily.

"I sacrificed myself for you, and you push me away like some animal? Some monster? Do you push her away? You failed her. Give up on her, I will be your salvation! She doesn't deserve you!"

"I failed Bree?" Tiger said, unsure and fearful.

He had promised her that he would protect her from harm, that he would die before he saw harm come to her. He believed in her. Saw the kindness in her eyes, deep behind the crimson shadows of her vampiric legacy. He cared for her.

"I saved you from being abandoned, forgotten, unloved. Repay me in blood, give me life."

"No," Tiger said. Gritting his teeth, he forced the dread rising in his throat down. It landed in the pit of his stomach with wrenching nausea.

"Feed me, join me in the sweet afterlife. Forget about the path you have chosen. Forget Bree, she has passed over into the abyss already," Hon'shu said, drawing closer to Tiger's soft and sweaty neck.

"NO!" Tiger yelled. He head-butted his father and whirled around.

Their swords clashed in the darkness. Anger and fear prickled his skin. His hands slick with moisture, he gripped the handle of his sword tightly. He stepped toward his undead father, his sword coming down and then across to catch the ghostly sword with the talon blade of the TigerClaw. They clanged together, and both men grunted with strain as they tried to push the other off balance.

Hon'shu reeled back. Tiger lunged forward with his sword raised. Their blades met in a clash that echoed off the stone walls.

Anger and guilt threatened to choke him. His hands, slick with sweat, gripped the handle of the TigerClaw, knuckles turning white. He pressed the attack, not willing to give an inch to the undead visage of his father.

Hon'shu recovered quickly, swinging his ethereal sword in a wide arc. Tiger ducked low, feeling the whoosh of air as the blade passed overhead. He countered with an upward slash, aiming for his father's midsection. The apparition parried, their weapons locking again.

They circled each other in the dim light.

"You fight like a cornered beast, boy. But you'll tire soon enough."

Tiger ignored the taunt. He feinted left, drawing his father in, then spun right with a downward strike. The TigerClaw skittered off Hon'shu's guard and nicked the ghoul's arm.

Hon'shu growled and thrust forward. Tiger sidestepped, bringing his sword across in a swift motion. The talon blade of the TigerClaw caught the ghostly sword, hooking it with a twist. Both men grunted with strain as they tried to push the other off balance.

Tiger's arms shook. With a quick twist of his arm, the TigerClaw wrenched and snapped the blade his father was holding in two. The broken halves dissolved into vapor.

Tiger didn't hesitate. He came back with a quick change of direction, his sword whipping through the air. The edge sliced clean through the apparition's neck, decapitating the ghastly head of his father.

Bree moaned and blinked rapidly, trying to clear the blurry vision and starlight that sparkled in and out of focus. Her ears were ringing, and she felt disoriented. How long had she been out? She staggered to a knee and then stood, as she scanned the pitch-black room they had entered. It was empty, and she couldn't sense Tiger's presence anywhere nearby. The statues stood stony black a few feet away, mocking the sudden lonely feeling she had. It was like being locked in the coffin all over again. The space around her was stifling. She felt panic bubble from the pit of her stomach, a sensation she had not felt in a long time. For the first time in her entire life, she felt as if she were being suffocated.

She whirled around to see if Tiger had exited the room, but she couldn't find the crevice that they had entered a few moments ago. She clawed at the walls as sheer panic began to take control. Her eyes felt as big as saucers; her heart, had it been beating, would have been pounding through her chest.

"Welcome to the abyss," a voice echoed behind her.

She spun back around to see several ghostly, pale visages of people she didn't recognize appear from the depths of the darkness. They were not alive, she could tell that much. They didn't radiate life or heat that she could see.

"What do you want?" Bree asked testily, forcing the panic down. Anger was an easier emotion to let loose than fear. She had no use for fear.

"Do you not know your victims? Do you not see our faces in your dreams, mocking you, teasing you as you lie awake each night in his arms?" the voices said as more bodies began to appear suddenly behind them.

"We are those you kill each night as you feed the disease you harbor," the lumbering bodies echoed coldly.

"Stay away from me," Bree growled as they approached. She flicked her wrist at a small group of them and watched as they flew away from her in a fiery explosion of energy.

"You are hungry now, aren't you?" they asked collectively. "You can no longer feed, while under the watchful eyes of the GateHar Clerics."

"Stay... away... from... ME!" Bree growled. She put her palm toward them, causing the surrounding air to explode with flames that just as quickly went out.

The ghostly apparitions shimmered, then solidified once again and advanced toward her, their blank expressions turning to anger and disgust.

"We know what you want. Your heart, though still from the curse of blood lust, you long for him. Tiger—You want him. Your hunger wants him, doesn't it?" The ghosts grinned evilly at her.

The crowd of wraiths parted ways, and Tiger walked toward her. She saw his body heat, warm and inviting in the black room. He drew closer to her, inviting her.

"Bree, what's wrong? You look hungry," he said worriedly.

"T-Tiger?" she asked.

"What's wrong, Bree?"

"I-I don't know. What's going on?"

Tiger touched her cheek softly. His skin was warm and soothing. She felt the pulse of life flowing in his veins.

Bree had promised herself that she would never drink Tiger's blood. It would cause too much pain to taste it, and he knew he would never accept that kind of life. He was too pure and valiant to be lured toward immortality. She alone would endure the vampiric tastes and would never want him to go through the same hell she lived in. Yet, now, here, alone with him, hunger raging in her throat and stomach, she wanted nothing more than to taste the sweet life in his veins. She imagined the crimson liquid, pulsing in her mouth, quenching her thirst, lifting her to ecstasy. She shivered with anticipation.

"Yes, Bree. Take me. Feed," Tiger offered, tilting his head to the side to expose the soft skin of his neck.

"N-no. Tiger wouldn't want this. The real Tiger would not want this. You are not Tiger!" she scowled.

She pushed the imposter back toward the crowd of ghosts, knocking him into the pedestal and landing with a soft thump.

"It is no use. The thirst will consume you. Feed now, on your willing friend. Or die here, alone and hungry for all eternity!" The disembodied voices echoed.

"Never!" she replied angrily.

The ghosts flooded her from every direction. She froze in terror, unable to move as the cold void of death's minions washed over her.

Chapter 20 – Revelations

Before Hon'shu's head hit the ground, it evaporated, along with his father, leaving Tiger in the dark once again.

He stood panting, his legs shaking as his adrenaline burned away. He'd just cut the head of his adopted father off. Even though it was all an illusion, he still felt like he'd dishonored his father's memory with the act of barbarism.

"Your convictions are strong, young one," a soft voice said.

Tiger looked above the statue to see a ghostly figure of a woman floating. The ghost was naked, hovering eerily above him like a goddess of pure light. She had long white hair that flowed down the front of her body, barely covering her supple features. She radiated power that filled him with peace, causing his breathing and heart to slow as if by magic.

"W-who are you?" he asked. He was drawn into her eyes, piercing orbs of pure white light that stretched on beyond time and space. He was lost in them, as if he were everywhere all at once.

"I am the spirit of love and passion, a messenger from GateHar. Only people gifted by the Goddess of Life can see or hear me. My name is Ife," she replied solemnly. She bowed her head slightly, a smile splitting her lips.

"Why? Am I dead?"

The spirit chuckled and shook her head. "No, my dear Tiger. You are very much alive, more so than ever I would expect," she said.

"What happened?" Tiger asked. He was too preoccupied with the spirit that he didn't even notice the sword he had been holding was gone.

"Though there is much greatness within you, there will be plenty of temptation to stray onto dark paths. You were tested on how you would react to these distractions. Your faith in yourself and others is a great strength, but never let your mind stray to the shadows lurking in men's souls."

"What do you mean? I don't understand," Tiger replied hopelessly.

"Clear your mind of everything except the future. Your road will take you on many adventures; you will see many things in your time. But within your travels, there will be times when doubt, anger, fear, and death will cloud your judgment. Remember what you have learned here and know this: Your father, Hon'shu, gave you everything you need to conquer any obstacle. Let his light guide you."

"What should I do?"

The spirit smiled. "Your destiny is your own, young one. The Gods have no part in your life, much to their confusion. But don't fear, the Goddess will always be with you. You have nothing to fear."

"I live in fear because I don't want to die without leaving this world a better place for everyone," Tiger said heavy-heartedly. "How can I get away from that?"

"It is a noble cause, Tiger. Please understand that I cannot tell you how to lead your life, rather provide you with insight into what will occur," the ghostly woman said with a sigh. "There are abilities and strengths within you that have not yet been discovered. Believe in them, and they will assist you when you need them most. The Goddess has blessed you with amazing gifts; use them well.”

Tiger nodded, questions flooding his mind the longer he stood. He peered down to try and pinpoint his next question, but as he looked up to ask another, the apparition was inches from him. His breath was instantly knocked from his lungs as the beautiful being touched his cheek.

“Go, now, Tiger Darqlaw. Be at peace with yourself, with the world, and its people. Love those close to you, hold them closer, and never stray from the path you have chosen,” she smiled and kissed his forehead softly.

Darkness engulfed him as his vision blurred, and his thoughts narrowed into unconsciousness, his mind drifting to Bree. He hoped she was well and wished he could see her again.

Bree’s vision turned crimson as anger and fear raged for dominance. Blood lust thundered in her ears as it grappled for control of her soul. The cold bodies of hundreds of her dead victims piled on top of her, mocking her. Every one of them was a reminder of the sacrifice to the vampirism that flowed through her body.

Now, every single one of them clawed at her, tearing at her flesh and clothes. Their moans and pain-filled screams echoed through the darkness, drowning her, drawing her further into despair.

She felt trapped, hopelessly trapped. Fear exploded with a flash of energy that sent the bodies on her flying through the air, causing the room to shake with fury as she lost control.

She crawled to her knees and tried to stand. Her legs buckled under the weight of guilt, and she fell to her hands, panting from the exertion and panic. She sat back on her heels and looked around.

The statues on the pedestal shimmered with soft light, and slowly the silhouette of a naked woman with stark white hair appeared before her. She floated in the air a few feet from Bree, looking down at her approvingly.

"Child of the night, soul barer, rise, please," the ghost said calmly.

Bree's breathing began to pace into normalcy. The fear and cold terror she'd felt a moment ago receded.

"You are indeed an unusual specimen. Why this has been allowed to pass, I cannot say. You have an extraordinary ability to suppress the bloodlust that your kind thrives on. You would rather face death than cast your burden onto those you love and care for," the ghost explained casually.

"Who are you?" Bree asked respectfully.

"My name is Ife. I am the guardian of this cavern. I have seen many wayward souls come through this room, but none have been like you," Ife said with a gentle smile.

"W-what happened?" Bree asked.

"You were tested, child of death. You were given the choice to live, to free yourself from the bloodlust in order to thrive. But you forbid it and instead pushed it aside with your immobile will," Ife explained. "Your heart is pure, even if it doesn't beat with life. You can feel emotions, even though the curse you were burdened with should have stripped them from you. You do not take life needlessly, and you regret it. You feed, not for pleasure, but for survival."

Bree looked at Ife with confusion. Though she couldn't quite place the feeling, somewhere deep inside her, she understood what the spirit was trying to tell her.

"Go now, walk freely among the children of GateHar, for she has no fear of you further infecting the world with the vampiric curse you bear. Your soul is protected and will not fall into bondage."

"I am a monster!"

"No child, you are not a monster. A monster did this to you. You have shown great restraint in what you have to do, need to do, to live. And that's all the Goddess can ask."

"If you are the messenger of the Goddess, then please, heal me of this affliction!"

"To heal you would mean your death. Do you want to live? Or die?"

Bree thought for a moment. "I want to be free."

"You are free. You are free to choose your path. You are free to love. Your soul stirs in your breast, guides you, makes you. You."

"I don't want to be alone anymore," Bree said, bowing her head.

Ife floated toward Bree, stopping inches from her, and peering deep into her. Bree felt her probing her inner thoughts, hidden behind the wall she had built up around them over the decades, as if it was never there. But, she didn't feel invaded or vulnerable. She felt at peace.

"You are not alone, Bree," Ife whispered.

"Tiger," Bree said.

Ife smiled and nodded, then placed a soft kiss on Bree's forehead, causing her to fall to the ground in a heap. As the beautiful spirit floating before her faded from view, she realized that for the first time since becoming a vampire, she felt the warmth of a kiss upon her skin. It reminded her of her mother. A single tear crept its way from behind her eyelashes and trickled down her cheek.

Bree stirred as she felt cold, icy wind whipping at her robes. She opened her eyes and bolted upright. She was lying outside the room where they had entered, seemingly hours ago. She looked to her side and saw Tiger moaning, covered in sweat, and shivering convulsively.

"Tiger, wake up," she said, pushing his arm gently.

Tiger quickly opened his eyes and sat up, screaming.

"Tiger! You, okay?" she asked, sliding next to him and putting a reassuring hand on his shoulder.

"Huh? Uhm... Yeh. I think so," he replied. "Let's get out of here."

Bree nodded and stood, helping Tiger to his feet. They hurried across the chasm to the winding tunnel that led back up to the crack in the wall. Moments later, they emerged into the brazier-lit room where they had started down into the Passage of Revelations.

Tiger and Bree's eyes adjusted to the new levels of light, and they saw that the chandeliers had fallen into heaps on the ground.

Opposite the passage, they noticed Kendrick, half-buried under one of the metal works of the chandelier.

"What happened?" Tiger said.

"I-I think I caused this!" Bree replied. "When I was down there, I lost control. I was scared. I lashed out."

"It's okay," Tiger said.

The two began to fling debris from Kendrick's body, tossing them aside, heedless of where they fell.

The cleric moaned as the last piece was removed.

"Shhhh! It's okay, be still," Tiger said, looking him over. He looked at Bree, who was concentrating on the pool of blood under his body. "Bree?"

She didn't respond. Instead, she sat, frozen, in the flickering light of the room, the reddish ooze in front of her, tempting her to take a sip.

Tiger frowned and turned his attention back to Kendrick. "I don't know how this works, but I'll try," Tiger whispered.

He set his hands on Kendrick's forehead, remembering what had happened when he'd healed the barkeeper back in Xonthian City. He tried to recall what was going through his head, but couldn't remember. Suddenly, he felt it, without even knowing how. Warmth spread out from his hands, and a soft light highlighted his fingers. Kendrick grunted and grimaced slightly, just as Lio had done. Then his features cleared, and he lay motionless. Tiger watched him and saw his eyes slowly begin to flutter open.

"What-What happened?" Kendrick groaned, placing a hand on his head as he sat up.

Tiger shrugged. "We came out to find you lying under a pile of stones and the chandelier," Tiger said.

"An explosion somewhere under me shook the entire temple. The next thing I knew, a rock the size of my fist had landed in my lap, and then I was out cold. I think bigger chunks hit me," Kendrick said. Picking up a rock in illustration, he tossed it aside. "How am I healed, though?"

"Back away from him this moment!" Iro said from behind them, his sword leveled at Tiger and Bree.

Tiger went for the sword usually strapped to his back, but it was gone once again, like a phantom limb.

Tiger looked over to Bree, who had closed her eyes upon hearing Iro.

"I said, back away!"

Tiger stood in front of Bree. Iro lunged at him, his hatred blinding him. Tiger sidestepped the thrust and pushed him off balance. This further enraged the Paladin. He turned around, slashing across Tiger's midsection, but he was faster than the bulkier knight in armor.

"How did I—what did you do?" Kendrick asked, narrowing his eyes at Bree, then Tiger. "Am I bitten!?" He pressed a hand to his throat fearfully.

"I'll kill you both!" Iro said.

"No," Bree said under her breath. "I am not a spreader of the disease that's in me. I am its avenger," she growled. Bree stood and squared her shoulders at Iro.

"Enough!" Kendrick commanded.

The Paladin, eyes blazing with anger, ignored the older man and lunged at Bree. Iro propelled Tiger aside with a swift, brutal shove and landed heavily on Bree. She made no move to keep him from running her through. She knew it'd hurt, but he wouldn't kill her.

Tiger scrambled to his feet and pulled the torch from its holder in the wall. He ran at Iro, smashing it across the Paladin's head, causing sparks to fly through the air. Iro growled, his hand feeling the back of his head.

"You'll pay for that, boy," he said as he regained his composure.

Tiger dropped the torch and drew his sword. His heart pounded. Iro charged, his own blade swinging in a vicious arc aimed at Tiger's chest. Tiger parried, the clash of steel ringing out like a smith's hammer. The force jarred his arms, but he held his ground.

Iro slashed high and then low, forcing Tiger to dodge and weave. Sweat stung Tiger's eyes as he countered, thrusting forward. The tip of the TigerClaw grazed Iro's armor, scraping metal with a screech. Iro roared and kicked out, his boot slamming into Tiger's gut. Air exploded from Tiger's lungs, and he staggered back, gasping.

"You think you can stand against me, whelp?" Iro snarled. He brought his sword down in an overhead strike. Tiger rolled aside, the blade embedding in the stone floor with a crack. Seizing the opening, Tiger surged up and drove his elbow into Iro's jaw. The Paladin's head snapped back, rivulets of blood seeping from a split lip.

Iro wiped his mouth and laughed. He yanked his sword free and spun, slicing toward Tiger's side. Tiger blocked, but the impact sent him skidding across the floor. Pain flared in his shoulder.

Tiger lunged forward and slashed at Iro's arm. The Paladin dodged, but not fast enough; a shallow cut opened on his forearm, blood running down it. Iro's eyes widened in rage. He barreled forward, tackling Tiger to the ground. They tumbled in a heap, swords clashing to the ground.

The fight grew frantic, blows raining down as they wrestled for dominance. Tiger's vision blurred from a stray elbow to his temple. He was losing the fight.

Suddenly, from where he lay on the ground, Kendrick reached out with a powerful arm, grabbing Iro's ankle and yanking hard. The Paladin stumbled, his grip on Tiger loosening. "Iro, that's enough," Kendrick growled. He extended a hand to the Paladin. "Get over here and help me up."

Iro's face flushed red under the torchlight. He held his position atop Tiger for a long moment, knuckles white around a fistful of his tunic. Then, with a low grunt, Iro released his hold and pushed himself up.

Tiger rolled to his side, coughing, one hand pressing against his bruised ribs. He watched Iro turn toward Kendrick, his sword still clutched in his other hand. Iro hesitated as his gaze flicked to Tiger, eyes narrowed. With a sharp click, he sheathed his blade. He reached down, clasping Kendrick's extended hand, and hauled the older man to his feet with an irritated jerk of the wrist.

Kendrick steadied himself, his expression stern as he met Iro's glare.

Tiger pushed himself upright, wiping blood from his lip. The room fell quiet.

Tiger ran to Bree, who was standing, blood pooling around her from the wound Iro had caused.

"You okay?" he asked.

"I'll heal," she said.

"We are in the house of the Goddess; you know better than to draw your blade here!" Kendrick said, looking first at Iro and then Tiger. "You two will respect that, am I making myself clear?"

The muscles in Iro's jaw tightened, his rage barely contained, as he sheathed his sword with a harsh, metallic scrape.

"We should report your return to the Lord and Lady," Kendrick said, his voice regaining its calm authority. He gestured for them to follow, turning toward the grand staircase that spiraled up into the shadows above.

Tiger watched the elder cleric's retreating form, his mind racing with thoughts of the recent conflict. Bree, her expression now unreadable, fell into step behind Kendrick. Iro brought up the rear, his face still flushed with anger, his eyes burning with a silent fury.

As they ascended the stairs, the air grew warmer, the light dimmer, and the shadows deeper. The house of the Goddess seemed to close in around them. The tension among the group was palpable, ready to ignite again at the slightest spark.

Chapter 21 - Reluctant Blessings

So, you are able to heal," Kendrick said, examining Tiger.

"Be thankful we returned when we did, or you would have died," Bree replied coldly.

Kendrick looked at her but said nothing.

"She's right, though. You felt pretty far gone if that's even what I was feeling," Tiger said, looking at his hand. "I'm not sure how I heal, but I do, I've done it once before."

"Yes, I'm aware. Supposedly, Carv was healed. Is that right, Iro?" Kendrick asked as they ascended the stairs.

Iro only grunted.

"Yes," Tiger replied. "I was surprised. I ran home, scared I'd be caught."

Iro snickered. "And here you are."

"But you completely healed me, no after-effects, and I was still able to walk out of there as if nothing happened. Only high-level clerics and Paladins can heal that quickly and extensively," Kendrick replied.

Tiger had no response for him. He didn't know any more about his healing powers than Kendrick did. They were as much of a mystery as the rest of his latent abilities. His mind remembered what Ife had told him. He had many such latent talents.

Iro snorted derisively. "The idea that this half-breed, vamp lover is a Paladin of the Holy Goddess, fills me with sickness."

"It is not up to us to judge his calling, or the will of the gods," Kendrick said.

The cathedral was bright, causing the stained-glass windows to sparkle brilliantly against the darkened sky outside.

As they entered the cathedral's main palisade, they were greeted by several guards like those in Davin's office several days ago.

"This way," one of them said, leading the group down the center aisle toward the altar.

Tiger followed behind Kendrick, with Bree close beside him, and Iro lagging behind. As they approached the altar, Kendrick bowed before Davin, who was waiting in front of the steps, with two other stately-looking clerics.

The woman had long, flowing, silvery gray hair and stood slightly taller than her companion. Her features were soft, with gentle amber eyes that straddled a sloping, knife-edge nose. She wore plain white robes that covered her body down to her ankles. The man beside her was older. Both had deep lines under their eyes and across their faces. He wore white robes but had short gray thinning hair, with strands of brown that reflected his former youth.

"Lady Acacia, Lord Eros," Kendrick said, bowing before them.

They held themselves with an air of importance and holiness, which caused Tiger to shift his weight uncomfortably.

The main chapel around them stretched out. High vaulted ceilings curved overhead like the bones of a leviathan. Light poured in through tall stained glass windows behind the lord and lady, splashing reds and blues across the intricate tiled floors that ran down the aisles, their scenes were a mix of storytelling and divine warnings.

Tall pillars of carved limestone lined the nave, octagonal in shape, each with slender attached columns rising up to meet the arches. Pews of dark wood filled the sides, leading toward a grand altar at the far end, where the group now stood.

The air felt thick, laced with the faint smell of wax, dust, and incense. The two priestly rulers bowed respectfully and then returned their eyes to Bree and Tiger behind him.

"Is this them?" Lady Acacia asked coldly, her kind eyes suddenly darkening. "Tiger Darqlaw and Bree Sangmu?"

"Yes, your grace," Kendrick said, turning to look at their guests.

"They passed the tests," Lord Eros said, mildly amused. "The Goddess has either a weird sense of humor, or they cheated."

"I assure you, we didn't—" Tiger began, but was cut short by Lady Acacia.

"Pass or fail, I would rather see these two heretics die, than allow them to roam free across the world," she spat.

Tiger arched a brow and opened his mouth to protest, but was cut off when Kendrick jumped in.

"Your holiness. If I may? They saved my life at the passage. Tiger shows great potential to heal; he was able to mend my wound with a Paladin's touch," Kendrick explained.

Lady Acacia looked at Tiger and Bree calculatingly before responding. "A Paladin's touch?"

"Yes, your holiness," Kendrick replied.

"Blasphemy," Iro spat. "There has never been, and never will there be a half-breed Paladin."

"Are you calling Kendrick a liar?" Lord Eros asked.

Iro glanced sidelong at the elder cleric. "I believe he is mistaken. I don't think he was in any danger. The charlatans made the story up to make themselves look good."

Bree started toward Iro, but Tiger put a gentle hand on her arm and shook his head ever so slightly. He saw her jaw muscles tighten in repressed agitation.

"I know I was injured. Look!" Kendrick held up his robe in illustration; a large amount of his right side was tacky and stained a darker color. "And they did survive the trials."

Iro stared at it as if trying to come up with an explanation.

"But he is a half-elf, that's impossible," Iro said. "Their healing is elemental-based, not that of pure light."

"I understand," Kendrick said. "However, I know what I saw. I would have lost my life if it weren't for him. I am sure of it."

"What about her?" Lady Acacia growled. "Her kind is a disgrace to all that GateHar stands for."

"From what I know about GateHar, she stands for Life," Tiger said levelly.

"She is not alive," Lord Eros replied crossly.

"She is a vile creature!" Iro interrupted.

"She breaths, she feels, she has whatever it is that makes the rest of us alive. She can walk in the sun, she does no evil willingly, she shows emotions," Tiger replied.

"Walk in the sunlight? Th-that's not possible, vampires can't—" Lady Acacia sputtered. "Iro?"

The Paladin opened his mouth to contradict Tiger, but couldn't. He closed his mouth again, his face turning red as he did. "She is able to travel in the sun, yes."

Kendrick nodded.

The two rulers convened with one another for a moment, then looked back at Tiger and Bree.

"It looks like we may have to bow to the wishes of the divine. I don't know what they have planned for you two, but there must be some reason you walk among us," Lady Acacia said.

"Make no mistake, you two will be watched," Lord Eros added.

"No! I forbid this! This is blasphemy of the highest!" Iro spat, taking a step forward. "If a half-breed and a vampire are blessed by the goddess, then my covenant, all our teachings, and sacred rights are all for nothing!"

"You are out of place, Iro," Lord Eros said, glaring at the Paladin.

Iro reached up and unstrapped his breastplate. It fell to the floor with a loud clash. "If I am not able to show my discontent, then why are we even here? What has my life been for, if not in the service of GateHar?"

"She teaches us more than what is written by mortal men and women," Lady Acacia said.

"But those teachings are based on the Goddess's divine gospel. I refuse to bow before the lies and hypocrisies anymore," Iro growled. He withdrew his sword from his scabbard and plunged it into the floor with a crack that reverberated through the room. And with a twist, the blade shattered, leaving the point embedded in the white stone floor. Iro whirled around and stormed from the hall.

Lady Acacia shook her head and glanced sidelong at Lord Eros. "There will be others who question their faith. This has changed so many lives. What has been done can no longer work. We must trust in our belief that the gods have a plan."

"This very well may be the beginning," Lord Eros said, jutting a chin toward Tiger and Bree.

"Very well. You may leave and go where you wish, unhindered by the Clerics of GateHar. I will spread the word through our clergy to leave you be and aid you should you need it. But only because you saved Kendrick's life, and your quest to purge Xonthian of the vile Fire Isle Mages is a righteous one. If you step out of line, however, our wrath will be swift and unforgiving," Lady Acacia explained bitterly.

Tiger started to ask her about how he could heal if it wasn't based on the elven magics, and if she could help him learn more about it, but decided that in light of recent events, he should leave while they could. The guards escorted them out of the cathedral to sparsely furnished and private sleeping quarters just outside the entrance to the cathedral's main portal. It appeared to be part of the monastery and shared a hall with another, larger steepled building nearby.

Bree entered her room, and Tiger was shown to another opposite hers. He sat down on the thin bed and bowed his head. His soul felt tattered. Despite the heaviness in his heart, he was thankful they were both alive. He wanted to leave as soon as possible.

A knock on the door broke Tiger's thoughts.

"Come in," he called.

Kendrick opened the door and stepped inside. "I am bringing you your weapon. And, I wanted to have a word with you. If I may?" he asked.

"I don't see why not," Tiger said. He took the TigerClaw and cradled it protectively in his arms.

Kendrick nodded, then shut the door as he entered.

"Thank you for healing me," Kendrick began, "Though your methods are untrained, you were able to channel vast amounts of healing power through your hands and into my wounds. I want to offer you my training, teach you how to be more efficient with your ability to heal."

Tiger raised an eyebrow. "Won't your Lord and Lady frown upon this?" he asked.

"Perhaps, but they need not know. I will train you as a gift for saving my life," Kendrick replied.

Tiger bowed humbly. "Thank you," he said.

"Their holiness is very interested in how and why a half-elf such as you has been gifted with the power to heal so easily," Kendrick said with a wry smile. "You've set the hall ablaze with inquiries and prayers."

"I wish I had the answer for them."

"Their calling you a Paladin is a very high honor in our order. I've never seen them so beside themselves with confusion," Kendrick said with a shocked, amused expression. "That is likely the reason Iro had an issue with you. On some level, he knew that would be the case."

"Well, then, they don't get out much. Life is confusing," Tiger snickered.

"Ironic, isn't it?" Kendrick chuckled. "I've lived in Xonthian City for most of my life, and I've seen how the gods don't exactly play by any sort of rule."

"So have I," Tiger replied, remembering the lesson he'd learned from Bree regarding the bartender.

"Well," Kendrick added, "take your Paladin status and use it for the betterment of mankind and you'll do alright in my book."

"I intend to," Tiger replied.

"Good, then let's begin our lessons," Kendrick said, clasping his hands together.

After several hours of practicing the healing arts through meditation and concentration, Tiger began to feel a greater connection to his powers.

"You learn fast," Kendrick mused as he sat cross-legged on the floor beside Tiger, who was meditating quietly.

"Thank you," Tiger whispered. "Does the healing hurt?"

"Not unless you are undead," Kendrick said. "Why?"

"Because each time I heal someone, it's like my touch pains them."

"That is likely caused by the strain on their own life energy. It's more of a shock than actual pain," Kendrick explained.

"I see," Tiger said, looking down at his hands. "So, healing the undead hurts them?"

"It has been known to, from time to time. That level of pure energy is rare, though," Kendrick said, scratching his chin thoughtfully.

"Tell me more about the undead," Tiger stretched his legs out and leaned against the wall.

"What would you like to know?"

"How does that magic work?" Tiger asked.

"It starts with a very high-level magic-user, usually a Fire Isle Mage who studies the arts of death, called Necromancy. Once they obtain a certain level of skill, they can cheat death and create Liches. These Liches are kind of a node, if you will, that channels pure magical energy and directs it to the dead creatures it controls." Kendrick scratched his cheek, "Sort of like the strings of the marionette, with the puppet master being the Lich."

"I see," Tiger said.

"That's it for tonight. I must be off," Kendrick said as he stood with a groan.

"Good night," Tiger said as he too stood.

Tiger watched as the old man left, closing the door behind him. He thought back to their attack on North Kelsa, remembering how Bree had killed her parents. They were all puppets attached to a single Lich, marching against them because they were bound by a magical string. He shook his head in dismay and lay down in the bed to fall slowly into slumber. His dreams were plagued by death.

Bree sensed Kendrick enter Tiger's room shortly after being left to her own devices. The sparsely furnished room resembled a cell more than a bedchamber, one she desperately needed to escape.

She had to eat, though she knew feeding here among the villagers was out of the question. She paced the small room idly, trying to think of something she could eat without raising alarms. As she did, she recalled the deer they had seen on their way to the Cathedral.

"Perfect," she thought.

It was better than nothing, and she would not make it back to Port Orlynns without satisfying her hunger.

She cracked the door open and peered out. There were no guards, and as the night progressed, fewer and fewer people wandered the streets.

Bree slid from her room and darted down the hall to exit the building. Upon reaching the cool, comforting darkness, she jumped to the roof and quietly glided along its peak.

She followed the roof till it ended, then she leapt and landed soundlessly on the next building.

After a few minutes of dodging torch lights, open windows, and the occasional priest, she finally reached the edge of town.

She raced to the open plains around the village, bound for the area where they had seen the deer. After what seemed like hours of hiking, she finally caught their scent.

Bree stalked her prey, her senses picking up their smell like a wolf, looking for its next meal. She caught sight of their body heat, a slightly discolored area in the darkness several yards away.

As she drew closer, the hunger in her belly grew, anticipating the blood she would soon have on her lips.

She continued to stalk them, growing closer with each step she took. As Bree drew near, she could see them more clearly. Their spotted hide was within striking distance. She could almost taste them.

The deer's ears twitched toward her position, but they made no attempt to move. It felt at peace here.

She started toward the creature and froze.

A sudden wave of clarity washed over her. She wasn't a mindless predator driven only by hunger.

She had been so preoccupied with her hunger that everything else had faded. Her name, her identity, her reason for being. Realization hit her hard.

Bree stepped back. Her breath came ragged in her throat, almost in a panic, as if she had forgotten how to breathe.

The deer didn't notice. They kept grazing, tails flicking lazily, calm in the quiet. They had no idea how close they had come.

She stared at them. Everything felt constricted, as if the clothes she wore were tight. What was she doing? She had to feed, right? Why was there a sudden doubt lingering?

Bree fell to her knees. The weight of her uncertainty pressed down on her like a heavy cloak. She buried her face in her hands, the turmoil within her swirling like a storm. The forest was silent, except for the soft rustling of leaves in the gentle breeze.

She felt something shift nearby.

Bree lifted her head, slow and unsteady, as if it were weighed down by guilt. Her eyes burned from unshed tears.

The deer had moved close beside her, watching her with wide, dark eyes. Curious. Unafraid.

It stepped forward, one careful hoof pressing into the grass. Its nose twitched as it sniffed the air between them.

Bree held her breath. She didn't move. She was afraid the smallest twitch would send it running.

But the deer didn't bolt. It lowered its head and pressed its soft muzzle to her shoulder.

Warm breath touched her skin. The lump in her throat tightened.

She raised a shaking hand. Her fingers met the animal's dappled coat, light as a whisper.

Still, it didn't flinch. It just stood there. As if it understood her pain and conflict within her. The acknowledgement of needing to feed, but not wanting to take an innocent life. It felt as if it forgave her.

She breathed in slowly.

"I'm sorry," she said.

The words wern'te for the deer. They were for everything and everyone she had ever killed in the name of her hunger.

She wasn't a monster.

Chapter 22 – Return Home

The city looked different in the twilight. Xonthian's towers caught the last of the sun, lit up like dying embers. Smoke drifted over the rooftops. The smell of bread lingered in the streets, strong enough to stir something in his gut. He heard a blacksmith's hammer. Laughter. Horseshoes on stone. All of it was familiar. But none of it felt right.

Tiger sat straighter in the saddle as they passed through the southern gate. One of the guards gave him a nod, and he returned it out of habit. Bree rode beside him, quiet under her hood. He couldn't see her face, but he felt her tension. It matched his own.

The square opened up around them. He glanced at the Stone Flame, then scanned the side streets. Nothing unusual, but the air felt tight. Like the whole city was pretending things were fine.

When they reached the apartment, his jaw clenched. The door had been repaired. New hinges. New lock. Curtains in the window. Someone else lived here now. Disheartened but undeterred, they returned to the Stone Flame, where they left their horses to the capable stable lad and his crew.

"We need a room," Tiger said, his voice tinged with weariness.

"Of course," the innkeeper said, "How many nights?"

Tiger pursed his lips. "It will be at least a few weeks. Will that be a problem?"

"Not as long as you have coin."

"Of course."

Tiger handed over the coins, scribbled his name in the guest log, and took the key without looking the innkeeper in the eye. No need for talk.

The stairs creaked with age and wear as they ascended to the rooms. Tiger peered around, dropping his bag on the floor. It was a modest room. Water basin, chair, bed, and stand, with a few candles. Bree shut the door with a soft click behind her, drawing her hood back and spilling gold hair down around her shoulders as she did. "It's strange being back," she said. Her voice was soft, while her eyes lingered on something far off in the distance.

Tiger slipped off his sword and hung it by the door. His shoulders ached from carrying it all day.

"Yeah," he said, sitting on the edge of the bed. "Doesn't feel the same."

A long breath left him. He ran a hand through his hair, fingers catching in the knots.

"We haven't had a real moment since… all of it," he said. "I need to talk to you." Bree turned to face him, her pale features illuminated by the flickering light. She peered at him with a quizzical look, her brow raised in silent question.

"I'm sorry, Bree. For everything. For getting us caught. For you getting tied up and… put in that coffin. I'm so sorry."

"Tiger," she said quietly, her voice steady and calm as she walked toward him, "Why do you think that was your fault?"

He lifted his head and looked at her, his green eyes shadowed with guilt. "Because it was my decision to go to North Kelsa," he said. "I didn't care what anyone thought about us. About you and me. I thought… I thought we would be fine. I didn't think…"

Bree knelt in front of him, her pale hands resting lightly on his knees. Her crimson eyes, usually so guarded, shone with a rare tenderness. "You have nothing to be sorry for. Nothing. Yes, I hated being tied up. Yes, I was scared. But there was nothing you could have done to change what happened. I could hear you, you know. Talking to me, describing what you saw. That kept me going. It gave me hope. You didn't abandon me. You could have, I'm sure. But you didn't. You are not the monster here. You took a risk because you believed in us, in what we're doing. You didn't fail me, Tiger. Not then, not now."

Tiger's chest ached, but he couldn't tell if it was from guilt or the relief of it lifting from his shoulders. He had carried it ever since their arrest. He lowered his head again, his forehead almost touching Bree's.

"I just hate that you got hurt," he murmured.

Bree smiled faintly, her fangs glinting in the light. A genuine, gentle gesture that he sorely needed to see. "Tiger, I've been hurt before. And I'll get hurt again. That's part of what we do. What matters is that we're here now. Together. And, I forgive you. You have nothing to be sorry for. Hells, it's my curse that put Iro on our scent to begin with, I should be the one who's apologizing. Not you."

"You have nothing to be sorry for," he said. "I know you had no choice. None of this is your fault. You were trying to show me that taking a life isn't easy, right? That's what you've been trying to show me, isn't it? How can I fault you for that?"

Bree's crimson eyes glistened as she nodded. She rose to her feet and took a step back, drawing her cloak tighter around her. "Our time on Angelic Island showed me something," she said. "It showed me that I don't have to let this curse control me. It's okay to feel guilty for taking lives. I should feel guilty. Sometimes, I need to feel it, because it makes me more than a monster. It makes me human again." She paused, looking away as if searching for the right words. "When you were talking to Kendrick, I snuck out of the monastery to feed. I found a deer; I was intent on slaughtering it like some feral beast. But I couldn't do it, I hesitated, frozen by fear and disgust. I knew I had to feed, but didn't want to take its life. The deer came to me. It just… came to me. And in that moment, I felt as if it forgave me. It looked at me, looked through me. I-I can't describe it. I don't know if you understand. When I fed through, it was almost like... Like I would be ok. As if I weren't some monster. For the first time in a long time, I didn't feel dirty for feeding.”

Tiger watched her closely, his heart aching at the vulnerability she rarely showed.

Bree gave him a faint smile that held a hint of sadness around the edges. A bitter smile that didn’t hold mirth, but rather self-loathing.

Tiger held her gaze. He wanted to take all the pain away, and knowing he couldn’t, caused the lump of guilt in his gut to grow.

“You’re stronger than I’ll ever be,” he said. “I’m glad you’re here. Glad we’re together.”

She didn’t speak, but the look in her eyes said enough. It wasn’t the first time that a mutual glance held more than enough to convey what they wanted to tell one another. And it wouldn’t be the last.

For a while, they just sat there. Each one lost in their thoughts, their emotions tangled around their hearts, as if trying to bandage the pain. Tiger shifted, causing the old wood to creak under them. Outside, the city murmured with distant voices and the clatter of carts on stone, drowning out the silence around them.

Tiger let the stillness settle between them. It wasn’t uncomfortable.

Finally, he stood and peered down at Bree. "You can have the bed, I'll sleep on the floor."

She said nothing, leaving Tiger to wonder if she had heard him. He shrugged and began to attend to his sleeping bag.

Night fell over Xonthian City, blanketing the streets and rooftops in a deep, velvety darkness. Soft laughter, clinking glasses from the tavern below, drifted up through the floorboards, lulling the two occupants off into deep slumber.

A few days later, Tiger awoke to the warm, golden light of the morning sun filtering through the thin muslin curtains. The room was quiet. He noticed Bree was nowhere to be seen, having likely slipped out during the evening to feed.

He stretched, muscles tight from another night of broken sleep on the hard ground. He wasn't sure if he would ever get used to it. His back ached from too many nights on the road and the continuous weight of tension that had settled there.

The floor was cold under his feet. He dressed quickly, not bothering to fix his hair, and headed downstairs.

The common room was already busy. Voices rose and fell in uneven waves. Someone laughed near the hearth. A child ran between tables. The smell of bacon and fresh bread hit him as soon as he stepped in. It made his stomach growl.

He slid into a corner seat and ate without fuss. Eggs, toast, and a slab of something close to ham. Nothing fancy, but it did the job. The innkeeper gave him a nod as he passed, and Tiger nodded back. No need for words.

When the plate was clean, he wiped his mouth, stood, and left a few coins on the table.

He departed the inn for the waking streets of Xonthian City. Carts already began to roll along the avenues on their way to farms, warehouses, or wherever they were needed. The morning sun, although bright, held no real warmth. It was almost chill, as if the sun hadn't yet warmed the earth. The air carried the faint smell of hay and tilled earth, mixed with the usual brine of the nearby ocean.

There was no urgency in his steps. For the first time in a while, he didn't feel as if he were running from something. It had been days since he and Bree had returned to the city, and the tension from their journey finally began to melt from his muscles and his mind. Each step became easier, as though the weight of it had become bearable.

The cemetery gate loomed ahead, an imposing structure of black wrought iron. Vines clung to its lower reaches, their green tendrils weaving through the metal like earthy veins. The gate was old but well-maintained, its artistry both inviting and solemn. Tiger paused, his hand resting on the cool iron as if steadying himself before entering. It had been years since he'd come here; he wasn't sure if he was ready.

He pushed the gate open, the hinges groaning softly in protest. A patchwork of headstones and crypts nestled beneath the shadow of the hill spread out before him.

The air was heavier here. Not just cold, but thick in his lungs, like it didn't want to be breathed.

Gravel shifted under his boots as he walked, slow and steady, between rows of worn stone. A few graves had flowers. Most didn't. Just names, faded and crooked, like the earth had started to forget them.

He kept to the north side. It was quieter there. Old trees loomed overhead, their limbs twisted like bones, leaves casting shadows that moved when they shouldn't have.

His father's tomb stood under the largest oak. The sight of it stopped him cold.

He hadn't meant to look away, but his feet stalled a few steps short. His chest tightened, breath caught halfway up.

Something sour drifted past his nose. Sharp, chemical, wrong. He frowned, glanced around, then let it go. Not now.

He stepped closer, slow this time. The stone looked smaller than he remembered. Moss crept along the base. The name was still there, carved clean into the surface. He ran his fingers across it. The letters were cold. Familiar.

Tiger knelt. Rested his hands on his thighs and let the silence wrap around him.

The breeze moved through the leaves. He stayed still. Let himself be quiet for once, forcing the noise in his head down.

"Morning, Father," he said. His voice cracked halfway through.

"I've missed you. It's been... hard. We're back in the city, but everything feels off. Bree's holding it together better than I am. We don't know where we're going yet."

He reached into his bag and pulled out a small leather-bound journal. "I've been keeping a record of everything that's happened since…

since you were taken. Maybe it'll help me make sense of things, or maybe it's just a way to keep you with me. I don't know. I wrote down all your strategies, all your military wisdom. Life lessons, anecdotes."

Tiger's fingers traced the binding with a finger. "Bree and I, we've been through a lot. We've been caught in a web of power and politics, while the Fire Isle Mages threaten everything we know. And while we try to navigate all of this, I find myself often questioning what I'm doing. Where am I going? Kendrick—do you remember him? He wants us to meet with the king tomorrow. He wants us to tell the king our secret. Bree's not too thrilled with the idea. I think she's only doing it because I said I would go. She's a good person, I feel... I feel like you'd like her."

Tiger took a deep breath. That smell again, he furrowed his brow, then shook his head. "I've been thinking a lot about what you would say if you were here. About how you always taught me to face challenges head-on, to stay true to myself. But things have gotten so complicated. I've become a Paladin." He laughed, though there was no mirth in his eyes. "Even saying that out loud seems ridiculous. Although I'm sure it's more of an honorary title, as I don't think the GateHar Clerics really think of me in that way. The clerics are not too thrilled with it. You should have seen them when we left Angelic Island. It was as if someone had kicked an ant hill."

Tiger's voice faltered as he continued. He didn't feel any happiness in the chaos their presence had caused, and here, now, giving confession among the dead just felt... Wrong. Like he was desecrating their memory. "I suppose there's something to be said for irony, isn't there? I was never the most devout or the most disciplined. And yet, here I am, caught up in something much bigger than I ever imagined. Burdened with the magic of all things, magic I don't even understand yet. I've been blessed, even, can you believe that? I tried to follow you, though. Follow your example of being a great military man. I joined the Swords of Justice, but… it held no answers for me. I tried to find ways of embracing the arms of death. Yet I was denied at every turn. You're the only family I ever knew, ever had. I am grateful for that, for the life you gave me. I had everything I ever wanted or needed. And now, all I can do is whine about how I don't have you." He sighed and shook his head. "But I do have you—you are always there. Even when…When… I never questioned where I came from, really, came from. I was always your son. That was enough. And... And now that you're gone, I wish I had told you more often that I appreciated everything you tried to teach me."

He picked up the journal and tucked it back into his bag, his hand lingering on the tomb. "I'll keep trying to end this war, Father. I'll keep getting better. I'll keep fighting for what's right, and I'll do my best to protect those I care about. I'm sorry you're not here to see that. I'm sorry I wasn't strong enough then. Hells, I may not be strong enough now." He sighed and shook his head again. "But that's the point, isn't it? That's why I could never beat you when we sparred. We were both growing stronger, wiser, better. Both of us. I understand that now."

Tiger rose slowly, brushing the dust from his hands as he looked down at the grave one last time. The words he had spoken still echoed in his chest, raw and unfinished. "I miss you. I love you," he repeated, softer this time, more to himself than anyone else.

He turned to leave, but something in the brush near the tomb caught his attention. A dark shape, half-covered by dry, tangled bracken. He paused, frowning, then stepped closer and crouched down, carefully pulling the brittle plants aside.

His breath faltered.

A dog lay curled among the roots, its body stiff and long dead. The angle of its neck was wrong—unnatural—and the ground beneath it was stained with dried blood, dark and rust-colored against the earth. It wasn't just any dog. Recognition stirred, faint and unwelcome. He had seen it before. Years ago. Around the time his father died.

A chill crept along his spine as he straightened. His eyes shifted back to the tomb.

Carved into the stone were rough, angry letters slashed across the weathered surface: Sins of the Son fall on the Father.

He stared at the message, the meaning slamming into him all at once. There was no mistaking it. This wasn't some forgotten threat or cruel coincidence. It was meant for him. Left here for him to find.

And he knew exactly who had written it.

Chapter 23 – The King and his Men

Tiger and Bree were led into the palace hall by a pair of solemn guards. The pair had bought new clothes upon their return to Xonthian City. They wanted nothing to do with the robes given to them by the clerics. The money the king had promised had been kept in a trust by the Merchants Guild and kept safe until they had returned. No one knew where they had gone, and during that time, they had accumulated a small fortune since their arrest.

"You sure it's Iro?" Bree asked. Bree wore a black and dark purple shirt, pants, and a jacket that included a hood. She had lost the cloak she'd had prior to her arrest, and on several occasions lamented its loss during their trip home.

"I'm positive. Who else would have?" he replied. Tiger wore simple cotton pleated black breeches with a white shirt and red vest.

"Defiling a grave like that, even for a disgraced Paladin, seems egregious," Bree said. "Should we tell Kendrick?"

"What will he do? Iro made his position clear."

Bree shrugged.

The double doors swung open, and Tiger and Bree were escorted inside. King Si'ann sat on his throne at the end of the hall. Beside him stood Kendrick, his expression blank.

The room sprawled ahead of them, with a high ceiling supported by massive wooden beams that crisscrossed like the ribs of a great ship. Light filtered in through narrow windows set high in the walls, casting long shadows across the space.

Suits of armor stood sentinel along the sides, while racks of swords, axes, and spears hung in orderly displays. Guards stood between them, keeping a watchful eye on the pair as they were escorted in. At the far end, a raised dais held a sturdy throne of dark oak, carved with patterns native to Xonthian, and its history. Banners and shields adorned the walls behind it. The royal crest, a sword flanked by flame, was embroidered on the dark blue banners. The air carried a musty scent of aged wood and polish.

The king was an imposing figure draped in regal robes of dark purple and silver. Something Tiger had never even considered before today.

King Si'ann's gaze fell upon the two travelers as they approached, his eyes flickering with a mix of curiosity and wariness. "Welcome home, Lord Tiger," he said.

Tiger's gaze met King Si'anne's. Although the king's greeting was genuine, it felt somehow accusative. Maybe Tiger was imagining things that weren't there. Had the king been told of their arrest? Did the king already know about Bree? He peered around the room at the guards and other court staff lingering in the hall. "Your Majesty, if it's acceptable, I would request that we speak privately. The matters we need to discuss are of a sensitive nature and require discretion."

King Si'ann's eyes narrowed slightly, but he nodded after a slight pause. "Very well. Guards, please ensure that only Lord Tiger, Lady Bree, Sir Kendrick, and I remain undisturbed in the hall."

The guards bowed and marched from the grand hall, closing the heavy doors behind them. The muffled sounds of the palace faded away, leaving the room in a deep, expectant silence.

Tiger took a deep breath, his gaze shifting between King Si'ann and Kendrick as he seated himself. "Thank you, Your Majesty." Tiger glanced at Bree, who nodded. He stepped forward, his voice low.

"We both have been given the blessing of GateHar. And I have been formally recognized as a Paladin. This title is both an honor and a responsibility. I will do my best to honor the title."

King Si'ann's eyebrows arched in surprise. "A Paladin? That is quite significant. But, not altogether a surprise, you are, after all, your father's son. You said we? Has she become a Paladin as well?"

"That is a bit more delicate, I'm afraid, and is the reason I cleared the room, your grace," Tiger said. "My friend here is a vampire. Of a different kind."

King Si'ann's expression grew more guarded, his eyes narrowing as he absorbed Tiger's words. "A vampire? That's impossible, it's midday. No vampires can live in the sun."

"Correct; however, because of her will to live, her soul, she is able to." Kendrick stepped in, adding to Tiger's stumbling explanation. "We're not actually sure how it happened. She has been spared the full brunt of the vampiric curse."

Tiger watched as the face of the king grew increasingly red. He leaned forward in his throne, fist clenched. "So the rumors were true. There is a vampire in my city. And she is standing before me?" He whipped his piercing gaze to Kendrick. "And you, have you fallen under her spell too? Has all Angelic Island been desecrated?"

"No, your grace," Kendrick said. "Please, my lord, nothing has changed."

"Changed? You," he said pointing a finger at Tiger, "brought this creature to my court, and asked to be this kingdom's saviors. You wanted autonomy to move unhindered by the Fire Isle Mages, and I agreed. Now… Now you bring this news to me and expect what, exactly? For me to understand?"

"It's not been my intention to deceive you," Tiger said, shaking his head. "We never expected this secret to get out. Or, at the very least, if it ever did, we were hoping that our actions, our contribution to stopping this war, would bury it. Would over-shadow it."

The king snorted, but there was no amusement in his eyes. "Perhaps it might have. And the worst part of this is that I can't exactly do anything about it. Everyone within my command, hells, within the city, knows there is a special team of individuals currently working to destabilize the Fire Isle Mages. I can't exactly go against that now, can I?"

"Nothing's changed, your majesty. Bree and I plan to do exactly that," Tiger said. "We don't ask for special favors; we never did. I didn't even want your stipend, remember?"

"What would Hon'shu say if he saw you. Knew what you were doing with this… monster?"

"I would believe he would let me forge my own path," Tiger said, bowing his head, then looking at Bree beside him. "But, she is no monster. She has proven herself over and over. First at North Kelsa. And then… the pirates. And again on Angelic Island."

Kendrick nodded. "Your grace, she has not enslaved our minds. I speak freely, by the Goddess's grace. She has, as Tiger has explained."

Bree put a hand on his arm and took a step forward, drawing her hood back as she did. "Your… Majesty. I am not one to stand on titles. But my parents did, and they were loyal subjects even when the war tore them away from me. We would not be here now if we didn't believe we could change the course of this war. We cannot, however, do it if we have to look over our shoulders. Betrayal lives in the very essence of war, wouldn't you say? You have enough deserters clambering away in mud and filth, right under your nose—"

"Enough," King Si'anne said, cutting her short. "You've made your point." The king rapped his fingers on the arm of the throne, his eyes darting between the two before him. "You speak of betrayal. And, Kendrick, you vouch for these two?"

"I do, your majesty," the elder cleric said with a bow.

"What is it you want from me?" The king asked, narrowing his eyes between Bree and Tiger.

"Nothing, your majesty," Tiger replied.

Silence hung over the court, nearly to the point of being seen. After a long moment, the king sat back in his throne. "Fine, I'll see to it you are given leave to conduct yourselves as you see fit. But mark my words, Tiger," the king said, though Tiger noticed the title of his name had been dropped. "If you interfere with the current war efforts, those at the wall, without consulting my generals, it will lead to consequences. This war has stakes, real, people's lives hinge on every aspect of it, as your friend there so colorfully pointed out. Since you've brought me in on this secret, I have to now keep it between us in this room. Because if I don't, it very well could mean the end of this very throne. The Clerics of GateHar may have given you their blessing, but the people who live here certainly have not. If your secret gets out, I cannot protect you. You will be on your own. And I will avow no knowledge of her affliction or your actions."

Tiger bowed, his jaw clenched in irritation. Bree was right. Betrayal was born in war. And the king had made that point very clear.

"We'll let you know what we decide to do," Tiger said, then continued, "when we have studied our options carefully. We only want to help end it, not impede your efforts. We are grateful for the discretion. We do not take your trust lightly, your grace."

The king nodded with finality. "Then go in peace and may the Goddess guide you."

They turned to leave; the king's blessing was more than either of them had expected. Yet it was a relief. The palace corridors seemed to close in with each step, a reminder of their precarious position. The shadows of war loomed over the country. That much hadn't been forgotten. Every decision from here on would affect not only their path, but that of an entire people.

As they passed through the castle, Tiger glanced at Bree. She seemed to understand. They knew that success would not come easily and that the cost of failure could be catastrophic. And yet, they had one more person to confess to. One more thread of deceit to clear up before they could truly be free.

The gates to the Swords of Justice compound stood swinging open in the breeze. They were never left open. Tiger felt gooseflesh prickling his skin.

The courtyard was chaos. Men were shouting, stumbling over each other. The place that once had discipline drilled into its bones had been cracked wide open. Something terrible had happened, and Tiger felt the dread growing in the pit of his stomach.

Two soldiers nearly barreled into them, panic in their eyes, one yelling over his shoulder to fetch the city guard.

At the center of the yard, a crowd had gathered. Not curious. Afraid. Hushed voices rippled between them. Bree touched Tiger's arm, a silent warning to tread carefully. Maybe now wasn't a good time for confessions.

As they neared, Tiger saw what the others already had. A body lay twisted in the dirt. Blood soaked the ground, spreading thick and dark beneath the broken frame. Limbs bent the wrong way. The head—

His breath caught. It was Aldrani. His sword lay a few feet away, its blade wet with blood.

The wound was vicious. Deep. Whoever had attacked him had almost taken his head clean off. Tiger's pulse hammered as bile climbed up the back of his throat. This wasn't just an accident during training. This was something worse.

"What in the hells is this?" Commander Sworren's voice rang out, cutting through the murmurs. He shoved through the cluster of soldiers. When his eyes landed on Tiger, his stare turned to confusion, demanding an explanation Tiger didn't have.

One of the younger soldiers stepped forward, trembling. "We—we found him like this, sir. He was already gone."

Sworren crouched beside the body. His jaw clenched as he studied the mess. "His sword…" he muttered, reaching out to touch the hilt. Blood smeared his glove. "Did anyone see what happened? Hear anything?"

The only response was silence and shaking heads.

Bree's voice came quietly, barely more than breath. "Iro." She met Tiger's eyes. Since finding the dog murdered in the cemetery, he'd had a suspicion. This made sense. Aldrani had lied to protect Tiger and Bree when Iro came looking for answers. The dog? Just an innocent bystander in all this. Iro had completely fallen from grace. No longer the saintly warrior of GateHar.

A soldier pointed. "Sir—his mouth. Something's wrong with it."

Sworren moved fast. "Back," he barked. He knelt again and turned Aldrani's face. Blood smeared across the jaw as he pried it open. A wet, awful sound followed. Then something slid out and hit the ground with a sick thud.

Tiger stared. He couldn't move. Couldn't breathe.

It was a tongue. Ripped out at the root. Jagged and still leaking blood into the dirt.

Sworren didn't speak right away. When he finally looked up, his face was like stone. His eyes met Tiger's, and something passed between them. Fury. Horror. And a question that hadn't been asked yet. Tiger knew this wasn't going to be easy to explain.

"This wasn't just murder. This was a damn message. You two have something to do with this?"

Tiger nodded. "Sir, we need to talk. In private."

Tiger and Bree followed Commander Sworren into his dimly lit office, the air inside heavy with the scent of old wood, parchment, and candlewax. The door shut behind them with a low thud, sealing them away from the grisly scene outside. Sworren turned, his shoulders squared like a man bracing for an oncoming storm.

"Start talking," Sworren barked. "What in the hells is going on here?"

Tiger hesitated, the words clawing at his throat but refusing to come out. He glanced at Bree, who leaned casually against the wall near the door. Her hood was pulled low, shadowing her face, but her posture was anything but casual.

Sworren's sharp eyes flicked between them, his impatience mounting. "Well? I've got a dead man in my courtyard, and you're standing here like you don't have a damned clue."

"I don't," Tiger said finally. "But I have a suspicion."

Sworren's frown deepened, and he folded his arms. "A suspicion. Fantastic. Care to share it?"

Tiger exhaled. He didn't want to share it. Not like this anyway. He looked at Bree again. Her head tilted slightly, the faintest nod of permission. That did not give him any reassurance.

Tiger straightened. "I think Aldrani's death has something to do with a Paladin investigating murders in the city."

Sworren's eyes narrowed, his stance shifting. "Murders?"

"Yes," Tiger said, his voice firm now. "A Paladin named Iro. He's been hunting down a... particular killer. A vampire. The victims were all criminals, thieves, murderers, and slavers. The kind of scum no one misses. Well, that killer was Bree here."

Sworren raised an eyebrow, his skepticism cutting through the air like a blade. "Bree is a vampire? Don't insult my intelligence, Tiger. Vampires can't walk in the daylight. Everyone knows that."

"Not all vampires follow that rule," Tiger said.

Sworren slammed his hand on the desk hard enough to rattle the ink pot. "Enough. I don't have time for fairy tales."

Tiger didn't flinch. "Do you remember when Aldrani told you I had control over a vampire?"

Sworren's eyes narrowed. "I remember. I thought it was just a ploy. You and Aldrani were always at each other's throats—I figured it was some twisted scheme or prank."

"It wasn't. Aldrani wasn't lying." Tiger turned, glancing at Bree, still cloaked in the shadows behind him. "The vampire he meant... was Bree."

Sworren's head snapped toward her. His stare was sharp, cutting. Bree didn't move. Didn't say a word. Her face gave him not even the slightest acknowledgement.

Then Sworren let out a bitter laugh. "That's insane. You're telling me she's—no. No, you expect me to believe that?"

"It's true," Tiger replied. "And Iro must've found out. Maybe he didn't say anything, and that was the problem. Either way, he's dead now. Tongue ripped out. That wasn't random. That was a warning."

The humor vanished from Sworren's face. He looked at Bree again. His gaze hung there, as if weighing her worth. Tiger saw the doubt shift into something colder. Hatred.

"If this is real..." Sworren began, but the words caught in his throat.

"It is," Tiger said. He stepped forward, fists clenched at his sides. "Aldrani wasn't just killed. He had lied, and to Iro, a lie is worse than anything else. Iro was once a proud GateHar Paladin, now he's nothing more than a murderer, taking his anger and spite out on those that he feels had wronged him."

Sworren's eyes locked onto his. Tiger didn't look away. He let him see every ounce of truth, every drop of vengeance burning in his chest.

Finally, the commander leaned back. His face turned to a stone mask. "Does the king know? Kendrick? Do they know what you've brought into the capital?"

Tiger hesitated, the weight of it all pressing against his chest. Then he nodded. "They know. We just left the palace." His voice cracked slightly, not from fear, but from... failure?

"Your actions cost me a man. A good man." Sworren said. "How do I forgive that?

As much as Aldrani had bullied Tiger, he hadn't given up their secret. Tiger bowed his head. "Nothing can forgive our actions; we must accept the consequences."

Sworren shook his head. "You say she's different. How can I trust her? You? After all this?"

Tiger, fixed the commander with a thoughtful stare, failing to come up with anything, he slung back down in defeat.

"Sir, if I may?"

Sworren narrowed his eyes at Bree. "Yes?"

"You saw the blood outside. You must know, I can smell it, even in here. And yet. I stand before you." Bree said, then glanced at Tiger. "We stand before you. Not asking forgiveness. But understanding that we are not the enemy. I can smell the blood outside, yet I make no move toward you or Tiger. My bloodlust does not control me. It never will again."

Silence hung between them as Sworren tapped thoughtfully on the arm of his chair. Finally, Sorren continued. "You went to Angelic Island then? Became a Paladin? Tell me about it."

Tiger blinked, as if clearing the derailed chain of thought from his mind. He recounted the events, omitting the more personal details that tied too deeply into his own guilt and Bree's struggle. He told him how Iro had arrested them and taken them to the island to be judged. How they came out of the Passage of Trials, how the Goddess had blessed them, and he was considered a Paladin.

When Tiger had finished, Sworren sat, his expression blank like an unmarred canvas. For a moment, the room was silent, save for the muffled sounds of the compound beyond the walls. The commander leaned back, his hand running through his hair as if to physically untangle the chaos in his mind.

"So, you're telling me," Sworren began, his voice slow, deliberate, "that a vampire was blessed by the Goddess. That the king knows, Kendrick knows, and now I'm supposed to just... accept this?"

"It would make things easier," Tiger said.

Sworren shook his head, clearly unconvinced. "Why now, Tiger? Why tell me this now, after all this time?"

"To come clean," Tiger said. "We need allies, Sworren. I'm not going to keep hiding things. You deserved to know. So did Aldrani. That's why we're here."

Sworren didn't speak right away. His jaw twitched. Then he turned toward Bree. "And you? You want me to just... forget what you are?"

Bree lifted her chin. "I trust Tiger. If he thinks this is the right move, I'll follow it. I'm not here to convince you of anything. The Goddess gave me a second chance, and I'm not wasting it. Think what you want."

Sworren exhaled through his nose, a faint smirk playing at his lips. "I'll give you this, Tiger—you've got nerve. More than I thought, anyway." He leaned forward. "I appreciate the truth, even if it's a bitter pill to swallow. I don't think Aldrani would have accepted it. Hells, I don't think any of those men out there would. You're lucky I knew you. Knew your father. But understand this—I will bow to the king's wishes. If the king trusts you, then so will I. I'll follow his example. But that doesn't mean I'll turn a blind eye to anything that threatens the Swords of Justice. If you or Bree get in our way, I won't hesitate to tell the king you impeded us in any way. Are we clear?"

"Crystal," Tiger said. We're not here to hinder you. We're here to make sure the future is one we can all survive. Bree and I will end this war."

Sworren nodded, the tension in his shoulders easing just a fraction. "And justice for Aldrani?"

Tiger glanced sidelong at Bree. She pushed off the wall, her movements fluid, almost feline. "He'll be dealt with."

Without another word, the two turned and headed toward the door. Just as Tiger's hand reached for the handle, Sworren spoke again, his voice quieter, but no less firm.

"Tiger," he said, "Don't make me regret this."

"You won't," Tiger replied. "And sir, for what it's worth, I'm sorry about Aldrani. He didn't deserve that kind of death."

They stepped out into the compound, the door clicking shut behind them. The conversation still clung to him, heavy and unfinished. He glanced sideways at Bree.

"We have to find Kendrick. Now."

As they passed through the gates, the city guards were already arriving, their boots thundering over the cobblestone. Tiger barely noticed them. His thoughts were elsewhere, locked on the last task left.

They had to find Iro. And fast.

Chapter 24 – Blood and Thunder

Tiger woke with a start. Something had disturbed him, and as he drew in his surroundings, realized it was the storm outside that had punctured his sleep. The room at the Stone Flame was dimly lit by the flickering light of a single candle across from him, melted down to nearly a stub of its former self. Bree was still asleep beside him, her chest rising and falling in a steady rhythm. He cast a glance her way, noting the peaceful expression on her face despite the storm's raging outside.

He slipped out of his bedroll, careful not to make a sound. He peered up at the bed. Bree appeared to be asleep. As he dressed, the thunder rumbled again, louder this time. The storm echoed through the stone and wood walls of the inn. It was somehow reassuring. The storms along the Irga Straight were frequent, and they always brought the scent of wet earth. But it was the sound they made. Like background noise that always, despite the thunder, calmed his nerves.

He opened the door and wandered down the wooden stairs. The common room of Stone Flame was deserted, save for the flickering candlelight casting long shadows on the walls.

Tiger approached the small hearth where a kettle was beginning to simmer. He poured himself a cup of the strong, bitter coffee that was the only offering at this hour. He sighed as he sipped the hot liquid. It wasn't the best in Xonthian City, but it beat not having any.

Suddenly, a voice pierced the storm's roar, cutting through the thick, heavy rush of wind and rain. Tiger froze, gooseflesh prickling his skin as he set the cup down on the table with a clatter. The voice was unmistakably familiar.

He ran to the door, pushing it open against the howling wind.

Rain slashed across the square in relentless sheets, turning the cobblestones into a glistening mosaic of puddles and rivers winding through cracks toward drains. The Goddess of GateHar loomed over the fountain at the square's center, her chiseled features as impassive as the surrounding storm.

Lightning split the sky, flashing across the rows of shuttered shops of the square. Their windows looked like dead eyes, dark and hollow, as if watching the pair of warriors. Tiger's breath caught when he saw Kendrick on his knees, slumped before Iro's imposing physique. His robes were soaked red. Blood streaked his face, his chin sunk to his chest like he couldn't even lift it anymore. The rain brought the stink of iron and ionized rain.

"Iro." Tiger's voice was drowned out by the wind, lost in the torrent around him, like smoke being whisked away. He stepped into a puddle without thinking. Cold water splashed up his leg. Iro stood stiff, armor dull and streaked with grime, eyes wide with accusations. He held a spear in both hands, the tip leveled at Kendrick's chest.

"Let him go," Tiger said. "This isn't the way. The Goddess wouldn't want this."

"You," Iro hissed. His voice cracked like the thunder above, full of contempt and anger. "You took everything from me!" The words came out twisted, loud enough to drown out distant thunder.

"I didn't take anything." Tiger raised his hands. His fingers shook. Never again would he let the strong tear down the weak. Not like all those years ago when he watched Bo beat down Carv in this very spot. "You left. You left the Order. That was your choice! There is no honor in killing, Kendrick. He was just following orders, just like you were. You think you can come back to the city and what? Summon Bree and I out here for a confrontation? Like we're some creature in a dark hole, waiting for a shining hero? Is that you, are you the hero?"

"You poisoned it! Sullied the very core of GateHar!" Iro's mouth curled. His face was all fury and grief and madness. "You and that creature you brought into our halls. That vampire. That thing. You turned us into a joke. A haven for monsters and heretics. You two need to be culled!"

His grip tightened on the shaft of the spear. Tiger barely had time to shout before Iro lunged. A flash of silver. Kendrick let out a choking gasp, short and sharp, and the blade punched straight into his chest. The sound of it, that wet crunch, hit harder than the thunder. Blood soaked his robes and ran across the stones toward the drains, a torrent of horror. Kendrick collapsed in a heap, unmoving. Eyes wide and empty as the windows.

Tiger's breath snagged in his throat. "No—" The word broke apart as he spoke it. He moved, but too slowly. The spear lashed toward him, and he flinched as the tip scraped his arm. Iro's face was twisted with pure hate.

"You're next," he snarled and came at him again.

Tiger dodged on instinct, the spear missing him by inches. Rain hammered the street. His boots slipped on the stone. He caught his balance and backed away, heart pounding so hard he could barely concentrate. No weapon. No plan. Just pain, noise, and the taste of fear lingering at the back of his throat. Like bile trying to rise unwanted from the depths of his stomach. The statue of the Goddess watched silently from her marble dais.

The spear came at him again, and this time it cut deeper. A line of fire slashed across his ribs. He stumbled, bit back a scream. Blood soaked into his tunic. He was slowing down. Iro wasn't. "Damn it, Iro!" Tiger shouted, trying to stay out of range. His feet slipped on the rain-slick ground, forcing him into an awkward retreat. "Listen to me! It doesn't have to be like this!"

"Shut up!" Iro bellowed, his voice thunderous, raw with fury. "You don't get to talk! You destroyed everything—everything! You corrupted the Swords of Justice with lies, sullied your father's honor, and even the court. "The king believes your lies!" Iro thrust the spear at him, the tip slicing the air near Tiger's shoulder.

Tiger staggered back, heart pounding, nearly drowning out the steady hum of the rain.

"You and that monster deserve to die!"

Each word he shouted was answered by a fresh attack, the spear jabbing forward with cold precision. Cuts bloomed along his arms and ribs, stinging where the rain hit them. His breath tore from his chest in uneven bursts, legs sluggish beneath him. One step too slow, and he dropped to one knee, soaked to the bone, the cobblestones biting through his trousers.

The doors of the Stone Flame slammed open behind him.

"Tiger!" Bree's voice cut through the storm. Tiger turned, his vision smeared with rain, and saw Bree charging into the square. She held something bundled tight in her arms. Without slowing, she hurled it toward him.

"Catch!"

His side screamed in protest, but he reached up anyway. The bundle hit his palms hard, soaked and heavy. With trembling fingers, he tore the fabric apart until they found the familiar hilt. The TigerClaw.

Tiger glanced at Bree. She was holding back. She could win this fight with a flick of her wrist. Send Iro flying across the square. She was purposefully holding back, and Tiger knew exactly why.

Relief cut through the pain. He rose, the blade whispering free of its wrappings. Even in the storm, its edge gleamed, sharp as memory.

Bree moved fast, faster than his eyes could follow. She closed the distance in a blink and drove her fist into Iro's jaw, snapping his head to the side. He staggered, then swept the spear in a wide arc aimed at her waist. Bree bent back just in time, the blade slicing the air inches from her ribs. The swing forced her to retreat, water splashing beneath her boots as she caught her balance. Tiger watched her adjust her stance. She wasn't trying to win. She was holding him long enough for Tiger to strike. This wasn't just about her, this was about the both of them. This was about their collective honor. Together. Neither of them were perfect, far from it. Tiger knew Bree could easily end this fight, but it wasn't about that. It was about choice. They were giving Iro every opportunity to back out and run. To find the faith he had lost. To rise above being the monster that Tiger now saw him as. If they didn't give Iro that choice, what hope was there that they, too, could rise above being the monsters? The outcasts they were.

Tiger rose. The adrenaline was carrying him, urging him up. With Bree keeping Iro occupied, he charged, his renewed attacks forcing the spear wielder to split his focus. The sound of steel on steel rang through the square as the battle grew like a tempest.

Together, they pushed Iro back. Tiger's strikes were relentless now, each swing of the TigerClaw forcing Iro closer to the fountain. Bree darted in and out, attacks glanced off the edges of Iro's tarnished armor. The tide of the fight was shifting; Iro's movements were growing slower, his strikes less accurate.

But just as hope flared in Tiger's chest, Iro let out a furious roar. Feinting left, he spun and drove the spear forward, the blood-stained tip pierced Bree's chest, and slamming her against the wall of the Stone Flame. She gasped, her eyes wide with shock, as blood spilled from the wound.

The rain mixed with the blood pooling beneath Bree, her eyes squeezed shut as she struggled against the spear pinning her to the wall.

Tiger's grip tightened until his knuckles ached, the TigerClaw trembling in his hands. Every nerve screamed for him to strike, to silence Iro before another word could leave his mouth.

Iro faced him fully now. Rain clung to his armor in streaks, the metal catching flashes of lightning like a warning sign. His smile didn't hold victory. It was small and bitter, carved deep by whatever he'd been carrying for far too long. Wordlessly, he reached behind him and pulled a short blade free, etched in runes that caught the grey light of the storm with a dull shimmer.

"You look at me like I'm the villain," he said, his voice almost quiet enough to miss beneath the wind. Too calm. As if the outcome had already been written and he was just walking it out. "Tell me something, Tiger. Have you ever seen an undead creature healed?" Tiger narrowed his eyes. Rain streamed down his face, hot where it mixed with the blood on his skin. The question didn't make sense. "What are you talking about?" he asked, his voice sharp. He stepped forward, slow and careful.

Iro raised the blade, holding it between them. The motion stopped Tiger cold.

"I fought through the horde once," Iro said. His tone shifted, carried by something old and angry. "They weren't just corpses. Some of them remembered who they were. They screamed when we cut them down. Begged. But their eyes were gone. Their souls were gone. I had nothing but the blessing of the Goddess and my own will to survive. They outnumbered me. I was wounded, alone. They kept coming, no matter how many I cut down."

"What does that have to do with this? With her? Let her go," Tiger said.

"I prayed. And with the strength the Goddess gave me, I called down the heavens. I healed them. One by one, I restored their corrupted flesh, killing them in the process." His voice grew cold, his words cutting through the storm like the blade in his hand. "And I will do it again."

As Iro's words faded, he lifted his hand toward Bree. A brilliant white light burst from his palm, radiant and focused like a holy flame. It struck her squarely, divine energy crackling against her skin. Her scream tore through the air, sharp and panicked. Her body jerked against the spear, limbs shaking under the weight of the magic. The light blistered her flesh, searing her through every layer.

"Stop it!" Tiger shouted. He charged forward, the TigerClaw slicing in a wide arc toward Iro's side. Steel met steel with a violent crash. Sparks scattered into the rain as Iro deflected the blow and shoved him back, boots scraping against the wet stone.

"You will not interfere," Iro said, his voice steady. The light in his hand burned brighter, flooding the space between them with a cold, white glare. Bree's screams faltered, slipping into hoarse gasps. Her body sagged, but the spear held her upright. Her skin was scorched, her breathing uneven.

Tiger's heart pounded, his grip tight around the hilt of the blade. He scanned for any opening, some gap in Iro's defense, but the man had only one thought, one purpose. There was no hesitation in his stance. No fear. Only conviction.

Tiger saw that Bree was slipping away with every breath. Every second felt like an eternity, every breath a struggle, the pain, and the overwhelming fear of losing Bree.

Tiger's breath came in a final, desperate attack aimed at Iro's chest. The TigerClaw glinted in the storm's fleeting light, slicing through the rain with deadly accuracy. Iro spun to parry, but the force of the strike knocked him off balance, forcing him to pull back his hand. The white light ceased, and Bree collapsed forward against the spear with a sharp gasp.

Freed from the burning pain, Bree seized the moment. She gritted her teeth and gripped the spear, forcing herself to move despite the agony. Pain was etched on her features. She walked the length of the weapon's shaft, inching it out of her flesh. With one final stumble, she fell to her knees, the spear sliding free with a wet, sickening sound. She braced herself against the cobblestones, panting but alive.

Tiger darted to her side, standing guard with the TigerClaw poised between him and Iro. His eyes burned with fury and determination, even as his arms trembled from exhaustion. Iro, bloodied but unbroken. For a moment, none of them moved.

Bree rose shakily to her feet, clutching the wound in her stomach. She met Tiger's gaze and gave him a single, resolute nod. It was all the assurance he needed.

Tiger turned his focus to Iro. "No more."

Bree stepped forward, her hand outstretched, blood dripping from her fingers. With a flick of her wrist, Bree unleashed a wave of energy. Iro's body lifted off the ground as if struck by an invisible force and hurtled backward into the fountain. His face collided with the jagged stone, shattering it with a sickening crunch. He crumpled to the ground, his face a ruin of blood and broken bone, his breath shallow and labored.

Tiger and Bree stood in the rain and watched in amazement as Iro staggered to his feet. His gaze flickered between them, hatred burned in his eyes, his body was too broken to fight. He stumbled backward, then turned and ran into the veil of rain, disappearing from sight.

Bree made to follow, her hand rising instinctively. But before she could act, Tiger placed a firm hand on her arm. "Let him go," he said quietly. "He's not worth it. You're not a monster. We can be better. Leave him to whatever the fates have in store."

"Our actions here may have consequences later," she said. Almost as if to remind him.

"I know."

Bree stood frozen, her chest rising and falling as she fought to hold back the storm inside her. Bit by bit, her hand dropped to her side. She turned to Tiger, her eyes softer now, the fire in them dimming. "Not anymore," she whispered.

Tiger bent to retrieve the sheath, half-submerged in a puddle. The fabric was soaked, the leather warped from the rain. He slid the TigerClaw back into place. Around them, the rain began to wash the blood from the stone. The crimson trails thinned, fading as though the gods themselves were scrubbing the city clean.

His gaze drifted upward to the statue of the Goddess of GateHar. She had once stood for protection, for mercy. But now, beneath the bruised sky and flickering torchlight, she looked more like a mourner carved from stone. Her face was streaked with rain, and in the dim light, it almost seemed like she wept.

Outcast. Heretic. Monster. The titles came back to him like a litany of disgrace. Bree, damned by her blood. He himself was cursed by birth with magic he'd never asked for. And yet, as he stood beneath that silent goddess and thought of the Clerics of GateHar, along with their rigid rules, their blind faith, he finally saw it. The real monsters weren't the ones they had hunted. They were the ones who refused to see beyond their doctrine. Those who didn't believe in their fellow man, those who didn't protect the innocent, and spread hope.

He thought of Iro, swallowed by hate. Of Kendrick, who had died trying to change something too broken to bend. Maybe the war had lasted so long not because of evil, but because of fear. Fear of change. Fear of what peace might demand. And maybe that fear had cost more lives than any blade ever had.

Tiger approached Kendrick's body, the weight of everything pressing down with each step, the resolution to stop the war was even more demanding than it had been a few hours earlier. The elder cleric lay crumpled, blood mixing with the rainwater that pooled around him. Tiger crouched beside him, his hand hesitating over the old man's shoulder before finally settling there. Kendrick's face, lined with years of wisdom and faith, was now etched with pain and silence.

Tiger bowed his head. "You deserved better than this," he murmured.

Bree stood silent just behind him. She made no move to stop Tiger as he slipped his arms beneath Kendrick's lifeless form and carefully lifted him. The elder's body was heavy. Bree was right; their actions would cause ripples in people's lives, and Kendrick had paid the price. The square seemed hollow. Once, it was a crowded gathering place under the watchful gaze of the goddess, it now felt defiled.

"We should report this to the king," Tiger said. His eyes met Bree's, and they shared an unspoken understanding. The weight of what had happened here was theirs to bear. Together. Kendrick's death was a consequence of the fractured world they were fighting to heal.

Bree nodded. "We owe him that much."

Tiger adjusted Kendrick's body in his arms, careful not to jostle him, and began the slow walk toward the castle. Bree fell in step beside him.

The streets were still empty, between the rain and the early hours of the day, people were indoors. Hiding. Lightning split the sky in the distance, briefly illuminating the castle's silhouette. Tiger's footsteps echoed on the wet cobblestones, each step a reminder of the duty they now carried.

Chapter 25 – Bringer of Death

The chapel felt oppressive, the air thick with the mingling scents of old incense, aged wood, and the faint metallic tang of blood that clung to Kendrick's shrouded body. Tiger stood still, his boots planted firmly on the stone floor as he regarded the cleric's body. The stained glass window of the Goddess loomed above, her crown of stars catching the flickering candlelight, casting fractured rainbows onto the chapel's gray walls.

Tiger's gaze lingered on Kendrick's form, barely a shape beneath the dark shroud. A flicker of respect passed through him—brief and muted, like a wind brushing over dying embers. Kendrick had been a man of conviction, a man of faith who he'd known only briefly. But Tiger wasn't here to mourn. He was there to take on whatever punishment the king saw necessary.

The king knelt beside the body, his grief palpable. Tiger shifted uncomfortably, watching as Si'ann's trembling hands rested on the shroud. The king's voice was low at first, rough with emotion, and Tiger had to strain to hear his words.

"Kendrick was there when I was crowned," Si'anne murmured, his tone thick with memory. "He was there when my son was born. He stood at my side through every storm, every doubt." The king's fingers curled into fists, his knuckles white. "And now he is gone. Struck down in my city. In the chaos you brought here."

Tiger's jaw tightened. The words weren't unexpected, but they still cut deep. He glanced to his side. Bree stood near the wall, her pale face emotionless as her eyes roamed the stained glass window above them.

The King rose. His grief was turning to anger now, his voice trembling with it. "You brought this hate, this vengeance, this uncertainty to Xonthian City. For what? To pursue your own battles? To destroy the fragile sanctuary we have left?"

Tiger straightened. "We didn't want this," he said, his voice steady despite the tension in his chest. "We never intended for Kendrick to pay the price. Kendrick was a good man; he vouched for us when he didn't have to. I respect him for that, owe him even. We're here because of that respect. But make no mistake, we did not intend for this to happen."

The King's glare burned into him. Then his voice dropped, quieter but no less harsh. "Is Iro dead?"

"No," Tiger said.

The single word hung in the air, colder than the stone beneath their feet. The King closed his eyes, his breath escaping in a shudder. He pinched the bridge of his nose, his shoulders sagging under the weight of everything he had lost. "Then this is not over," he said bitterly. "It will never be over, will it? It will get worse even. The hate that festers in this world, between the kingdoms, the clerics, the mages. It is all connected. It poisons us all, corrupts us from the shadows, even."

The silence in the chapel stretched, heavy and unyielding. Tiger exhaled slowly, the weight of the moment pressing down on him. He looked to the King, still standing by Kendrick's shrouded form, grief etched into every line of his face. "I'm sorry for your loss," Tiger said.

The King waved his hand dismissively, his eyes fixed on Kendrick's covered face. "Your apology won't bring him back," he muttered. He glanced at Tiger, his gaze hardening. "Commander Sworren came to me the other day. Told me about a soldier he lost at the Swords of Justice compound. Was that Iro as well?"

Tiger nodded solemnly. "Yes. Aldrani died protecting Bree and I. He... he lied to Iro."

The king bowed his head and murmured a prayer, his voice steady despite the rawness beneath. The words were soft and reverent, a plea to the Goddess for Kendrick's peace and guidance.

When he finished, the King turned, his expression now colder, more resolute. He pointed a finger at Tiger, his tone firm. "You and Bree need to slink off into the shadows, disappear for all I care. Xonthian City has endured enough. I'll send word to my men to search for Iro, and I'll send a message to Angelic Island. They deserve to know of Kendrick's death—and Iro's crimes."

Tiger inclined his head. "We understand."

The King took a step closer, his gaze burning into Tiger. "Do you?" he said, his voice rising. "Do you understand, Lord Tiger? I don't want to see you again—not until this war ends or you are dead. You've brought enough suffering and secrets to my city. I won't tolerate anymore."

Tiger's jaw tightened, but he nodded. The king's words stung, but he couldn't argue with them. He had no defense.

King Si'anne turned away, his shoulders hunched under an unbearable weight. Tiger glanced at Bree, who still stood by the wall, her face unreadable. She moved without a word, following him as they exited the chapel.

The faint creak of the chapel doors closing behind them echoed through the stone hall. Once outside, the cool early morning air greeted them. Tiger didn't look back, his steps heavy as they moved away from the castle's heart. The king's words lingered like a shadow over him, a bitter reminder of the path he walked.

Chapter 26 – Gifts of the Heart

Bree crept across the room, trying to avoid waking Tiger, who was sleeping on the floor beside her bed. She didn't want to be pent up here, not while there was a world outside where people were killing one another. She had to feed anyway, and now was a good time as any.

She slid out of the balcony and disappeared into the shadows surrounding the Stone Flame before heading toward the gate leading to the streets beyond. The smell of a storm drowned out the usual smell of the ocean not far away. She would need to hurry before the deluge hit.

The GateHar moon was glowing brightly in the east behind a thick blanket of clouds. The air around her was cool and clean but still held a scent of despair and fear.

Bree wandered the streets for a while before seeing anyone else lurking around in the darkness. A few yards away, crouched over the body of a dead guard was a muscular man with a sword strapped over his back and several daggers hanging from his belt. He was cleaning a small, curved blade on the cloak from the guard's back. His eyes scanned the street, making sure no one was watching.

Someone was watching, however, Bree thought ironically as she slipped from the shadows and drew closer to the man. She saw he was dressed for war, and she wondered why he would be out here on the streets, slaying city guards. She shrugged to herself and slid beside him in the darkness.

"Killing a guard is grounds for beheading," Bree mused as she emerged into the glow of the nearby streetlamp.

The man paused and then looked up at Bree. "And being as beautiful as you are is a crime against humanity," he said, clasping a hand over his heart in mock appreciation.

Bree laughed hollowly.

"I wasn't being funny," the killer said, resheathing his dagger.

"So, then, why are you killing this one?" Bree asked, taking another step toward him.

"If you must know my name, it's Thurm. I am a Merc," the man said with an evil grin, "and I was killing him because I was hired to do so."

"Well, Thorn," Bree said, "too bad you've killed your last guard."

"No, that's *Th-urm*."

"Whatever," Bree growled as she lunged the remaining few steps and grabbed his throat.

"My, you're strong. Maybe you should grab me a little bit lower—rrrk!" he spat, realizing too late and letting out a pointless scream as Bree sank her teeth into his neck.

She drained the life from him, allowing his muscular body to slowly sink to the street. She licked every last drop of blood from the wound on his neck and then sighed in relief. The warmth she felt from his life prickled her skin, teasing her senses.

"Well, thank you for getting rid of Thurm. He was starting to be a pain in my backside," a voice said behind Bree.

"Who?" Bree said, whirling around, dropping the lifeless mercenary to the ground with a thud.

"Easy there, killer," a brown-haired Atticatten said, holding up her hands in submission.

"Who are you?" Bree asked, eyeing the woman suspiciously.

"Yatáki. And I'm going to take a guess, that you're Bree," she said, leaning against the wall of the building she stood next to, her arms crossed.

"Yatáki, huh? Tiger told me about you," Bree said, walking over to her. "Well met."

"Aye, and you," Yatáki said, shaking Bree's hand. "Nice work there."

Bree looked over her shoulder at the dead merc and grinned. "He had it coming," she said with a bloody grin.

"No doubt," Yatáki said. "He's been trying for weeks now to find our hideout. Thanks for taking care of him."

Bree shrugged.

They stood facing one another, privately sizing the other up. After glaring noncommittally for a few moments, Yatáki finally cut in.

"You guys have been gone for a while. Everything okay?"

"We're fine," Bree replied.

"Glad you're back. I found something of yours when I noticed the door had been kicked in. I'll send someone with it."

"Oh?"

Yatáki only nodded.

The silence between them grew heavy.

"Tiger's a nice kid," she said finally, breaking the uneasy silence.

Bree nodded. "He is, has a lot of hope for this world despite his losses. A lot of faith in its people," she said.

"Aye, he does," Yatáki said, glancing up the street toward the castle. "And in you, too."

Bree arched a brow, but then shrugged.

"I mean, he looks up to you quite a bit," Yatáki corrected. "Look, I don't mean to get into your personal life, I was just making an observation."

"I know you were," Bree said, turning to walk down the street toward the Stone Flame. "He's spoken of you, too."

"Oh yeah?" Yatáki asked, watching her leave.

"Yeah," she called over her shoulder, stopping a few feet away. "He said he wishes you would join us in fighting the mages. He said you were wicked at stealing purses."

Yatáki giggled and watched the vampiress disappear into the darkness.

Tiger walked the streets of Xonthian City, the storm that had swept through the morning before had left behind a city washed clean, but still damp. Puddles lay scattered across the cobblestones, reflecting the remnants of the stormy sky that had given way to a fleeting, fragile calm. The air was fresh, carrying a scent of rain mixed with the earthy aroma of wet stone and blooming flora.

He had set out with a single purpose: to find a present for Bree. The city's grand market square was alive with early-morning shoppers, with merchants shouting over the clatter of carts and the sizzle of morning food being cooked by street vendors. Stalls and shops, their awnings and signs dripping with the last vestiges of rain, offered everything, from rare spices like crimson firepepper and moonbloom petals to exotic fabrics woven from spider silk and silver elf thread. Tiger's gaze swept over a herbalist's booth laden with bundles of whispering willow bark that gave off a spicy, yet acrid stench when crushed. There were vials of phoenix tears for healing potions, although he doubted they came from an actual phoenix. Jars of mandrake root that seemed to twitch faintly as if alive sat on shelves, while nearby, a weapons stall gleamed with rune-etched daggers, with promises of being ancient. Of course, anyone should know better, since magic was forbidden. Yet, there were plenty of fools standing around appraising them as if they held anything but the promises of words. Further along, a food cart steamed with skewers of yak meat basted in honey, spiced with the hottest pepper in all western Xonthian. A trinket shop displayed orbs that looked as if shifting colors floated just inside, alongside puzzle boxes carved from elderwood that only opened for those who knew the correct sequence of buttons to push. Tiger's steps were light, as light as his feelings for Bree. He passed by a vendor displaying a collection of hand-carved wooden figures, each one unique and finely detailed. His fingers brushed over a delicate box crafted from dark mahogany, its surface adorned with swirling patterns. He considered the possibility that it might hold some special significance for Bree, but something about it felt too impersonal.

Further along, he found a shop specializing in rare herbs and magical components. The fragrant mix of dried flowers and enchanted roots filled the air; while she didn't dislike nature, it wasn't her, she was much more than what nature could provide.

As he continued his search, he was drawn to a stall, where an elderly man displayed intricate jewelry, each piece glowing with a soft, enchanting light. Among the collection, a pendant caught his eye. And the symbol was perfect.

"Can I help you?" the merchant asked, glancing up from his counter.

"Uh, yes," Tiger replied, pointing to the golden Ankh on display. "I'd like to buy that."

The merchant's eyes flickered with interest. "One hundred and fifty silver."

Tiger's eyebrows shot up. "Wow, that's quite a lot."

"It's a fine piece," the merchant said with a nod. "Are you sure?"

Tiger sighed and placed the silver coins on the counter. "Fine, I'll take it."

The merchant's demeanor softened. "Thank you, sir. I'll wrap it for you."

"Please," Tiger said.

The merchant worked quickly, wrapping the Ankh in soft cloth. A few minutes later, Tiger left the shop with the small package securely tucked in his pocket. A sense of excitement and anticipation bubbled up inside him; he couldn't wait to give Bree the gift.

He hurried through the market, grabbing a few more things: tonight's dinner, a bottle of mead, and a dozen fresh roses. He felt a surge of spontaneity, eager to express the depth of his feelings for Bree. It was a gesture of gratitude and affection, a way to bridge the gap between their worlds.

Panting slightly, Tiger bounded up the steps to their room at the Stone Flame and called out cheerfully, "I'm back!"

Bree's response was a tired moan, but it made Tiger's heart lift. He set the food down and turned to her, still holding the small package and the bouquet of roses.

"I brought dinner and a present," he announced, his face beaming with anticipation. He noticed a package at the edge of her bed. "Oh, what's this?"

Bree slowly rolled over and glanced at him with curiosity. "Oh? What IS this? Wait, how did anyone—"

"Yatáki," Tiger chuckled.

Bree opened the large package on the bed and unfolded a large, black piece of cloth. "My cloak. The one I thought I had lost when we were arrested."

"Is it special?"

"Have you noticed it absorbs light?"

Tiger peered at it, then glanced at the window. "Wow, I hadn't actually noticed it before."

"It's a long story, maybe one day I'll tell you about it," she said with a smile, then glanced at him. "You said you brought a present?"

"Indeed," Tiger said, kneeling beside her on the bed. He presented the wrapped gift and the roses with a flourish.

Bree's eyes widened with surprise. "Thank you. You're spoiling me."

"I hope so," Tiger said with a grin.

She set the roses down and picked the small package up. She glanced at it, and then him, a look of confusion on her face.

"Open it," he urged.

Bree nodded, her curiosity piqued. She carefully unwrapped the gift and revealed the choker, the golden Ankh dangling from it.

"It's beautiful, Tiger," she said, holding it up. "But why—"

Tiger interrupted gently, "The Ankh is a symbol of life. I want you to see it as a symbol of the life you bring to me, to yourself, and to the world. It's a reminder that you embody everything I hold dear and a reminder that you are not a monster. Though the world may not fully recognize it, I see it in you."

Her lips met his in a tender kiss, soft and fleeting, yet full of unspoken promises. Tiger's heart raced with a fervor that filled the room, the rhythmic pounding echoing in his ears with an intensity that left him breathless. He held her gaze, hoping she felt the depth of his emotions, the way his heart thudded in response to her presence.

Bree settled back into the bed, her eyes closing briefly as she absorbed the gift and the gesture behind it. Tiger sat beside her, his hand resting gently on hers, his thoughts drifting to the future and the uncertain path they walked together.

"Where are we going?" Bree asked.

Tiger sighed. "Yatáki has a lead for us. Smugglers are arming the Fire Isle Mages."

Bree nodded. "We'll worry about that tomorrow."

Tiger's smile returned. "Tomorrow." He poured a glass of honey-colored liquid into two goblets and handed one to Bree.

Tiger's mind was awash with the simple joy of the moment, the calm after the storm, and the hope for what lay ahead.

As Tiger watched Bree, his heart swelled with a quiet, hopeful certainty. The day's gifts, both tangible and emotional, had brought them closer, reaffirming their bond amidst the chaos of their lives. And in that serene moment, with the promise of more to come, Tiger knew that despite the storms that lay ahead, they would face them together.

End

Glossary

Atticatten (\at-i-ˈka-tən) - The Elder Race in the Xonthian fantasy world, often described as cat-like humanoids. They are fair, lanky, and agile, with pointy ears atop their heads, tails at the base of their spine, long slender arms and bodies, wide almond-shaped eyes with vertical slits, and typically long flowing hair. Created by the Greater Being Attin Yente from severed tails infused with his blood, they inhabit the forests and trees of Xecutran. With an average lifespan of 507 years, height of 5'7", and weight of 120 lbs, they sustain themselves on fish, plants, and hunted game such as deer.

GateHar (\gāt-ˈhär) - A deity in the Xonthian pantheon, serving as the mother of several gods including Sha'anne (Goddess of Water and Life), Gaisa (Goddess of Wind and Storms), and Fi'ra, paired with The Creator to birth these divine beings amid cosmic energies. The faith dedicated to GateHar emphasizes healing, magic, and protection, with followers including prominent healers, magic users, Paladins, and clerics. Key structures include the Tower of GateHar in Cettera, the tallest building in Xecutran, featuring a cathedral with stained glass depictions of heroic acts, housing the largest hospital on the northern continent and extensive archives.

Hon'shu (\hän-ˈshü) - Tiger's father in the Xonthian fantasy world. Fought in the One Hundred Year War and was a trusted military advisor to the King of Xonthian City. He's friends with the merchant guild, and the family of Der'handler. Took in Tiger when he was a baby, and raised him into young adulthood before his untimely death.

Xonthian (\zän-ˈthē-an) - The name of a fictional fantasy world and setting, featuring a diverse array of races including humans, elves, dwarves, Atticatten, orcs, and ogres. It includes various landscapes and locations such as the Shadow Mountains (home to dwarven communities), Juan'kij (an elven island retreat), and undiscovered eastern lands blending magic, swords, and gunslingers in desert landscapes. The world is rich in history, involving elements like ancient prophecies, guilds, kingdoms and conflicts such as the hundred-year war.

Yatáki (\yä-ˈta-kē) - A character in the Xonthian fantasy world, full name Yatáki "Kitt" Sothmore, who is a masterful thief and leader of the Xonthian branch of the Anarchs guild. She belongs to the Elder Race (likely the cat-like Atticatten), characterized by her slender, agile build, sandy-colored tail, cat-like ears and eyes, sharp claws, and long brown hair. Born into the Thieves House in Yente before the hundred-year war, she has a carefree, mischievous personality, enjoys trouble and joking in tense situations, and forms deep bonds with companions like Tiger.

Acknowledgment

This novel. This series even, has been decades in the making. Over the course of that time, the story has grown and matured. With that, has come a plethora of individuals who have helped shape and influence the novel and its characters. Many of them know who they are, while others don't. Mostly because I've lost contact with them over the years or never really had contact with them in the first place. As is the case with those responsible for creating some of the most fantastical worlds and media, I've had the pleasure of consuming. I can't exactly go around telling other authors, producers, game developers, how much their work has affected me. That'd be weird. I wouldn't feel right, calling them out here, I'm sure, through the course of my adventures in writing novels, meeting people, and speaking about these stories, the truth might come out. Eventually.

For now, though, I want to thank everyone involved in getting this novel where it is today. My friends and family have all played a part in seeing it come to fruition. Thank you, one and all for your support and love.

About the Author

Daniel Dickinsons' writing first appeared in an annual publication with his short story "Escape from Ogre Island." He has self-published two other stories "Gathering Tide", "Aggression Factor" and the newly released "Ember of War." He is a frequent contributor to the Arizona Author Association's quarterly newsletter.

At the age of ten, he began creating a realistic realm, Xonthian, in which his characters come to life, allowing the reader to become a part of that diverse world. Xonthian continues to evolve. The heroes Tiger and Bree, begin their sagas alone until circumstances bring them together. Future projects include a weird wild west tale, set in the world of Xonthian, and a novel featuring the titular heroes Tiger and Bree.

Daniel is a proud father with a beautiful wife. He enjoys traveling and photography, as well as food and art. One of his many hobbies is taking his daughter and grandkids camping at least twice a year

Three heroic tales from the kingdom of Xonthian
EMBER
OF
WAR
DANIEL DICKINSON

AGGRESSION FACTOR
GO AWAY
DANIEL DICKINSON

Visit me for More information

And be sure to follow all my social media

Don't miss out on updates!

Sign up to receive my Newsletter

THANK YOU

www.ingramcontent.com/pod-product-compliance
Lightning Source LLC
Chambersburg PA
CBHW070157310726
48976CB00001B/120